G000300715

The Odyssey of
Samuel Glass

Also by Bernard Kops

Novels

Awake for Mourning
Motorbike
Yes from No-Man's Land
The Dissent of Dominick Shapiro
By the Waters of Whitechapel
The Passionate Past of Gloria Gaye
Settle Down Simon Katz
Partners
On Margate Sands

Television Plays

I Want to Go Home
The Lost Years of Brian Hooper
Alexander the Greatest
Just One Kid
Why the Geese Shrieked
The Boy Philosopher
It's a Lovely Day Tomorrow
Moss
Rocky Marciano Is Dead
Night Kids
The Survivor

Stage Plays

The Hamlet of Stepney Green
Goodbye World
Change for the Angel
The Dream of Peter Mann
Stray Cats and Empty Bottles
Enter Solly Gold
The Boy Who Wouldn't Play Jesus
David, It Is Getting Dark

It's a Lovely Day Tomorrow
More Out Than In
Ezra
Simon at Midnight
Some of These Days
Sophie! Last of the Red Hot Mamas
Dreams of Anne Frank
Who Shall I Be Tomorrow
Playing Sinatra
Call in the Night
Golem

Autobiography

The World is a Wedding
Shalom Bomb

Poetry

Poems and Song
Anemone for Antigone
Erica, I want to read you Something
For the Record
Barricades in West Hampstead
Grandchildren: And other Poems
Where Do People Go
This Room in the Sunlight

Other works

Neither Your Honey Nor Your Sting
Bernard Kops' East End

And many other plays for radio

The Odyssey of Samuel Glass

Bernard Kops

DAVID
PAUL

First published in 2012 by David Paul
25 Methuen Park
London N10 2JR

info@davidpaulbooks.com

www.davidpaulbooks.com

A catalogue record for this book is available from the British Library

ISBN 978 09548482 8 6

Front cover design by Sarah Barnett.
copyright © Sarah Barnett, 2012
www.inkyfairy.co.uk

Printed and bound in the UK by the MPG Books Group,
Bodmin and King's Lynn

For Erica

1

"Do the dead know that life still exists, somewhere?" The thought was bugging him, piercing and twisting around in his brain when he heard his mother call his name, repeatedly. Sometimes he felt like strangling her. He loved her of course, but she simply would not pull out of her depression.

Sam had to get away from the doom-laden cloud that pervaded the house. He would skateboard down the Elysian slopes of Muswell Hill and never return.

He banged his forehead against the window glass and was jolted back to that terrible evening.

Slightly drunk, on half a lager with his mates after school at the Minstrel Boy, he had returned home and was astonished to see the living room crammed with people. At first, he thought there was a jolly party celebrating something. He had mistaken their anguish for joy.

But all that was almost a year ago. That Friday evening was indelibly stained in his brain. But this was another Friday and the pall of his dad's death was still hanging over the house. He was starving, but he could not escape from staring out of the window where he was imprisoned, as usual. Again and again, the sequence never changed. He imagined how it must have happened.

The beautiful Saab 9-3 Convertible drew up outside the house. His lovely dad smiled at him, and came inside. He was grasping the usual bunch of red roses for his beloved

Lisa. They kissed their usual Friday night kiss and then – and then – he fell on the floor.

The silence! That dream in slow motion; again and again! And then the screams! That sudden massive heart attack as Ben Glass kissed the carpet. He was dead. Very dead.

Sam thought his mother was smiling. She was stuck in horror. Her mouth opened wide. He had played all this over and over again. Maybe it would come out differently if he did it often enough.

Outside, the same lifeless, semi-detached sleepwalkers of London N.10 were trudging homeward. He laughed. It was terrible that his father had the audacity to die young; but at least he had escaped from Muswell Hill.

Sam was seventeen; and six long months to go before he was free, released from education. But even that didn't relieve his despair. It would be his last year of being alive. After the cosy joys of school there would be nothing except university and death. The thought of it was too hard to think about. University would prepare him for this decaying world by shovelling tons of shit into his brain. Oh! The world of work! The conspiracy! Those endless paths to ravenous suburbia, that wait to swallow us all. And then, finally, "Hoopla!" Hoop Lane Crematorium. Such an appropriate name. He went to his room.

Sam loved words. Words were his daggers; the gift of the gab as you negotiated and staggered your way through life. And no-one could get out of this life alive.

"Sam! You alright?" Lisa, his mother squeaked plaintively in endless lament. Lisa, his pathetic mother! He loved her to bits but sometimes he could bite her to bits. Life alone with her was as dark as death. No wonder he hated her.

The way she criticised him; trying to give him advice day after day after day.

Then he sighed. He also happened to love her. "How can you hate the person you love?" He mumbled at the angry reflection in the glass. It was his father's face, staring back at him.

"Dad! How could you do this to me? You madman! How could you leave me all alone in this sterile suburb? How could you leave your Saab outside, still mourning for you?"

He wasn't going round the bend. He was already round the bend.

She called again. "Sam! Be nice! Be like other boys. Please!"

Then her tone of voice did a back somersault; "Sam! Do come to the kitchen. The chocolate brownies are ready. You've been in there for over three hours."

She meant well, even if she was a prisoner of suburbia; his heart went out to her. She too was in pain. "Can you wonder I hate this world?" He stood sideways, glancing, grinning at himself in the mirror.

He smiled as he posed and felt good, suddenly. "Nice! Good aquiline profile." He would slip off soon; to see if any of those posh, uptight, leggy, giggly girls of Channing were dawdling outside the school, with their teasing tits blossoming through their tunics, and their yearning innocent eyes crying out for divine de-virgination.

But where could they do it? Waterlow Park? There were no empty, derelict houses behind Highgate Hill. Where else could he impregnate them and show them a glimpse of paradise? Anyway he was bound to be caught and his smirking face would be spread all over the *Journal* next Friday morning. And the entire Glass tribe would sing

9

litanies over the telephones. "What a lovely boy he was! So clever! An original mind! How could he do such a terrible thing? Who does he take after?" Sam groaned. He would be done with them all. Soon!

He would never become a lawyer with a filthy, bloated belly; or a simpering, whimpering architect; or a chartered accountant with a ravenous prick; or a sadistic dentist enjoying drilling into your soul. He had declared war long ago on all those so-called respectable gits. To hell with their future! He would become an existential nomad. Anyway, in the end nothing exists, so it can't get worse. Nothing gets worse when you are not there.

And then it all came true; stinking death and his insatiable appetite. That day the world ended. Ben Glass was nothing now. His ashes were still within that obnoxious urn, staring down from the mantelpiece, in the living room. When would she find the courage to scatter him?

All he wanted out of this life was to ride alone on his skateboard. His beautiful skateboard. He knew he should have grown out of her years ago. But putting it to one side was saying goodbye forever to his happy childhood when death had not yet entered the ring. Of course, his mother did not qualify for total rejection. He really liked her, sometimes.

But there was another person in the tribe that he truly cared for; his wonderful grandfather, Maurice! His mother's totally bonkers father. How often he journeyed to Stamford Hill with his parents. And how he loved being there, enjoying the constant chat about the past. "I talk about the past because there's no future." He loved just listening to the old man who would never dream of growing old.

Maurice would close his eyes to revisit his past; relating his incessant tales over and over again. The General Strike. The Battle of Cable Street. The Aldermaston Marches. The same old stories of protest. Sam had heard the stories so many times, that he could quote them, entirely.

"Ah! I see you've rung the doorbell with your elbow; cos you always come with such beautiful delicatessen. What have you brung me today? You're the best daughter in the world; even if you do have your pish-posh car bored and impatient, outside. So why not? You've earned it. Marvellous! Pickled herrings! Black bread! A half a pound of the best quality smoked salmon! Some cream cheese and a chunk of cheese cake."

Maurice was always on the edge of death, the great *gornisht*; always sighing and promising that this day was going to be his last. His son-in-law, Sam's dad, Ben, sat there as usual, a smile fixed on his face, never uttering one word. The menu never varied.

Maurice always turned to Sam, smiling. And he would give such a bear hug that it almost stopped him breathing.

"My wonderful, brilliant grandson! You will make such discoveries that will change this world and the hearts of people." For Maurice, the cataclysm was going to happen any minute now, after lunch. Tomorrow noon! Yesterday! "Go! Go now! Go! So what's new? Nothing's new. I'm tired. Thank you Ben. And Lisa my beloved daughter. Come, let me squeeze you."

Sam could see his mother's gentle sigh as she complied and surrendered to his gorilla cuddle.

"Goodbye, my lovely ones. It's a pleasure to see you, Sam; you're growing up fast. I hope I'll be alive, next time you

11

come to visit. Next time? No thanks. Save the petrol. I'll be dead by then. Thanks for the lovely provisions."

It was always the same. "You came to visit me? A miracle! You never come to visit me. Now go! Please. I'm dead tired. Thank you for coming." That's when he would belch wind from both ends and nod off, rehearsing for you know what.

The death of Maurice was the passing of a world. Maurice was the very last of his tribe.

At the burial ground, two days later, Lisa laughed as she threw earth on her father's box. "Life never tamed him."

"Thank God for that." Sam replied. Then he shook his thoughts away. It was now. It was always now. When other kids asked him about his politics he always replied. "I am a Nowist!"

Sam in his bedroom looked out at his father's car; that beautiful car with its layer of bird shit getting thicker and thicker by the day, by the month – by month after month. The beautiful Saab, now almost an old carpet; unloved, unused, uncared for. Just like himself.

How he wished his mother would get round to selling it. He loved that car, as much as his father did. Not for Ben Glass a shitty four by four black Mercedes; that was more suited to chauffeuring a gang of relatives to the crematorium.

"Goodbye! Oh beautiful Saab 9-3 Convertible. You ought to have been in that same oven where my dad was turned into gravel." He wiped his stupid tears away on his cuff. No longer would he ever ride in any car ever again.

"Sam! Are you alright?" Her soft voice tinkled through the door. "Sam! You've been in there for hours."

"I'm reading. Studying!"

"May I come in?" She tried to hide her concern. He truly, really loved her, but she was driving him up the wall. She entered without waiting for his reply. His stunning mother, Lisa, her perfume wafting before her, but her mascara slightly smudged. She was definitely not looking after herself.

Every night, since dad became a package of gravel, Sam heard her crying a whispering of tears. And bloody hell, now she was even crying in the daytime. Only the day before, he was with her in Sainsbury's, and her tears started flowing at the fish counter.

But now she stood pale and lifeless. Like a marble antique statue in the British Museum. "Sam! You must get on with your life. Your dad is dead. Right? And we both have a life to live. Right?"

He almost doubled up with laughter. "You can talk!" Perhaps he would run away from all this. Peru. Or maybe Baffin Land. "When are you going to get rid of the Saab?" She didn't respond.

"Mum! When are you gonna find someone, and have good sex and be happy again?" Again, she did not reply.

"Mum! Can I smell your hair?"

"Sam! You really must grow up one day." She was such a beautiful woman. Too bad she kept him in thrall. This was the ritual he loved the most. No-one's hair ever smelt so special; it was the elixir of life; the one thing that stopped him leaving home. He went close to her, pushed his nose deep into her nest and sighed.

"My darling madman! By the way, did you have a bath this morning?"

"Mother! You amaze me. I had a barf last Wednesday.

Four days ago. Right?"

"Sam! Be good. Please don't get angry but you smell a little high. Take a bath now."

He sniffed both his armpits. "You're mad. I smell fine. What's the problem? Alright! To placate your ridiculous middle class urges I shall take a shower, tonight; just before bed."

She gently slapped his cheek.

"Come out into the garden and breathe some fresh air. By the way I've made your favourites."

"Chocolate brownies? Yeah! Fanks."

She took his arm and led him out onto the grass.

"Look! My myrtle bush! Just rub the leaves between your fingers."

He did. He always did as he was told just to placate her.

"Lovely! Beautiful! Your hair smells like no-one else."

"Thanks. You are a strange young man. Don't you just love Japonica? Sometimes I wish I lived far away from this place. If only I could get away. Shall we try to move? Somewhere! But maybe not too far! Totteridge, maybe?"

"Mum! There must be some decent guys out there. Blokes who missed out! Desperate for a prize, like you! You could light up their dreary lives. Get happy again. There are some great agencies."

Lisa Glass shook her head. "My impossible son. Who would love you if I didn't?" Her eyes were so full of sadness.

"Incidentally! Where have all the lovely sparrows gone?" She shuddered. "Someone just walked over my grave."

"Mother! A poem still haunts me. Can I read it?"

"Of course! I just love the sound of your voice, especially when you read to me. But please! Just a few stanzas!"

"Please sit while I perform." He sat down on the swing. He cleared his throat.

When I was but thirteen years or so
I went into a golden land.
Chimborazo Cotopaxi
Took me by the hand.

My father died. My brother too,
They passed like fleeting dreams.
I stood where Popocatepetl
In the sunlight gleams.

The houses, people, traffic seemed
Thin fading dreams by day.
Chimborazo, Cotopaxi had
Stolen my soul away.

I dimly heard the master's voice
And boys far-off at play,
Chimborazo, Cotopaxi
Had stolen me away.

"Samuel! That was beautiful. Thank you. But it was four stanzas. I'm cold. Let's go inside." She brushed a kiss on his cheek; he moved away, trying to fight back the tears in his eyes.

"Poetry is the zenith of all things; it takes me away from everything, everywhere. It's so beautiful."

She hugged him, burst out crying and ran inside. He followed her into the house and went straight to his room. He simply had to get away. He took up the opened book on his bed and entered the dark world of Franz Kafka; one of his gods.

"A somewhat precocious read for a schoolboy, don't you think?" He said to himself. "Definitely!" He dived into the beginning again and spoke the threatening opening.

Someone must have been spreading lies about Josef K.,
for without having done anything wrong, he was arrested
one fine morning.

He didn't care if some called him precocious and morbid for reading Kafka. He had been reading *The Trial*, slowly, for more than a month, and didn't want to finish it. The genius book of no hope. He loved no hope. Everyone hoped in this world. Nobody dared to go against the tribe.

Then he enjoyed a long Jewish sigh. "Sam! You'll never get out of life alive!"

He closed his eyes and shook his head and drifted over dark Prague. The River Vltava was flowing over its banks, engulfing him and drowning the world, so he quickly joined his mother in the living room. "The living room." He laughed. Now more like a dying room. And she was the principal mourner.

The doorbell rang. "Darling! The doorbell."

"What's the point answering? Opening the door is never to my advantage." He opened the door.

Katie with her soft smile stood there; fluttering her mournful eyes, just for him.

"How are you Sam?" She uttered the words with such concern. Katie lived opposite; sometimes they waved across at each other; especially when the parents were on the warpath. That slight shaking of the head. The soft groans, the plaintive wave of concern.

"Had a good day?"

"I've had a fantastic day. I want to die!" He replied.

She laughed. "So pleased you are yourself today." She touched his sleeve; looking somewhat plaintive.

Katie had such beautiful, soft inviting pink lips. He quickly dismissed his darkest of thoughts regarding the flaming foliage between her legs. An area he had not yet explored. Would she groan or slap him if his fingers slowly infiltrated up her dress and into her holy of holies?

She was the very last dessert on his menu called life. She was gentle and sweet and she had such beautiful, Medusa like, golden red hair. How often, he wondered, if it was quite the same on her undercarriage, crowning her sweet virgin orifice. That would be truly marvellous. One day, perhaps he would do all the things she longed for. But first he needed to get away and explore other places. He just couldn't afford to get into mutual heavy breathing at the moment.

"Sam! I like you. I'm very fond of you. But you are so complicated. Please! Just say something."

"Katie! I don't like myself or anyone. But if I did it would be so cool to like you."

"Thanks for the crumbs."

"I mean it. You're beautiful. A real friend."

"Thanks." She tried to smile.

"I'm trying to love myself. My mum says if you love yourself everyone will love you. Sorry Katie! I'm hopeless. I feel a bit shitty."

His mother interrupted them; "Here you two. Hot from the soul! Chocolate brownies!"

He shook his head, but his arm had a mind of its own and reached out. Soon they were both munching away.

17

Both now were lost for words. He had to get away from Katie's innocent, subtle clutches.

"Sorry Katie. I want to be on my own." She nodded. She was always so understanding. He hated understanding people. He went through the French windows into the garden that was strangling itself. No-one had tended it since his dad slipped away so silently, all those long months ago. "How could he do that to me? I hate him. Hate him!"

He wandered to the small pergola and stared into the sky. Day or night, he couldn't get away from that nicely turned out gathering of people in their expensive chic death clothes who had crammed into that auditorium of death. Sam was turning into Hoop Lane again, that same waking dream! That same moving image, the crematorium. The hush! The speeches! Extolling gentle clichés, about the goodness of the man! His generosity; his love of life and family. His verve for living. It was all a load of shit. Etcetera!

What did they know? Only he and Lisa knew how marvellous the man was. So he decided to stand up and slip away from that theatre of death. He could not bear to see his dad slide away into the ravenous flames. He rushed out and he could see the shock surprise on all their faces. And his mother turning to him; pale and astonished.

"Sorry Mum. I need fresh air. I'm choking. I don't know who I am." She cuddled him and sobbed. "You're all I have left."

God! How he hated those words. He gathered himself together and tore away from her; and walked and walked away. Anywhere was better than that palace of licking flames.

Suddenly, he was in the Holy Land of Temple Fortune,

where the kosher cowboys hung out. Especially today, when it seemed the whole tribe were cheerfully gathering for the end of the world. Nattering; speeding, unaware of all the other tribes that also inhabited those streets. Fearful and anxious that they would miss the Messiah, dishing out doughnuts to all the ravenous faithful, outside Marks and Spencer's.

How lovely, how quaint they were, the Orthodox. What lucky sods to have such certainty; such faith. Oh to be blinkered and have no doubts. How fantastic to be free behind their walls in their blind tribal prison. Those *frummers* from outer space! From Stamford Hill and Temple Fortune. They belonged. He never belonged; but he longed. He just longed; but for what?

Sam, still on his bed could not eliminate that terrible day, the dreaming again and again; the wide open mouth of eternity. There was his father, not there; not anywhere. Falling off to sleep or waking in the morning he would never be there, ever again. The taste, the smell of death clung to his mouth, his clothes. The coffin, again and again, slipping unto the fire. He sat up and looked out of the window at the tall, mourning, poplar trees. Then she tapped on the door.

"May I come in?" She cooed.

"If you must!" He groaned.

His mother entered. "Sam! Am I disturbing you?"

"No! I'm disturbed enough already."

"Why are you torturing yourself? And me! Sam, my darling; you must grow out of this."

"I am. I'm going to kill myself. Tonight!"

She stroked his face. "Sammy! We must get on with our

lives." She was a dam holding back the floods that would drown them all.

"Or maybe I'll postpone my suicide for the week after next."

"Thank you. Good boy!" She was about to leave the room, but then came the admonition. "It's those books you read. Those dark poems that clutter your brain." She hurriedly left his room.

"Thank you mother! Goodbye mother."

She was gone and he went diving into Palgrave's *Golden Treasury*; a book he loved. Bound in leather; genuine Victorian. He pushed his nose against the cover and smelled its antique aroma. It comforted, that special present from his father, the once Ben Glass, two weeks before he fell, dancing his last Saraband onto the carpet. Sam felt his dead father deserved to be read to, aloud. "Any excuse to hear my own mellifluous voice once again."

> *I met a lady in the meads,*
> *Full beautiful—a faery's child.*
> *Her hair was long. Her foot was light,*
> *And her eyes were wild.*
> *I made a garland for her head,*
> *And bracelets too, and fragrant zone;*
> *She looked at me as she did love,*
> *And made sweet moan.*

"Oh! How much I love thee John Keats." He snuggled down into his pillows. Sam felt marvellous. He smiled and intoned. "Here lies one whose name is writ in water." Then he decided not to hold back the dam, so he cried and he cried; then sated and satisfied he lay back on his pillow.

2

He felt unusually happy in this dream, shooting down the slopes of Muswell Hill on his skateboard.

Gone was yesterday and tomorrow; gone were memories and promises. "Down! Down!" The top skier of the London slopes. He passed Queens Wood "I am the King of Skateboards." He shouted into the rushing air.

Soaring, sailing, gliding, floating, descending. And the whole world spread out before him. But suddenly he felt conspicuous. People glared upward as he whizzed past. All the passing faces, sneering with such disdain. "Aren't you getting just a trifle too old to be still obsessed with a skateboard?"

Before his father escaped from this rotten world, Sam was a child, and here he was, stuck, somewhere else in his head. It all seemed to happen overnight. The past was dead. He somehow had to face it! Things!

"For God's sake, Samuel. You're in your eighteenth year. Grow up. Face the world. Life!"

Down, down, he could go anywhere in his dreams. He hurtled into Temple Fortune. Into the bustle of life. A pinch of East Europeans: Poles! Lithuanians! Ukrainians! Russians! Latvians! And worst of all, the cursed Croatians. And, surprisingly enough, a sprinkling survival of the English.

And there it was. The reason for his descent. "Manny's Fresh Bagels." And he was absolutely starving. And the smell! The smell of those newly baked, universal bagels. The wonder, the joy, desirable as that beautiful part of every virgin's anatomy.

A bagel was even better than the bliss of those spellbinding orgasms he created in the bath. Manny's bagel bakery was the synagogue of fressing. Bagels were holy; created by God alone, to displace and satiate his holy desire for the worship of the precious vagina. Life without bagels would not be worth living.

"Yes please!" He shouted near the top of the queue. He had to shout or he would be trampled upon and shouted down and lose his place, forever.

There were piles and piles of them, just baked.

"Hey! Save some for me." And then the pretty little delectable Polish girl smiled. He was sure she fancied him. "How can I help you?" Her voice drove him to the edge of the precipice of wet dreams.

"I know how you can help me." He said to himself. "One superb, sensuous bagel; to eat now. I'm ravenous."

Oh yes; he could eat her; she had something far more desirable even than her concealed bagel.

"Yes please! With lashes of you know what, and your best quality wild smoked salmon." She gave it to him, warm and waiting to be devoured. He held it in the paper bag, close to his heart and left the hall of frenzy.

All was quiet now. He sat outside on the chairs reserved for the starving bagel seekers and began to explore the boundaries of self-pleasure. This was the answer. This was what life was all about. The existential bagel.

"Take your time." He uttered. This was serenity.

"Dad! Where are you taking me? Where is this supposed to be?" Ben Glass was rowing his son in a boat on the Thames, a tributary of the Lethe, going east. This was a mission with a purpose. And there above them was Tower Bridge, her arms open, welcoming in the masses of hungry Jewish immigrants of Eastern Europe.

"This was the harbour that gave hope and succour, home and sustenance to our people. And this was the first glimpse of London your great grandfather Aaron cherished, when he arrived with his Essie, and landed in this country; finally, escaping the frozen tyranny of pogroms in the Land of Baal, otherwise known as Russia."

Ben was dead; he was ashes, and he was smiling at his son and you had to believe him.

"Why are we on a boat? Where are you rowing me?"

And his father replied at last. "Fine my son, my beautiful son; we are escaping from Charon and we are on a mission to the Aldgate Pump, and environs; for a fitting; remember? I'm getting you a new suit for your bar mitzvah from Mr Adler, the bespoke tailor in Brick Lane."

Dad led the way into Mr Adler's cluttered den and the little tailor came smiling, his tape measure around his neck. He nodded and the ghost father nodded when the tailor started his measuring.

"Funny. People go to Savile Row and spend thousands on a sprauncy suit. Barmy, shithouse bastards! Little do those posh geezers know that I make their bespoke shmutter right here for a pittance; in this my lovely hovel; my own private sweatshop in the East End, and they sell that same suit in the West End, for a fortune. The gonifs, the thieves!

"Tell me young man, what are you going to do in life?"

"As a matter of fact Mr Adler, I hope to become a poet."

His dead father said nothing.

"A poet? A shmo-ett. Mendel! Mendel! Gay cuck in the fendel. Have a shit in the fireplace. Nice!"

"Nearly finished measuring, almost done. Mr Glass, your son is a very polite and pleasant young man. Now we must choose our cloth. But tell me young man, will you become a night poet or a day poet?"

"What do you mean?" Sam replied.

"Rilke was a day poet. Baudelaire, a night poet. Schiller, a day poet. William Blake, a day poet. Rimbaud, a night poet. Shakespeare, a day and night poet. And Shelley and Keats and Federico Garcia Lorca. All, day poets! And what will you be? What will you become?"

"I will become like William Blake, a day poet!"

"Congratulations Mr Glass. Your son knows his onions."

Sam chose his cloth and Mr Adler showed them the door.

"Wonderful to oblige you. Trade is a little thin these days. Most of my erudite customers are dead."

"So am I Mr Adler. I'm very dead; but what can you do when your son needs a new suit. Goodbye!" Ben sighed and sighed. And Mr Adler scythed and sighed.

"Goodnight and goodbye! Don't let the river rats bite." Mr Adler waved; lethargic, in slow motion. Sam took the plug out of the bath and Mr Adler went swishing down the plughole with the whirlpool of water.

"Memories." Dad said, with a sad laugh. Sam knew in the dreamless world he would never see his father again. That bagel he devoured in Temple Fortune was all there was.

He decided to wake up, and so he did. He looked in the mirror, and splashed his face with holy cold water. That surely would suffice and please and pass his mother's scrutinising stare when he faced her in the kitchen.

And there it was; the cage of his life, the kitchen seemed

to have come to him.

"I love you Sam."

"So do I."

"I love you and only you, with all my heart."

"I would have thought you still love your husband."

"Shut up! My husband is dead. Against all my desires, my anger, I still love you so much. Samuel! I have something important to discuss with you." She dried her tears.

"Sorry! Very sorry." He did not desire to turn her into a pathetic mass of blubber.

"You are the only one I have. You are my love, my life."

"Oh God!" He said to himself. "How embarrassing." Then he found the exact quote to cover this ridiculous moment.

> *What is love? 'Tis not hereafter;*
> *Present mirth hath present laughter;*
> *What's to come is still unsure.*
> *In delay there lies no plenty.*

"Quote! Quote! Quote! You marvellous, ridiculous boy."

She was right. Quoting covered a multitude of the things he could not deal with.

"So, what's the crisis? What is this important thing you need to unload on me?"

"Sam! I have a terrible dilemma. Please sit down. I need to talk it through with you." She sat at the table opposite him. He knew her words would not be to his advantage.

"Please Listen! And don't interrupt." She said. "I've met someone. A man; a very nice man!"

She stared at him, looking for some reaction. His face gave away nothing. But Inside there was turmoil.

"Really? That's nice." He replied, flatly.

"His name is David. He's very nice. Gentle. Patient! I feel all mixed up; I feel guilty. It's only a year since your father died. But I know what he would say. 'Good! Lisa, get on with your life. You're still a young woman.' I turn it over and over in my brain; in the middle of the night, in the middle of cooking, shopping; with company; at a concert, a play. I can hear him. 'Lisa! Do not bury yourself.' Samuel! I need to know what you think. Don't you think I deserve a life while I'm alive! Say something. Please!"

"David? Nice!" He smiled ice.

She had stabbed him through the heart with a poisoned dagger. She tried to maintain the hint of a smile, but she too was very close to tears. "He said he might be popping over today."

"I see." He replied. "You must do what you must do."

"Samuel! I try hard to understand what's going on in your impossible head. Please try to be nice. He'll be here quite soon."

"Terrific! Thank you mother! It's your life. Whatever makes you happy. Good luck." He yawned. "I have so much revision to do. See you later."

He strode to his room. Maybe it was the best thing. Maybe it was the worst. His beautiful, dead father was dying, over and over again. When would he stay dead? There was no real safe security with parents. His books were his true parents; his best friends. He grabbed a book from the shelf. *The Love Song of J Alfred Prufrock*! Hmm! How he loathed Eliot and how he loved him. He knew each honeyed word and slowly spoke and coloured them.

I grow old ... I grow old.
I shall wear the bottoms of my trousers rolled.
Shall I part my hair behind? Do I dare to eat a peach?
I shall wear white flannel trousers and walk upon the beach.

The door bell rang. He jumped from the bed, and slightly opened the door, and caught a glimpse of the man as she led him into the living room; the room of Urn. That ghastly urn!

And David, the man who was trying to worm his way into their lives, seemed absolutely obnoxious, with his neatly trimmed beard. He hated him on sight.

He was waiting for her call, and it came. "Samuel darling! Can you spare a few moments? Please!"

"Sorry mother. I'm too deep into this. Sorry. Maybe soon. Maybe another time. Sorry."

"Sam! Are you alright?"

"Ye...sss! Oh Mother! I am perfect, in absolute ecstasy and life is fatal. That's all."

"Please, do try." She went away.

Rosie, his mother's mother, entered his head from all the woes and ghosts of Europe. His dear old grandmother. "Alas! Poor Rosie! Where are your jibes now?" Death had led her all so slowly, gently across to the bathroom, that stinking anteroom of that Cursing Home in East Finchley.

Sam wondered how she could manage being dead and not going any more to Brent Cross at least once a week. Rosie went so quietly, with all her marbles rolling around in her head. Her puckered lips covered with vermillion lipstick and her deep, brown eyes swimming with mascara. She turned and spoke her last to Lisa, her pale, weeping daughter, a few moments before she deflated.

27

"You know what Lisa? I still feel sexy. I still fancy a bit. And all those dirty rotting old men still think they're in with a chance of getting their end away. Some hopes."

The nurse opened the bathroom door. "Come on darling, do your pinky poos!" Rosie went in, but she never came out.

Sam returned to his book, but there was a gentle tapping on the door, putting paid to his sad reverie.

It just had to be Katie. At seventeen, she might feel the need to devote her body to the ravenous aspiring genius from over the road. God knows they both needed it. Today might well become his most auspicious day. And he would also be doing her a great favour.

"Sam? Are you in there?

"Yes! Where else would I be? Enter!"

She did, and stood there, before him, frail and nervous; as if she was having the same thoughts. She might be dying to help him get his end away.

"Ah Katie! How marvellous to see you. May I read you the best poem in the whole universe? Listen!" He didn't wait for her reply.

He took up Omar Kayam, still open on his bed. He almost sang it to her.

> *A Book of Verses underneath the Bough,*
> *A Jug of Wine, a Loaf of Bread—and Thou*
> *Beside me singing in the Wilderness—*
> *Oh, Wilderness were Paradise enow!*

She was sure that he wanted to grab her but he was too lost in another world.

"Poetry! I am sick of your poetry," she cried. "I'm never

28

going to see you ever again." And she stormed out.

He was surprised. He liked her. Girls were a very strange species.

Sam was starving for another quatrain:

> *Ah, make the most of what ye may yet spend,*
> *Before we too into the Dust descend;*
> *Dust into Dust and under Dust to lie,*
> *Sans Wine, sans Song, sans Singer, and – sans End.*

He was sorry for Katie. She was so nice; but she was so, so boring. He could have provided her with such joy. He looked into the mirror; he was quite handsome.

Then came the deafening row; like the grand organ in the Royal Albert Hall. A crashing, booming voice shuddered the whole room. And the source of the vortex was coming from somewhere within the bookcase.

> *'Oh ye of little faith hear this.*
> *Balaam shall curse the children of Israel.'*
> *'Go to Hell!' God thundered.*
> *'In that case and despite you I shall bless those Israelites.'*
> *The dreaded Balaam replied.*
> *God remained adamant.*
> *'Give them neither your honey nor your sting.'*

The bookcase swung open.

Sam was spread-eagled. He had been blown backwards on the bed and a strange man-creature appeared and hovered over him.

"Shmuel! These are the key words. Remember them. Think for yourself. Survive by not relying on others."

"Who are you?" Sam was definitely not afraid.

"What are you? Why are you here?"

The man did not respond. Sam spoke to himself but also to the ravenous, ragged apparition invading his space.

"Keep cool Sam. You are the King of cool, the epitome of cool. You are the coolest." But Sam's heart was beating double time. It was wonder. It was wonderful.

A blinding light pierced his brain and changed everything. His mouth gaped with fear.

"Do not move Sam. Do not dare to move." He commanded himself. He was surely about to find himself in the land of dust where his father was wandering.

The creature laughed. He had two, searching, incredibly thin, long hands with red, bitten fingernails. He was quite tall with bushy, black, overgrown eyebrows. He wore a terrifying smile and a bedraggled, black and red cloak, covered with twinkling stars. He stank to high heaven. And the silence was shouting.

"Are you death? Are you the end of everything?"

Sam tried his nonchalant touch. "What do you need? Money? Something to eat? Do you play chess? Are you after my body? Because if you are, you can fuck off!"

The silence was supreme. He clenched his eyes tight. He was merely having a brainstorm. Maybe the spectre had dissolved. He opened his eyes again. It was still there.

"Shmuel, known in these parts as Sam, trust me."

Those words shivered through Sam's body and his heart turned to ice when the creature roared his name. "Please! I'm only seventeen. Have mercy on me. My mother couldn't bear another death."

Now, the man from another world, looked almost human.

"Boy! Take it easy. Listen to me. I am a friend and I have

come for you."

"For what? Who are you?"

"I am the Red Rabbi."

"Sorry mate. Don't understand; they've closed all the asylums. Try A and E."

"You and I are inextricably bound from now on."
The man came too close and stroked the boy's head.

"These bloody journeys take the *kishkers* out of me. Shake hands, my darling boy."

Sam calmed. It was obvious that this man thing had not come to violate his body and have his way with him. He took the shrivelled hand reluctantly. The rabbi hooted and closed his eyes with audible contentment.

"Nice! Nice. Nicely nice! Samuel Glass! How do you do?"

"I'm afraid I don't know."

"From now on until the end of the world I shall call you Shmuel, your original Jewish name. I know all about you Shmuel. You are an atheist. So am I. There is no God, thank God, and thank you for allowing me this ease." He sang.

"This is Muswell Hill! A God-forsaken suburb. What are you doing here? What do you want?"

"I am the fisher of outstanding men; a youth like you. I am come for you. It is writ in the book, the Holy of Holies; the Kaballah! The deepest mystical book that guides us through this dark labyrinth of life."

The rabbi pulled off his knee-high leather boots and danced a jig on the carpet. He wore no socks, and he raised a big black and red toe to his mouth, and chewed away at his curling, overgrown toenail. "That feels better. In fact, perfect. At last I find you. The one I seek."

31

"Please! Sir, I've been praying for a miracle; not for you. Life has been so dark, recently. I hate life. Please find someone else."

The thing breathed out foul breath. "Life is a celebration and also fatal. I love this life, but sadly I am destined to live forever. But we all live in hope. Who knows? Maybe, one day, I shall sleep the sleep of a million billion years. I am not important. You are. But enough of that! I am merely obeying orders. I have done my duty and found you. Now you must come with me."

"What! Why? My nightmares are enough. Go to hell."

"I am the Red Rabbi of Vitebsk. You are safe in my hands. I have my accreditation on my person. I keep it in my secret hiding place." He winked as he fumbled open the flies of his trousers. He pulled out a thick and ancient leather book, and started a frantic search through its contents.

"Who'd want to go with you? Where on earth would you want to take me?"

"You'll know when we get there. Hang on."

Sam felt sick. He was hanging on alright for dear sanity. Hanging on, hovering over the sheer cliffs of existence.

"Rabbi! I fear death forever; the billions of years without me."

"I fear life, forever." The Red Rabbi still fumbled through the massive book. Then he held it high and kissed it and hugged it as if he were partnering a lover. "All my books are lovers! But this is the very best of them all."

"You and I have a singular and rather important appointment."

"Really? Who with?"

32

"Someone you will be pleased to know as soon as you meet her."

"Where have you come from?"

"Prague. Centuries ago. Long before your time or my time."

"Why do you keep looking in the book?"

"This is the holiest book. The way to move from one sphere to another. It is an offshoot of the Kabbalah. I know it well, but my forgetfulness likes playing tricks on me. Shmuel! Please be silent for a few moments while I search."

He started rocking backward and forwards and belching. He whipped through page after yellowing, crumbling page; as he mumbled a fervent, whining, piercing song, high up in his head. He was well away.

Sam could hear his mother moving around in the sitting room. He went to the door and pressed his ear against the wood.

He could hear her talking quietly. She was beautiful, passionate. He hated her.

It was obvious, the man who seeks a lonely, trusting widow can only want to get into her knickers. The imposter, the dreaded accountant or chartered surveyor, was coming into their lives in order to destroy her. If all that was going on, he wasn't going to stick around and see the end; her humiliation and devastation.

He had to get away from his moaning, morose and innocent mother and that urn on the mantelpiece containing his father's ashes. "Can you assure me that I am not dead already?"

The rabbi's response was a snigger. "Sorry!"

"Can I at least phone my best friend, Albion Krichevsky; or text him?"

He clutched his mobile, hard in his pocket. No answer was the loud reply. "Okay! Let's go. Take me far from Muswell Hill. Open my eyes with visions of joy and destruction."

"They said I should expect such courage from you."

"Who are 'they?'"

The rabbi was intoning, mumbling.

"My lovely mother! She will be left all alone. I love her."

"Shmuel! Love and cruelty go together. Come! No more time to waste, but all the time in the world to wonder."

"Can I have a piss please?"

"Yes but double quick! The past awaits. No more time to waste. Come! But don't forget your skateboard."

Sam took a slash and quickly grabbed a few of his most favoured books, shoved them into his rucksack, snatched his skateboard and followed the old wizened wizard into the closing bookcase.

"Follow me!"

"WHOOSH!"

The rabbi's voice echoed, gathering volume.

"Into the Tunnel of Return." He boomed into the hungry mouth of eternity.

Sam laughed and shivered.

"Gather energy, my dear boy." He shouted. "We are about to enter a very cold and dangerous world, that once was."

"It will make a change from Muswell Hill Broadway."

The rabbi farted. "Come; into the dark to find the light." And his farts rumbled on and on, into the land of eternal nowhere.

"*Gornisht mit gornisht*, nothing with nothing." The old

man uttered; then everything went silent.

"Goodbye my son, my only son." His father left him on the bank and got into the boat. Ben haggled with the hooded man who nodded and embraced him. The boat slipped into the fog that hovered above the waters of Whitechapel, and he could now just about make out his father, sitting beside the hooded man, rowing towards a far shore.

"Goodbye Dad!" Sam's voice echoed into the mists of nowhere. How could a father do that to his only begotten son? His devoted, loving father. Fathers like Ben Glass were hard to come by. Sam held up the urn of grey ashes. And he was gone.

3

Sam walked slowly; through the tunnel; he knew the rabbi could not be far. He could smell him. There was a rich stench of garlic, melding in with the overwhelming waves of sweat. Or maybe he had landed in an old sewer.

The dark tunnel was making a strange pulsing, singing sound; like he was back in the womb and waiting to be born. He was definitely not afraid, but his stomach churned over as he continued slowly forward. When his eyes came to terms with the dark, he could see the grotesque old man not too far ahead.

"Red Rabbi! Wait for me. You move too fast." He shouted. The rabbi laughed. "Ah! Shmuel! There you are. I've been looking for you everywhere."

"I'm not too happy in the dark. When I sleep I like to pull the cover right over me. I am not afraid, but may I hold onto you?"

"Absolutely! Hang on to my cloak. We must get moving or we'll never get there."

"Where's there?"

"The oldest riddle in the universe."

Sam got onto his skateboard, grabbed the rabbi's cloak and they soared upward. Sam's eyes clenched tight.

"Where are we going?"

No answer was the loud reply.

The dark had been slowly receding and the tunnel

seemed to have no ending. The rabbi reassured. "Fear not my son. It will take a few more millennia before it loses its potency. Now grab my hand and march!"

William Shakespeare! William Blake!
We are marching for your sake.

Sam sang one of Grandfather Maurice's ditties from the misty past, long before he was born.

"Those were great days, Sam, when we decided enough was enough. At a place called Aldermaston where we won the day. And we chanted slogans:

Men and women, stand together.
Do not heed the tongues of war.
Make you mind up, now or never`
Ban the bomb forever more.

Sam was proud that his Grandpa was once a rabble-rouser for peace.

Water dripped on to his forehead. He looked up. The sky was spitting rain and a crescent moon beamed down.

"Red Rabbi? How can that be? We're in a tunnel. How can the moon shine down through a stone ceiling?"

The Red Rabbi shrugged and moved even faster, trying, to outdo the boy. If he was a rabbi where the hell was his congregation?

Sam shouted. "Rabbi? Where's your synagogue?"

Again there was no response. The rabbi was going too fast for comfort, and Sam, for safety, detached his hand.

And the Red Rabbi was soon out of sight.

His heart was pounding and he was shivering. Now he knew he was afraid.

"Why has this happened to me?" He shouted and could hear his echo bouncing ahead. Only one person could now calm him. His mother.

He took out his mobile and prayed he could get a signal in this gigantic worm of a tunnel. He tapped in his home and it rang and rang at the other end. He was certain she had to be there. She simply had to be there. That's where mothers were meant to be. There!

"Hello!" She answered. "Hello? Who is it?"

"It's me. My darling, wonderful mother." He shmoosed, as he trotted forwards. She loved shmoose.

"Hello! Who's there? Who's there? She sounded angry. Agitated.

"Mum! It's me. Sam. It's Sam!"

"Hello! Is there anyone there?"

"Mum! I'm alright. I'm with the Red Rabbi. Ever heard of him? He's extraordinarily strange but he's great. Don't worry, He's not a perve. He's strictly kosher."

Again her voice. "No-one again. This bloody phone is crackling again. Whoever it is or isn't, please go to hell." And she clicked off.

"How could she do that to me, her only child? I hate her." He cried without tears. "Just when I need her."

A rat ran past. "Lucky rat! You have no family ties." He placed his hands around his mouth making a megaphone. "Rabbi! Red Rabbi! Where the hell are you?"

The Red Rabbi was no Virgil, to lead him away from this dank dark. He hated his imagination. And now he was terribly lost. And God and his representative were fucking wankers; disturbing him from the eternal sleep of Muswell Hill. Life was a miasma of unanswerable questions.

But then, joy of joys! Music was playing. Dance music. So all was not lost. Someone was singing, so beautifully.

A girl's voice; a plaintive voice:

> *Dancing in the dark and it soon ends;*
> *We're dancing in the dark ...*

And he could see a small alcove busy inventing itself; lit up in the darkness by a single candle flame. But the smallness of the alcove seemed to stretch to infinity. He entered, and there was a girl, slowly moving. Dancing. Her back to him, with one arm outstretched and the other twisting her hair, and it was she who was singing:

> *We're dancing in the wonder of why we're here.*
> *Time hurries by, we're here and gone.*
> *Looking for the light ...*

She turned and smiled, as if she knew he would be there.

"Hello! Samuel."

"Hello! How do you know my name?"

"I think I heard someone calling you." She shrugged. "I don't know. But then I know nothing."

"But you know you are here?"

"Where is here? Here is somewhere else. Everywhere is somewhere else." She came close and shone in the darkness. He was confronted by her haunted eyes.

"Do you love owls?" She asked with expectation.

"Yes! I am deeply in love with owls."

"Marvellous. I thought you might."

"Are you Minerva, the goddess of wisdom?" He replied.

"I had an owl once; a barn owl. I opened the cage and she flew away. But she turned her head all the way round as she reached the clouds. Then I heard her screech:

" 'Goodbye Anne! Goodbye.' "

"So, what are you doing here in the dark?" He asked.

"I write."

"What do you write?"

"Words! I write words." Then she changed the subject.

"And what are you doing in the dark?"

"I am Samuel Glass of Muswell Hill and I think I'm on a quest."

"What sort of quest?"

"Ithica! You see! It's not the destination but the journey. Quests are the journey." He was out to impress.

"I see." She said, not seeing. He laughed. She laughed.

"Tell me about Muswell Hill."

"It's a sort of leafy suburb, high over London. It's the enclave for somnambulists." He could not help showing off. It was deep in his bones.

"Sounds wonderful." She replied.

"It's a lovely place to escape from; if you are as mad as me. I love it, therefore I hate it. Where do you come from?" He felt he had overstepped himself.

"A place I can't quite place." She closed her eyes, trying to force herself back into a forgotten strand of time. "I might have been born into a place called Pogrom."

Sam thought he could hear something rumbling in the distance. It was not the Red Rabbi.

"Can you hear something?"

"Yes! All the time. The boxcars! The cattle wagons. I remember now. My name is Anne. So I am Anne. I keep on telling myself. You were Anne and you are Anne!"

"You are very lovely!" He remarked. It just slipped out.

"Lovely? Lovely? Thank you." She replied. "Have you run away from home? Home ran away from me."

"Yes! But I didn't run. I skateboarded with someone who calls himself the Red Rabbi."

"Home? Home! There was a cat and a mirror. And other humans. And candles. Alight. *Havdala*! And the Messiah bumped along the ceiling; playing hide and seek in the clouds. So here I am, and I must go back soon. Or who I am will not provide me with bread and water. And my pen nib gets angry."

She pointed at her alcove, now coming into full focus, and the gleam of golden light coming from the one flickering candle on the table.

"That's Anne's table. That's Anne's folding chair. That's Anne's candle. That's Anne's ink! And that's Anne's writing paper." She spoke like a child of five.

He felt the need to give her something. "Before I go may I sing you a troubadour song? Your face needs a song."

"I would like that." Her eyes lost their lostness.

"My voice is not too awful. I am in the school choir."

She seemed startled by the word. "School," she said, covering her ears for a moment. "Please sing."

"Right! I am Ariel and for this role I have a rather high voice." He thought he could hear the sea, calling from afar as he sang:

> *Full fathom five thy father lies;*
> *Of his bones are coral made;*
> *Those are pearls that were his eyes.*
> *Nothing of him that doth fade,*
> *But doth suffer a sea-change*
> *Into something rich and strange.*

She walked slowly backwards, away from him, like a frightened dancer. "That was the most beautiful sound I ever heard. Goodbye." She was about to return to her alcove, but the rattling noise was fast approaching. Sam froze, dead still.

"That noise again. Can you hear it?"

She sighed. "Anymore for the excursion to the sky?"

> Boxcar! Boxcar! Burning bright,
> in the forest of the night.

William Blake would have understood what he could not.

"Cattle truck and boxcar! The animals are crying, mooing. moaning!" She said.

"They're trailing away now. That's a relief," he said.

"Left and right; and right and wrong. Then take a shower and say goodbye. Goodbye." She offered her outstretched hand. He took it.

"Shake hands Samuel, shake hands and never do it again. Only death is immortal. We are all borrowed from death, so stay alive as long as you can. And thank you for stopping here and singing to me."

She entered her alcove and the candle flickered out and the dark enveloped her.

"Goodbye Anne!" He shouted, and, then, almost in the same breath, the rabbi appeared.

"Here I am, Master Glass, at your side."

"Where have you been?"

"Forgive me, my dear, impatient, Shmuel. Nature must. I was having a most wonderful shit. I feel quite euphoric." He laughed from the depth of his guts and gently punched his young companion. "Don't be deterred by a turd."

42

He thought of his mate, Adrian Aaronson, whose toilet needs were of the infantile kind, and who was also a turd.

"Come Shmuel! Cheer up. We are well on our way."

"Well on our way to where?"

"We are well on our way to Vitebsk!"

"Vitebsk? Where is Vitebsk? And I don't have my passport."

"Dear boy, Vitebsk is in Belorussia. A beautiful pearl of town in the *shtetl*. It has even more Jews than Stamford Hill! When we get there it will be eighteen eighty one but it must not shock you. We will find ourselves in the mighty jaws of the greater Russian empire, the hungry wolf that gobbles up everything."

"Vitebsk? I don't like the sound of it."

"It is your birthright. Vitebsk flows in your blood. You are too full of questions. In my world there are no questions, only answers."

"Answer me this then. Don't you think you should clean yourself up?"

"Sorry my darling boy, I don't think I understand."

"You look a little dishevelled. There are soup stains all over your cloak. And you pong like a farmyard. If we are going to an important town and you look like this, won't it bring trouble?"

"My dear boy, thank you very much. I just smell the normal detritus of living. All decent rabbis are soup-stained; our minds and souls are clean and clear and far away in dreams and holy practices. But thank you very much for your kind words. Come Shmuel! We are well on our way. So cheer up."

The rabbi looked up at the sky and clicked two bony

fingers together, and the sun came blazing down; drenching them with light.

"*Emet* is the magic. Emet is truth. Truth is world. What is world? World is existence. What is existence? It is phenomena. What is phenomena? It is life. What is life? Life is truth. And what is man and what is woman? We are magic! Emet! We are the miracle, torn from the bleeding thigh of a dying god."

"Thank you rabbi. I love all this."

"Then love my soiled soup-stained cloak." They laughed and marched on; taking long rhythmic strides. Sam rolled back along the years to when the beautiful young girl, his mother, diffused by golden sunlight, shouted and giggled when he sucked her breast too hard. And she had laid him in his cot and sung so softly:

> *How many miles to Babylon?*
> *Three score and ten.*
> *Will we get there by candlelight?*
> *Yes, there and back again.*

"We shall reach Vitebsk tomorrow morning." The Red Rabbi said. "And we owe ourselves a good night's sleep. It is all arranged. Look! Down that slope! Can't you see it? There! That inn! The Halfway Inn. Strictly kosher, of course. And tomorrow morning we shall reach Vitebsk! Where all my friends are, living or dead. There you will discover who you really are. Trust me."

The words sent a chilling bolt of ice, all the way down his spine.

"What are we waiting for?" Sam said, covering his

trepidation, living each uncertain moment. Here he would not find the safety of the suburb. It was living; it was adventure. It was a fantastic and fearful journey of danger and delight. He was climbing the Everest of his dreams.

"Onward!" The rabbi shouted. "We are almost there. Just around that next corner, where we shall find repast, and grateful rest for the necessary night."

4

Sam wasn't sure if was day or night. He was tired and he was imagining things. The two halves of time were being married in the bed of the sky and were turning and melting into each other. The sun was shooting flashing tongues of fiery sparks into the mouth of the moon, his lover.

He followed the rabbi towards a yellow house with a blackened door that had just swung open for them.

"Remember! This is the year eighteen eighty one and Alexander the Second is on his bloody throne."

A rather sinister woman appeared, smiling and bowing. She had the makings of a moustache. The witches of fiction were just as fetching. She had the most grotesque pock-marked face and body he had ever seen.

"Ah! Just in time, my masters. I am, I believe, the housekeeper, and the beasts are all gone, hurried away before dawn. Thanks be to the God who loves us all. I knew you were coming and I know why you are here. So, welcome. Please, come inside. You will be wanting food and prayer no doubt."

"Leave out the prayer." The Red Rabbi joked. Then he kissed the *Mezuzah*, the ancient little box containing a copy of the sacred scrolls, fixed on every Jewish door. Sam followed, kissing his fingers and touching the marquetry case.

The rabbi poked his nose inside and breathed in the dusty air. "Ah! Things smell better now that the *Malacha Movis*, the Angel of Death, will not be visiting us tonight."

They entered. No other person was inside to greet them.

"You are the only guests tonight. Please sign your precious names in the book, my masters."

The book was almost a foot thick and bound in stained, red leather. The rabbi sang happily, mumbling to himself as he scrawled his indecipherable signature. Sam took up the hopeless quill and entered his sudden new name. "Ozymandias Percy Bysshe Shelley".

"How may I please you my masters, for your stomachs delight? Perhaps some yummy Blood Borsht with sprinkled matured gizzard for starters? And for tonight's main course I recommend a rare speciality; gently fried bulls' testicles with local wild mushrooms; garnished in vodka, rosemary and garlic."

"Thank you, but no thank you. My young friend and I are dead tired and must go straight to bed." The Red Rabbi yawned.

"My pleasure, sir." She chuckled and bowed again, with theatrical flourish. "Have fun and behave yourselves for a good, sound sleep."

"Have fun and behave ourselves? We can't have both." Sam said wearily. His brain had largely shut off, but he managed to follow the creaking man up the creaking stairs to the attic.

The room was expecting them. The eiderdowns on the two made-up beds were pulled back, revealing two pristine white sheets. The coal fire crackled in the grate and the golden flickering flames sang a welcoming, yearning

Yiddish song, *Tif in Vedele*, Deep in the Forest.

"Why are we Jews so sad?" Sam yawned.

"This is the country for sadness." The rabbi replied. The rabbi kept his shoes and clothes on as he bounced into bed. Sam thought he would just keep his trousers and his boots on. Two essentials if he had to make a getaway in the night.

Sam soon didn't know if he was awake or asleep. "Life! It becomes more and more absurd. Are you asleep, rabbi?"

"Yes!" The rabbi whispered. His eyes were closed and his mouth wide open, and he held in his hand a pre-historic set of false dentures.

"Rabbi! Tell me. How many times have you almost died?" An avalanche of snores was the reply.

Sam desperately needed to speak to someone. His mobile lived in his inner pocket; sometimes it chirped with the beat of his heart. Without his mobile he would be truly lost. Maybe this time he would get through. He reached for his jacket and tried to ring his home again. But there was nothing. The mobile was dead. And he knew there were no batteries to be found in eighteen eighty one.

In a sudden fit, he hurled the mobile away. This was the end of the world that was.

"Only chicken soup can save me from a fate worse than life."

He laughed with tears. He enjoyed his sense of humour. It was his second weapon. He pulled on his first weapon; but it was into pathetic droop so he decided to retreat to the lost continent of sleep; where all his mates were waiting for him. All his friends had deserted him, even if he was the one who had been blown away.

48

He was drifting like a kite, high above Kite Hill on Hampstead Heath. "Rabbi! What is the answer?"

"The answer is shut up." The sleeping man turned over.

"The answer is there is no answer? I'm dreaming this! I'm dreaming that I'm dreaming. Oh, that clever God, who tries to convince you that tomorrow is going to be better than today."

Sam did a swallow, down, down into the arms of his mother. He was gliding across the silent fields of deep snow, to the land without words.

Next, the rabbi was shaking him.

"Shmuel! Shmuel! Wake up." The sun, the real daylight sun was streaming gold into the room. The rabbi was awake and doing handstands fully clothed.

"Shmuel! You've been talking in your sleep. Time to enter the day. Time is precious. Get up."
Sam leapt out of bed.

"Today is the day of days. Come, my son. Breakfast."
Sam went to the shutters and they opened and there was Vitebsk, unrolling before him. The dazzling sun crept out of the mist, daubing the sky with Crimson Lake.

"If I were a painter this would be my perfect day. Look! Mist is avalanching towards the town."

"That's not mist." The old man said. "That's smoke. Breathe in boy! Enjoy their dreams, their nightmares; the screams of all those creatures who were fed to the flames. It never ends."

He laughed darkly. His eyes became slits. "But that's all in the past, and the future."

Sam's stomach was punching from within. "I can smell food. If we don't hurry I shall die."

"Shmuel! I shall keep telling you, you are not the dying sort. Down my boy, down; down into the day. Last man down is a *schmock*. That is to say, something of a prick."

With that, the rabbi bolted and beat him down the stairs.

"Not bad from an oldish man born in sixteen sixty six or was it fifteen fifty five?"

The Red Rabbi let out a thunderous fart. "Better to have an empty house than a bad tenant." And they entered the dark hole of the dining room where huge saucepans were bubbling way.

The woman was already there, smirking, red in the face. "Good morning and welcome my masters. Help yourself to the breakfast I have laid out for you."

"Ah, wilderness is paradise, e'now." Sam was wildly in love with the feast spread before him. The long oak table was crammed with bowls of every possible kind of delicatessen.

He breathed in deeply. He was starving. This was the real thing. He concentrated on the holy act of controlling desire; the killing anticipation, holding off the endgame; like slow masturbation, so he could be deserving of the incredible crescendo; the shattering, falling into the climax.

"You must have been up all night, preparing this feast."

"I am always up all night. You know." She nudged him.

"Up! You know, young sir. A nice bit of up! Without a nice drop of up where are we?"

Being close to a crude and lewd woman was the worst thing that Sam could imagine in this life. He ignored her wide, popping and expectant eyes. But the food – what could be better? Better even than his hot weapon. What a way to die. Not from starvation but from stuffing yourself.

So where should he begin?

He savoured and smelled every dish. A mountain of salt beef. Enough to make one die of joy! Smaltz herrings! Latkes! Chopped liver! Egg and onion. The doors of heaven were opening wide. "Look! A grinning smoked salmon, amazing!" Everything here was keeping the wheels of this Yiddish world running and making even Jewish survival possible!

The woman, with her wobbling whoppers bursting out of her bodice, grinned and spoke with a watery voice.

"Excuse me, my handsome boy. I feel hot and weak and funny all over. I think I'll lie down; in the second room on the left. If you come into me we can talk about afters and I can make you welcome and happy."

Sam felt queasy. Then he noticed the Star of David on a thick, golden chain with a small skull attached, dangling from her neck.

"Wait! By the way, you are Jewish, aren't you?"

"I am anything you want me to be."

She could not be Jewish. He had never witnessed a Jew with warts. Her whole flesh was probably covered with warts.

She winked and smiled at him.

"I noticed that you were admiring my lovely Star of David. But have you seen these?" She lifted her hair to expose her ears. Each lobe had an earring; and on the earrings was a cross. "Not taking any chances. If I am not the daughter of God or the devil, I am the daughter of both."

Sam looked around to the rabbi, to share his derision. But the rabbi was too far away, somewhere in the universe, swaying, praying, mumbling a *niggun*, one of his people's wordless, timeless tunes.

51

"He's well away, your boss. So grab! Take! *Fress*! Eat, while you're alive. You never know your luck; you could easily be dead cold before the long night comes and comes again and fog descends and ascends and we all lose our dignity and virginity, thank the bloody Lord."

"I must eat" said Sam.

She held her open hand close up against her face. "*Toi! Toi! Toi!*" And she spat seven times through her fingers. "Eat while you can. Eat in good health. The Malacha Movis hovers."

She went close; the tip of her tongue almost in his ear. "I've got something special for you, when you've demolished this lot. It will make your pipik squeak. Don't forget. Second door on the left."

She moved backwards, slowly away, and hung on the edge of the door like Talullah Bankhead, an old Hollywood star, and with a final parting come-on look she disappeared. Sam shrugged. It was time to fall on the feast.

The Red Rabbi returned to the world. "Careful! My boy! She's one of those anti-Semites who needs to be close to Jews. We must go. Now! There are even kosher zombies in this world and we must go at once." He grabbed the boy and pulled him to the door.

"My breakfast! My wonderful breakfast. Let me go. I'll die without my breakfast."

"You'll die with it! Shmuel! It is all an illusion! From the spittle of the Evil One! Black molasses of magic! As potent as a universe without the holy *Hashem*."

"Let me go! Let me go!" But Sam could not fight against such sudden strength.

"This is eighteen eighty one. She will have your guts for

52

garters. Quick! Out! Out. Out of this place. Now!"

They were outside and Sam was sobbing uncontrollably.

"That breakfast! It was worth dying for."

"Away! Away, Shmuel! Be thankful you are still alive. Just breathe in this glorious morning."

They were not twenty-five feet along the road when they heard her shouting. She was trying to run after them.

"Come back! Come back. You Yid bastards!" She shouted. "You haven't paid."

The rabbi shouted back. "I never pay. I am the Red Rabbi. I have special dispensation from my Beth Din, my Jewish court that dispenses divine earthly justice."

There was no answer. They continued jogging along the sleeping road.

"We come across them occasionally. Those whose souls have no resting place, and are tormented by demons."

Sam was back into the world; emitting his first true Jewish sigh. "Conned by a zombie, who almost tempted me by smoked salmon to yield my manhood. Wicked, wicked woman!"

"She is one of those who belong to the other side; who ingratiate and harbour the lost."

"Then, farewell, sweaty lady," said Sam. "May flights of devils sing thee to thy death." They disappeared into the tight, hugging alleyways.

"Sam! Listen! Can you hear the Almighty, Hashem, laughing? He is pleased with us."

Sam nodded. "I thought you said God didn't exist."

"Sometimes we have to reinvent him, to keep him happy. Now we are truly on our way."

"Thank you, rabbi. Now can I finally know why I am here?"

"Shmuel! That is the biggest question of all." The rabbi marched on with remarkable speed and Sam had to mount his skateboard to keep up with him.

"And, voilà! Vitesbk!" The old man shouted with jubilation; as if he had created the town, opening before them.

A bunch of kids joined them in the town square, dancing around them, jabbering with wild delight at the sight of the two strangers racing over the dusty roads. They were pointing and poking and especially delighted by Sam's wondrous means of travel.

"You could become the richest man on this earth if you had toboggans for all these unfortunate and beautiful children in this mighty kingdom of Russia. Shall we rest here, Shmuel? Are you tired?"

"No! I can't wait now to get to where we are going. I have new wind."

They passed oddly shaped houses, jagged and sloping, nuzzling into each other as if afraid that time was on the rampage. Houses that should have fallen down long ago, but somehow managed to survive.

Few people were about. One or two diagonal groping skeletons slowly crossed the streets. And all was silence, except for the rattling boxcars coming and going in the distance, passing from somewhere to somewhere.

"I love Vitebsk. It was in seventeen eighty five when I emerged from the chaos of gornisht, out of the everlasting ocean of time."

"Rabbi! Sam groaned. "Make up your mind when you were born. A liar needs a good memory."

"What's in a sprinkling of few years? Come. We are almost there. To the world that once was."

The marketplace was a different kettle of pickled herrings. It was busy with people buying and selling in almost silence.

"They are not dead. They merely cannot face this wicked world. Can you blame them? But do not be misled by these ragged, beautiful, scum of the earth. One day soon they will all awake and rise up and change the world."

"I know where you are taking me. A journey across the forbidden, shrinking Aral Sea to Kazakhstan."

The rabbi shook his head.

"Then it must be the Golden Road to Samarkand."

The Red Rabbi shook his head.

"Where then? Where?" Sam cried as he continued running with his trainer, the Red Rabbi.

"I know why I came. Do you know why I came?"

The rabbi shook his head.

"I had to get away to find myself. I have to grow up."

"We don't grow up. We cover up. Who finds himself? You have to live long enough just to learn how to survive."

"Rabbi! This is my rite of passage. My odyssey for doomed youth. How fortunate I am. I am a dreamer. When I get home I am going to grab the urn and fling the ashes out of the window and watch the wind scatter them."

They marched on towards the countryside, at the far end of Vitebsk. The rabbi nodded. "Good boy. See that field? Sloping up to those gentle hills? That's where we are going. We are now truly on our way to where we change this world."

"Tell me more."

The rabbi turned his eyes skyward.

"I just want to understand." Sam uttered.

"He wants to understand. What impertinence." He stroked the young man's face.

"Shmuel, We have been invited to a wedding. It is important for you to be there. They are waiting for us. There will be food and drink galore."

"At last!"

"They shall be so pleased to see us. Things have got far worse. This much I can tell you. You are the final link. You will give us that extra insurance for the action."

Sam didn't know what he meant. But his stomach was rumbling.

"And you say there will be oodles of food?"

"More than even you could stomach. This is a celebration of magnitude. The marriage of all the pieces of the jigsaw. There will be champagne and food from all the continents of the world, and the world will rejoice after the cleansing of the murderers. This much I can tell you."

"Rabbi, with all your words you have told me nothing."

In the distance he could hear klezmer; a swooping clarinet and the heart strings of violin.

"It is our music Shmuel, born out of sadness, a gift from God to face and ease our journey."

"But you do not believe in God, you old bastard." Sam teased. The rabbi ignored him and jiggled up and down.

"You will soon dance the Kazatsky with me," he said. Then he hunched down on his knees. "We are the *Chutzpah* Comrades. We invented this Jewish dance long ago; long before it was pinched by those Cossack gonifs, as their own creation. Those thieves couldn't even create a smile of snot. You don't believe me? Be fearful. Be vigilant. In this world there are but two creatures. The Jew and the Jew-hater."

56

Sam was pleased to see a crowd before him and the old man and the young man went straight in amongst the jolly mass.

The rabbi scooted off, as if he had forgotten his charge.

"Wait for me! Rabbi! Wait for me" The icy wind froze on his face and sang its own piercing song.

"What a funny day for a wedding in the open," thought Sam.

The party continued around him, and the smiling ladies held up bubbling glasses to the cold sun; as they laughed Sam heard in the background the sounds of cattle in their bolted wagons.

The Red Rabbi put his arm around the boy. "Come! You'll warm up soon enough." He blew a kiss towards the *chuppah*. The wedding canopy had four poles, entwined with flowers, draped in cotton of blue and white.

"Shmuel! I quote directly three immortal lines from the Talmud. 'All brides are beautiful. Youth is a wreath of roses and the world is a wedding.' "

They were now close enough, for there was the bride, her back towards him beneath the chuppah, in her gown of glistening silver. They were just in time for the climax of the ceremony. The groom raised his foot and stamped it down on the glass goblet and smashed it to smithereens.

"*Mazel tov!*" Everyone shouted.

"This is to remember the destruction of the temple."

"Rabbi, I am not entirely ignorant; even if I do not dwell in tents, but in Muswell Hill." Sam whispered. "But why are we here? What has this got to do with anything?"

And everyone burst into song, wishing the groom and his bride good fortune.

And the couple embraced and were joined by their guests swarming like honey bees, under the canopy.

"These are my holy grandchildren. Sarah and Akiva! And this match is surely made in heaven; if heaven exists."

"Please tell me why we are here and what is going to happen to me?"

"Shmuel! It is not for me to enlighten you. I am merely the courier in this affair; but now you must meet the bride; the boss who will tell you everything. She is longing to meet you."

The bride was still busy hugging her husband; kissing him all over his face and flaxen head of hair. Sam could hear her excited words. "I am in heaven; I cannot believe we are one at last. You have made me the happiest woman in Russia, if not the world. I love you my darling one; my only one. Forever."

Her voice was so familiar; so terribly familiar. And then she abruptly turned her beautiful face towards him, smiling as if she already knew he was there.

"Samuel! My darling! My love." Her arms opened for him. "My darling Samuel, come to me!"

Sam could not believe his eyes. He had no words; there were all scrambled, lost in his mouth and his blood was draining away in his head.

"Rabbi. How can it be? She is my mother." These were his last words, before he fainted.

5

"Please wake up, my son. Please! My lovely son." Her sweet smile and soft, coaxing voice helped him to his feet.

"You are my mother! How can that be? I don't understand what is happening to me."

"I am Sarah! Be patient Samuel, all will be made apparent very soon." She turned to her new husband. "Akiva! So many of you were against me but now I am vindicated. Come and greet this amazing boy; the one I chose."

It was all happening too fast; if this was being awake he would rather be dreaming. Sam's mind was swirling in a whirlpool of confusion. "Chose for what?" And he grabbed another drink from a dwarfish waitress who wore a frightening owl mask.

He was drinking too much, and all the bubbles he was draining down unsteadied him. The young, handsome man, Akiva, came to shake his hand. Sam squeezed a weak, clammy hand. He could never trust a man with such a handshake. Akiva reminded him of someone he had met quite recently.

It was all coming back. Akiva was a cardboard version of David; the man who was trying to snake his way into his mother's body. The man he hated and despised.

He remembered those lessons he had learned at school; of how to cover up that cesspit of emotions, with a soft smile and a gentle, charming voice. "With that you will win the world," he was told.

"How nice to meet you Akiva! And by the way, mazel tov!" It was like that with some people. You could read them immediately. They were after something and not to be trusted. How could a woman with such radiance and beauty give herself to such a feeble human?

Sam turned to the young bride. "You are my mother, but younger." He was trying hard to appear at ease. "Please tell me who you are and what I am doing here."

"Akiva! Can you leave us, my darling? I need to speak with Samuel. Alone."

"Absolutely. I understand, my love." And Akiva wandered back down to the wedding party where many of the guests were a little less than sober. She took his hand and hers was warm, sending shivers of content all through him.

"Come! Samuel! Look! That seat on top of the hill. Let us go there. I will tell you everything." Her words calmed him and she took his arm. It was very strange and weird to be walking across a field with a bride clutching him.

They passed some stooping old ladies, who were clearing up discarded plates and glasses. It was getting cold and the rain was starting to slant down from out of a clear, cobalt sky. Except for a few drunken stragglers, most of the crowd had evaporated. There were some who refused to acknowledge that the party was over. And a few others were dancing alone with steps of introspective sadness.

Klezmer still swooned and swooped; creating a deep-rooted mood of Yiddish yearning. And the oblivious, ragged musicians were happy, meandering down the grassy slopes, playing for themselves.

"You are so cold." She said. "Your hands are like ice."

She stopped and rubbed them back into life and she kissed his fingers. Her closeness worried and excited him. He closed his eyes and breathed in the exact aroma of his mother's hair.

"How can you be my mother?"

A voice interrupted the reverie. "Sarah! Do you need me? Shall I come with you?" It was the Red Rabbi calling, struggling up the hill after them.

"Rabbi! No! I've told you already. Go back to my lovely husband Akiva, and keep him company. He will understand. Go! Now!"

It was obvious to Sam who was the boss.

The dejected rabbi turned. "I understand. Anyway, that vodka is potent fire. I need more." And he gambolled back down, downhill, skipping like a ferocious infant.

"Rabbi!" She shouted. "Careful! Take care. Don't fall and break all your broken bones."

When they reached the top of the slope he sat on the bench and she huddled beside him.

"Samuel! I've waited for this moment so long."

"Please. Just explain." He repeated. "How can you be my mother?"

She pondered, but smiled her radiance. And the air and the view were breathtaking. And he drained down the last of champagne and gasped for breath and his heart was thumping fast.

"I feel like running away. I don't know where, but I shall just run and run into nowhere, because my brain is about to explode from madness. And I need answers, quickly."

She put her arm around him to comfort him.

"I don't know where I am." He burst into tears.

"My dearest Samuel. This is the year eighteen eighty one and I am your great, great, great grandmother."

He did not dare to show surprise.

"Tell me more. NOW!" He wiped his tears away with his cuff.

She continued. "I knew of you from the day you were born. It was I who decided that you should come to us in our cause. It is all in the family, in the bloodline, somewhere, somehow, my dearest Samuel.

"Some are born to lead and actions need decisive leaders. And the dream of anarchism is my entire life. I am a leader of the *Narodnaya Volya*! The People's Will. What did your Percy Byshe Shelley exclaim: 'Rise like lions after slumber'? That's exactly what we are doing."

"You are very beautiful," he whispered. The fragrance of her body was more sweet, and potent as any bottle of champagne. She possessed a ring of certainty, a halo of strength and a will of iron.

He closed his eyes and laughed. A great burden had been lifted. He could help change the world. He was an anarchist.

"I am an anarchist. I am an anarchist." The words had magic when he shouted them aloud. He was wanted and loved.

"Yes Samuel! You are to help make this world a better place. Now let's go to my dacha. Come, you must be hungry."

The sky was now purple dark and he floated with her. Everyone had vanished except for silver silhouettes of the Red Rabbi and Akiva, dancing and embracing, laughing at nothing, and trying to remain perpendicular. Sam and

Sarah walked downhill towards the forest of foliage.

"Oh look. Look!" She said. "Look at those barn owls circling above us."

He stopped and stared and she glistened in the night.

"I remember I was desperate, lonely and sad after my father died. You know, Sarah, I loved him, and I hated him for dying. And he was gone. And the bookcase opened and here I am."

"Yes. Perfect timing." She responded. "Thanks to the incredible, irascible Red Rabbi, our impossible courier. He begged to go on this mission. How could I deny him, the only immortal I know?"

"He brought me here, to do exactly what?"

"Samuel. Everything is connected. We were destined to meet at this precise moment in time. No more questions."

And she kissed his cheek and he sailed to the owls in the moon.

"And here we are. My dacha! My home. My haven! You will love it. There's food laid out for you; and books to read."

The white palatial house was substantial, but you could not see the windows, because of the entangling foliage. It was fit for a queen – or a witch.

"After you've had a bath and we've eaten I will tell you how we intend to change our world."

She took a key from between her illuminated breasts. She opened the green door. And they entered.

"We will go straight to the feast." She said.

"Thank you. You are so kind."

"Shmuel! Sarah! What kept you?" The Red Rabbi shouted from the dining room. "We've been here for hours."

"And I'm famished." chimed Akiva.

"How did they get here before us? They were miles behind."

She shrugged.

The smell of the food was amazing; intoxicating. He breathed in deep and became dizzy. He could barely stand.

"My poor darling. It is all too much for you." She hugged him close and steadied him from falling over. The men came. "What's wrong?"

A sudden narcolepsy was engulfing him, like a giant wave of an ocean. He was ready to collapse into deep sleep. Food would have to wait.

"Have I a bedroom?"

"Samuel! Of course."

"Careful! Careful does it. I'm taking you upstairs."

And there was the door of the bedroom, opening for him and the bed ready.

"Please go," he gasped. Then his head hit the pillow and he hurtled down, spiralling into sleep; safe and deep, into the arms of Morpheus.

He was soaring over the dacha and then down, down to the soundless garden, where arum lilies and roses were vying for attention. "Look at me! Look at me!" They demanded. And in the pond the reflection of mauve irises rippled and swayed in the dark green water. And the scent of the blossoming myrtle bush enveloped him. A girl came slowly from the distant horizon towards him.

He was dreaming and poetry enveloped him. He was going deeper and deeper into a world where he wanted to be. And the words of Coleridge came to him.

Weave a circle round him thrice,
And close your eyes with holy dread,
For he on honey-dew hath fed,
And drunk the milk of Paradise.

She was close, and floated a few inches above the grass.

"Hello Anne." He said.

"Hello Samuel." She replied.

"Why are you not in your alcove?"

"Such a lovely day! And why are you not in Muswell Hill?"
She went straight to the myrtle bush, breathed in deeply,
snapping off a branch, and then she lay down beside him,
waving the magic frond.

"'A damsel with a dulcimer in a vision once I saw....'" He
began.

"Make love to me." She said.

"My pleasure!" He replied.

"And I shall wave the myrtle branch." She shook the blossom
over his face and body.

"It is my first time." He said.

"It is my first time." She replied. "Love me. Love me, before
I go down into the everlasting night and fog."

There was an absolute silence as they melted into each other.

And it was morning and the myrtle branch was lying on
the pillow, beside him. Someone was tapping on the door.
He returned into his body and to who and where he was.

"Samuel! Are you awake? We've been waiting for you.
It's breakfast time," said Queen Sarah, the hungry she-
wolf!

"I'll be down in a few moments." He replied.

"We've decided to breakfast at our famous watering hole;

the Café Cosmo. You will love it. Please hurry."

"Thank you! I'm there already." He opened the door.

"Oh! That warm, perfumed body will drive me insane." His thoughts contained no shame, no fear. He was not homesick any longer. She had changed everything.

"Guess what I found in my bed?" He held up and shook the myrtle branch.

"You extraordinary young man! This is myrtle from my sacred tree. How did you manage that?"

"It was Anne. She comes to me. She loves me."

"You have dreams that are out of this world. But remember we also have extraordinary dreams and our dreams will come true."

"Sarah! Where are you? We've been waiting and waiting and time is of the essence." It was Akiva, complaining, and now standing beside her.

Her anger flared. Her eyes were poisoned darts. "Akiva! How dare you! Get out of my sight. What we are discussing is of great consequence." He shuddered and retreated backwards pathetically, "Sorry." He said. "Sorry Sarah!" He backed away, almost bowing.

Sam was astonished. "I don't understand. You married him only yesterday; yet you seem so angry with him."

"I love him. And my necessary way of dealing with my beloved is called the 'Whip of Love'." She replied. And then she went.

He dashed to the bathroom, dripped a few spots of water on his face and did not bother to dry them. And there, as she promised, were the neat piled clothes. All this had been arranged; ordained. And he pushed his nose into the pile and breathed in their soft freshness; that special smell of

66

newly washed linen; a feast as good as newly baked bread.

He so wanted to speak to his mother and he reached into his bag, for his mobile. Then he remembered it was not there. He had thrown it away. The die was cast. There was now no way back.

"Shmuel! You need to come! We are all waiting." The Red Rabbi called out.

Sam rushed downstairs and through the open door and joined them in the street.

A cluster of ragged children yelped and followed. "The bogeyman! The bogeyman! The man who can't ever die." They chanted and the rabbi yelped: "Go home and get your mouths washed."

Sarah and Sam breathed in the dust. "I love this place," said Sarah. "Vitebsk! It smells like no other place. It is a womb of safety and joy."

Sam nodded. He felt at home amid the huddled houses and narrow streets that looked even older than time.

"We live here; we belong here; we long here. Pushkin the greatest writer of all time loved it here. The world that is and was will be gone forever."

The rabbi sidled close and whispered in his ear.

"Shmuel! We are going to assassinate the Tsar. That's all."

"WHAT? You've let the cat out of the bag. Idiot." Sarah hissed and raged at the rabbi. "How dare you? How could you? You know my orders! How could you be so stupid to speak of this? I warned you. And now I wish I could rid myself of you!"

Tears were welling into the old man's eyes. "Sorry. I'm so sorry. Sarah, forgive me. Please! It slipped out."

"I wish you could slip out. You *momser*, you old numbskull bastard." She hissed.

Akiva took her hands and stared close into her eyes.

"Darling Sarah! We are just a few streets away from the centre. People are watching. But no-one heard him. No real harm has been done."

Sarah drew back and went to the old man. "Rabbi, dry your eyes. It is unseemly for a rabbi to cry; even if you are immortal. We must not spoil anything by a foolish slip of the tongue. The tyrant's spies are everywhere. Even in Vitebsk."

Sam was agog; the Red Rabbi and Sarah had struck fear into his heart. This soft and steely Amazon ancestor was going to lead him to murder.

"Shmuel Glass! You are far too young and brittle to be carrying the burdens of the world. Rare intelligence often brings such raw vulnerability. Not to worry! We will soon toughen you up."

"Yes, please." Sam desired to be hardened on this odyssey into this dark world.

Then he noticed a very pretty young woman strolling towards them. She had a very sexy countenance; every female seemed sexy to him, but she stood out; she was special.

As she got closer she slowed down and went towards them. "Akiva! How wonderful to see you! I was just thinking about you." Akiva seemed puzzled. "Really? How nice!"

Her plump breasts captured the youth's eyes! "What wonders!" He swooned. They were riding free under her jerkin and her hips were ever so gently gliding, sliding from side to side. She was aware and proud of the enticing gifts that God had bestowed on her.

Akiva and the girl were now as close as love.

"Akiva! You don't remember me, after all those wonderful times together?"

"Sorry. You've slipped my mind." Akiva looked helplessly towards Sarah, who was using this moment to look at herself in her make-up mirror; she was not amused by this encounter.

"No! I just don't remember you."

She winked. "The marvellous naughty things we did together. In Minsk! Wasn't it? Or was it Pinsk? How could you forget your little playmate? Tamara Levinsky."

It was not a good start for a wedding of just a few days.

Sam's eyes shifted to her hips. The sight of them was enough to excite the sudden stretching weapon inside his trousers.

Akiva suddenly lit up. "Of course! It's all coming back. Forgive me. Tamara Levinksy. It actually was in Odessa! We had both just joined ... he slowly whispered his next words ... "The People's Will."

"I still belong." She whispered back. "You seem so careful now. You were not so careful then." She chuckled. "Going somewhere nice? Café Cosmo?" She laughed. "Where else? Akiva! You look so handsome, so strong. I never got over you. Give me a big goodbye hug, you handsome, powerful brute of a man."

A safety curtain of snow started gently falling on Vitebsk. Akiva was dancing away from the girl's embrace. Then in a flash the girl's right hand was free and she it held high. She was holding a glinting dagger and was about to plunge it into the carotid artery in Akiva's throat.

For a second, time was suspended, no-one moved, they were statues in the freezing street.

Then a shot rang out. And another! And another!

And Sam could see the horizontal body of Tamara Levinsky, lying on the cobbles, like a thrown away Barbie doll, oozing blood from her mouth. And the pure, white, snow carpet of the ground was stained crimson. Her eyes were open but they were dead and fixed forever.

"We must get away from this." Sarah said, secreting the revolver away, into her ample muff.

Sam had witnessed a shocking murder and he was astonished, and petrified, yet somehow elated; that two beautiful young women could be so deadly and act so coldly.

"Sarah! This is a terrible to thing to have done. How could you kill her?" She looked at him grimly but smiling.

"You saw how she tried to murder my lovely husband. What could I do? What should I say? 'Go ahead'. We have been married for just two days. That's quite enough. I am an anarchist and willing to do any deed to help the cause. Nothing must get in our way. Now let's go into the Cosmo and have a nice breakfast."

6

"My loathing for the greed of our society burns inside me, Samuel. I want to wipe this capitalist regime off the face of the earth." Sarah explained as they entered Café Cosmo. The Red Rabbi began a little jig. And they followed him towards an empty table.

The waiter shuffled slowly, slouching towards them, wincing at every step he ventured. He was well over retirement age and his feet were giving him lots of trouble.

"Ah my dear lady; may I be importunate enough to say you are a very beautiful woman. As for my handsome gentlemen, what can I do you for?"

Sam immediately recognised a certain likeness to his wonderful grandad; with terrible jokes but always full of chutzpah and shmooze.

"We're starving, as usual." Akiva responded. "Four traditional Russian breakfasts!"

"Perfect! What else?" Sam said, eagerly.

Sarah gently tugged his earlobe. "How very nice to be with you for breakfast, Samuel. You will love it. It's better than passion. Blinis, latkes and sour cream. What could be better? And lashings of black Russian tea."

The waiter came with his trolley of food and a silver samovar. "Your breakfast. Eat in good health." And he hobbled away.

They all tucked into the most important act of a Jewish

congregation, stuffing yourself, because the world could be coming to an end at any moment.

Akiva grunted, and then unexpectedly became talkative. "There is a Russian saying. Eat breakfast yourself. Share dinner with a friend, but give supper to your enemy. Breakfast is considered the most important meal of the day; it should not be shared or given away. One normally needs to eat breakfast silently; but we are here out of friendship."

"Not only friendship. We are here to clear the air and to tell Samuel what we intend to do," she said.

Sam was experiencing a minute twitch of ecstasy. Not just from the food. Fancy fancying your own flesh and blood; your very own great, great, great grandmother! How could he even think of crossing the forbidden line? He was in a sort of wondrous agony downstairs, in the basement of his daydreams.

All faces turned to Sarah. What a beautifully tough and ruthless leader she was.

"The waiting is over. Tomorrow we leave for Saint Petersburg to join our comrades. I have ordered a droshky from Nathan Leboff. But first, rabbi, I must be frank. You have succeeded as usual beyond expectation. But now we do not want to draw attention to ourselves or our mission will end before it starts. So you must clean yourself up and cut the jokes. We must all stay as silent as possible. The bastards who rule us are everywhere and if they find us we will be tortured and killed."

"Please!" Sam spoke with a hush. "You say the secret police are everywhere. Why then have you chosen such a public place for disclosing terrifying details?"

"Samuel, my darling! This is the best place. Believe me. Here, no-one is listening. Anarchists and bohemians are far too busy listening to their own voices."

But Sam wasn't entirely listening. "If this is a meeting place for anarchists why do they allow it? Why do they not pounce?"

"They like to know where we are, where we like to gather. So that they can pick us up any time, in one fell swoop."

"Very considerate of them." Sam responded. "Now tell me everything."

"Of course." She put an arm round him, drawing him close. She was loving and warm, and only twenty, a mere few years older than him, but with the mind and intellect of a mature woman.

"So let us go over the plan again. We, The People's Will, shall leave for St Petersburg early tomorrow morning. The assassination of Alexander the Second will happen the day after. We must not fail this time."

Samuel gawped with wide-eyed surprise.

"Our tyrant is the son of a tyrant. We shall end their obscenities once and for all. Akiva! Tell him what we have already prepared for our little holiday."

Akiva turned to Samuel! "You should know I'm a carpenter by trade."

"One of the best in all Russia!" said Sarah.

Akiva's eyes narrowed and he lowered his voice. "Last year, in early December, I was called to the Winter Palace to restore some old gilded wood carvings. I brought my closest friend Stephen Khalturin – another carpenter, and also a member of Narodnaya Volya.

"As part of our plan, we got to know the guards. They told

us there was going to be a banquet for foreign dignitaries and the Tsar himself was going to be present. We were working not far away from the dining room where the feast would be held. We were close, so very close!

"We went to work each day with sticks of dynamite, deep in our clothing, and found a perfect hiding place in the guards' room under the banqueting hall. There was more than enough to send the tyrant's bits and pieces to Hell.

"How could I forget that evening, that fifth of February, eighteen eighty? Stephen and I waited with comrades, in the Basement Café. Waiting. Waiting for all the bells of St Petersburg to toll, to ring out a dirge to the happy world. They remained silent. The explosion happened, but the bastard was late for dinner. Eleven people were killed but the Tsar was unharmed. God is a reactionary."

"What ingratitude! I hate their bloody God." Sam remarked, but Akiva hadn't heard.

"Those tyrants! Do you know Russia is the most anti-Semitic country on earth? With their Jesus Christ and their fearsome hatred of our small tribe. Kill one Tsar and another will take his place. All the way from the dark ages of Catherine the Great to Nicholas the Flogger to the even darker ages of now, with Tsar Alexander on the throne. Nothing changes all the time."

Akiva was madly in love with his own voice. And Sam, who knew about the Tsars from school, tried to stifle a yawn. But he also felt afraid when Sarah spoke.

"Jews can only live where the Tsar decrees," she said. "His horsemen come raping, pillaging our villages. We live in a world of pogrom."

"Samuel, it is time to set the people free." Akiva banged his fist on the table. "We will not fail this time! We will assassinate the tyrant once and for all. The date will become indelible upon the pages of history. March the thirteenth, eighteen eighty one. In two days. We shall have helped to free humankind of its manacles. And, incidentally, you shall need a mink fur hat with Ushanka flaps and an overcoat of bearskin, otherwise the North East wind from Siberia will finish you off before you start."

"Enough now, Akiva!"

Sarah resumed her authority. "The actual mechanics for the final moves will be given to you tomorrow, on the train; so that we shall all know exactly how we perform our separate functions. We must be on our way. Let's go."

"Wait! I need to go where no-one can go for me." The Red Rabbi was clutching his crotch as he hurried towards the toilet.

The old waiter came to clear the table. He stroked Sam's head. "What a lovely boy you are. I had a son just like you; snatched away by the Flogger. Go in good health."

When Sam and the Red Rabbi came out, they found Sarah and Akiva, waiting by the revolving door. They followed them into the street.

Funny! He thought. They entered into the café for morning breakfast, and now it was dark. He decided to discard all logic from now on; especially when a young woman sauntered towards them. She was smiling.

"Good evening," she said. It was Tamara Levinsky!

"It can't be! It's not possible."

The girl glanced at him, laughed saucily and went towards Sarah.

"Am I dreaming? Sarah! I saw her blood seeping into the snow."

"Our comrades always dramatise," she said, smiling.

"There are always murders on stage. And artificial blood is often the essence of drama."

"Sarah! You shot her dead. I saw you!"

"Samuel! They were blanks, my darling."

The two women embraced and laughed. But Akiva and the Red Rabbi were not laughing. They were both just as aghast and puzzled and waiting for answers.

"It was all a show, my dear, a dress rehearsal," Sarah answered. "Tamara Levinsky is one of us, a member of The People's Will. We all need reminding that we must be vigilant and keep on our toes. Anything can happen at any moment. Are you coming with us, Tamara?"

"No. Sorry. I have other fish to fry."

"Sizzle them well. My comrade. My beauty!"

"Farewell all. Have a nice evening. May we all wake up in the morning, not dead."

Tamara Levinsky breezed off, just as she had breezed in. Sam's eyes dreamed delight, magnetised by her hips, swaying into the distance. Then they walked through the frozen winds, along the huddled back streets. Sarah took his arm and soon they were far ahead of the others. The warmth emanating from her body was life enhancing.

"Vitebsk embraces me," said Sam ecstatic despite the cold. "I feel so safe here. How wonderful just to be walking with you. That alone would have been worth coming for."

"Do not be misled, Samuel. These peaceful empty streets are redolent with danger. This is Russia. The enemy are everywhere; all around us; in the past; the present and in the future. Unless we succeed! We are meant to be the Chosen. Well, we have certainly chosen our path."

"But Sarah, Why me? Why did you choose me?"

"I ordered you. I wanted someone of my lineage with the same strident, restless genes and ready for adventure. Someone I could trust with my life. Someone lost, yet looking for himself, willing to tear himself away from all the loving of his home. You had the perfect mixture of chutzpah, arrogance and courage for this mission. I am afraid my wonderful Samuel that it all fell on you."

"Thank you for my dark heritage. Very much obliged. By the way, I think someone is following us."

"I know. You are right; and astute; another reason why you are here." She grabbed his hand and dodged round a corner; Akiva and the Red Rabbi followed after. But they had not shaken off their pursuers.

"Don't quicken your steps." She said. "This is not new. They follow us everywhere. They know something is in the wind and about to happen. We are experts in this game. They are stupid and obvious. Don't walk faster; indeed my lovely, slow your steps. Like this. Good. They will not pounce I assure you. Put your hand into my pocket; for extra warmth but also for some other reason."

His heart was beating faster and faster. He did as he was told and brushed her thigh; and he felt – a revolver! He quickly pulled his hand out.

"Yes. But this time it does not carry blanks. Just in case. Isn't life sweet, my darling?" She brushed his lips with a kiss. She knew what she was doing. She was a terrible tease.

Sam walked but the gusting wind howled and tried to

pull them apart. His thoughts were swirling around in hilarious turmoil.

"It is eighteen eighty one. My father is not in his urn on the mantelpiece. He is not yet born. My mother makes her supreme chicken soup in the kitchen of a house in Muzzled Hill not yet built. And Grandpa Maurice is not yet even a twinkle in his mother's eye. But I feel too tired tonight to change the world. I barely have enough energy to change my socks."

"Is the man still following?" Akiva interrupted his thoughts.

Sarah shook her head and answered with a deep sigh.

"Look! The moon is piercing the clouds." The rabbi clawed at the sky.

"We are almost there. We all need our beauty sleep." Sarah pointed at her dacha, on the hill in the near distance.

Sam followed Sarah into the house, his arms open wide.

"Oh house! Come to me. I love you. You are edible. I shall fall on the feast of sleep at last. And St Petersburg, tomorrow."

He was mounting the stairs and she was holding his hand and opened the door for him and blew him a kiss. His mother of mothers! And, in his room, the fragrance of myrtle embraced him.

"Love of one's people can turn you to murder." He remarked to his reflection in the bathroom.

"Now straight to bed! Long journey ahead!"

Sarah was sitting down on a silver chair, watching him, to impress upon him, for the last time the logic and the need for those terrible actions ahead.

"Before I go I must impress on you words that guide us. And you love words. Remember! Your participation will make headlines in the English-speaking world. Help us reveal the tyranny that we are living under; a tyranny that will soon become a venomous virus over the whole world if it is not dealt with now. And we will declare that the anti-Semitic monster must be eliminated, once and for all."

"We are the *avant-garde*; and we seek out the pus, that threatens to poison us." Sam said, determined and inspired.

She went over and kissed him on the forehead. And then she left. He got straight into bed without removing his clothes or his shoes.

And he remembered another bedroom; another time, thumbing through some poems by TS Eliot, his hero. *Prufrock* was the greatest thing that ever happened to him. But now, he came across other words by the master. Words that had attacked him. He recalled them, like phlegm in his mouth and spoke them slowly, aloud.

> *The rats are underneath the piles,*
> *The Jew is underneath the lot.*

It shook his reflection in the long mirror. This could not be true. "My greatest idol!" He could not spew out such words. How could his best poet declaim such hateful, filthy detritus? Even God can let you down if you believe in him. How could Samuel, in the mirror still cry? Mr Eliot should have been tried at Nuremburg. He felt marooned.
Was he up for the tomorrow that he had somehow inherited?

He had never personally experienced one single act of anti-Semitism. He had never met an anti-Semite on the Broadway of Muswell Hill. The plague had passed over him, like the Angel of Death. He would die like everyone else. Death is the garden of unremembered things.

Before his flickering eyes had sailed him off into the depths of the cosmos he heard himself sighing. "Poor Katie! If only she had marvellous wobblies like Sarah the Princess or Tamara Levinsky, then I could love her for always." Primitive desire was bursting out of him.

And then it all changed and coalesced. There was Ben, his father in a small boat, crossing the water. And he thought at first that his granddad was the other figure in the tossing dingy, crossing the choppy sea. But now he could see it wasn't his grandfather; it was the boatman and the two men were haggling. Sam waved and waved. They didn't see him. They were deep in doing a deal. And soon they were out of sight.

Sam drifted onward into the darkness. Without sight or sound he entered the gaping mouth of all eternity.

7

They entered the station and went straight towards the ticket office. A long queue of ragged, silent and lifeless humans, were shuffling forward, one shoe at a time. It seemed everyone was trying to get away from Vitebsk.

The Red Rabbi sniffed several times, checking the atmosphere.

"I fear there is Pogrom in the air."

"There is always a pogrom in the air and more often on the ground." Akiva retorted.

The creatures in the queue seemed barely capable of rubbing two kopeks together. Where were they off to, and why? As they got closer to the ticket hatch some urgent whispered words started to circulate. The voices of the lumpen stragglers were morose and suddenly fearful.

"Did someone say 'pogrom'?" An old hag cackled.

"Yes! I see it with my own ears. 'Pogrom'."

"Yes! I heard it with my own eyes." A man of no teeth muttered.

"WHEN? WHEN?"

"Anytime! Anytime you like. Tonight! Tomorrow! Yesterday! It's all a tall story," uttered a heavily pregnant Jewish dwarf.

"Where?" Asked an over-pungent undertaker, in his highly polished threadbare suit and a silk top hat, that had seen many other centuries. "We can do with a nice healthy pogrom. Where is the pogrom party going to be?"

"Here! In Vitesbk."

"Who said so?"

"Izzy. The grocer."

"Nucham. My herring pickler!"

"Are you dead sure? Who said so?"

"My wife in her grave. Last night when I washed her body."

"Everywhere has endured and enjoyed this gift from our beloved Alexander. Why should he leave us out?" Said the dwarf woman, now smoking a cigar with her *sheitel,* her wig, all askew.

A long chorus of Yiddish sighs broke out, and the endless queue of the ragged became more and more restless.

"Where you going Rivka?" Shouted one toothless crone to another.

"I'm going to dread." She answered. The queue was no longer a queue. It was now an agitated phalanx of filthy, stinking creatures at a dried-up water hole; stamping and marching their feet up and down, getting nowhere fast.

Two women were on the floor tearing each other's hair out. Three men were pounding and punching each other, spouting red, black and blue. The words became mishmash.

"So what do we do when we reach our final ticket office?"

"Ask for a ticket to nowhere."

"Where will we find pogrom?"

"Everywhere! And blood. Our blood! We come from blood and we go to blood. Blood is our destiny. So bugger off, you bastard."

"And when will we be murdered? Tonight? Tomorrow night?"

A one-legged joker hit the pack. "Please God! Let it be tomorrow night! At least let us survive another day."

"Order! Order! The police are on their way."

"They'll kill us. They'll kill us all."

And a great cloud of *shtum* powder hit the mob, and silently.

In a black flash everything changed, and the long, snaking queue reassembled.

The rabbi strode to the top of the queue, reached the ticket hatch and sang for no reason. "I am Red! I am Red and I'll be Red until I'm dead." The astonished ticket clerk pulled back from the opening and lost all his indolent command. "Sorry sir, what can I do for you?"

"I am the Red Rabbi. You might have heard of me. It is ordained by God that I have priority over all others." He dived into his underwear and brought out some ragged notes.

"Four single return tickets to St Petersburg, if you please, my dear man." The transaction was completed.

"Quick! To the train." The rabbi shouted.

"No! We have two hours before the train. That way! To the waiting room!"

The sullen mob went silent and shuffled back to reform the queue. Only a few dared to shout.

"You fucking Yids."

"We'll have your guts for garters."

"Long live the Tsar! He's got your number."

"He'll have you all burning in hell."

"Yeah! Get a move on. Fucking Yids."

A middle-aged soldier hobbled on one leg. He was covered with medals.

"You've got your bloody tickets, so get out of our country before our Cossacks burn the lot of you."

"Thank you very much. I love you too." The Red Rabbi opened his fingers, and held them against his mouth and he spat seven times towards the soldier. "Toi! Toi! Toi! May the Malacha Movis pour boiling oil in your ears and may your brain turn to molten worms and devour your balls."

The *goyim* surrounded them, spewing a chorus of poison and hatred.

"Yids! Yids! Hack off their heads!"

"Vermin! Devils! Burn them!"

"Burn them."

Their obscene words chilled Sam. He quickly followed the others across the station. The waiting room was empty. Everything went quiet.

Sarah whispered to him "It's alright. The mob have moved on." She could see Sam's legs were shaking.

"I am not afraid," he said. "I am not afraid of them. It's just they are so hateful."

"There's something else. You don't seem too happy today, my darling."

"Sorry! I feel very lost today. I swear I am with you. But I'm thinking about my home, my mother. A new man has come into her life and I cannot bear it. And my father's ashes are in an urn on the mantelpiece. As soon as the deed is done I will have to go back."

"Who is the new man? Is he worthy of her?"

He wasn't answering her, but chasing his own thoughts.

"He haunts me."

"Your father?"

"He haunts me as well. But the new man haunts me.

How can she betray the person who was her whole existence? How can I live with it?"

She clasped her two arms around him and the smell of her flesh was music, and her tempo slowed him down, back to the reality of the waiting room.

"Life is a waiting room." Sam said.

"Life is the beautiful illusion between dark and dark. We are here, borrowed from darkness," said Sarah. "Life is the strangest place there is."

Having chucked his mobile away Sam decided that he would go no further with his skateboard. He would leave it behind, here in this waiting room. He had no time for it anymore. He had grown out of it. His childhood was now a mirage. That Sam had gone forever.

The Queen of the World and the Red Rabbi of timelessness were sitting together; she was whispering into his ear. The rabbi nodded and nodded, as if receiving instructions. He fixed Sam with a gaze he had not witnessed before. It was not cursory. It was magnetic, and determined.

Sam could feel the sparks of energy pouring into him.

Then the rabbi mumbled to himself, swayed back and forward. "A prayer to the mystical giver of life; the dead God that never was, and to my queen, my *shekinah*, that sits beside me in this wilderness called 'The Waiting Room'." He intoned, deep into his vibrating nose as he slobbered kisses all around Sarah's beatific face.

"They don't pray like this in Muswell Hill." Sam mumbled as he slipped into the arms of Murphy; the drunken God of Literature; and sleep.

He began dreaming about Delmore Schwartz, a great poet he'd stumbled across. He died, out of his mind, in a downbeat hotel in a stinking part of New York. Not before he had written *In Dreams Begin Responsibilities*. The words began reverberating around Sam's brain. And more.

May memory restore again and again,
The smallest colour of the smallest day:
Time is the school in which we learn,
Time is the fire in which we burn.

And he wanted to see Anne.

"Anne! Anne." Come! I'm calling you up. Appear to me."

But now there was no candle. No alcove. No Anne. He could smell the night and the fog.

"Anne! I'm back. Where are you? Anne! Anne!" He shouted and the echo took up his call and came back laughing. The dream tunnel was long and endless, a bit like life. Suddenly it was there and so soon it was all over.

There was no distance in endlessness. No beginning, no end. He stroked his face to feel the mask of age. He was an old man dragging his feet on the brink of the precipice.

"Anne?"

He thought he could hear someone. He couldn't be sure, because there was so much wailing, so much screaming, so many prayers and songs. And then he was sure it was her, dying. This dream was also the dream of poets. And he cried, suddenly overwhelmed by the thought that the death of every poet had robbed him of more of their words.

"Samuel Glass, get on with your life. Go forward!" He commanded himself. Then there was only silence. He hunched down and turned around to avoid the cloud of smoke rolling towards him. And there was the street and there was the house where he was suckled and loved; the woman he couldn't live without and couldn't wait to get away from.

And he realised his hand was numb from clutching the key too hard in the clenched fist of his hand.

And finally, when he opened the door, John Lennon was singing "Imagine." He was imagining. Without imagination where are we?

He was enjoying this dream; there could be a plate of chicken soup at the end of it. And there was his mother just coming in from the dark tangle of foliage, crying, and now, seeing him, translating her sudden smile into matzo balls.

"So, where have you been, clever dick?"

"Believe it or not mother, I ran into Anne Frank and we made excellent love."

"Nice." Lisa Glass nodded. "Nice. Very nice. At last you enter into decent company. Sam darling, your imagination will get you nowhere. I ask myself. How did you become you? Both sides of the family were comparatively down to earth. What will become of you?"

"Me! I am becoming me. Oh, by the way, I love you." He sauntered into the living room. She followed. He looked up at the urn on the mantelpiece. She kissed him.

"Your father's ashes! We must do something about releasing him soon."

"I dunno. Life is fatal, mother, but it's some consolation that our little lives are rounded with a sleep, as Prospero put it. I might be dreaming but a dream is a good way of escape a dreary waiting room that stinks of piss and sweat. And so is poetry."

"What are we going to do with you? Lisa sighed. "You

are such a clever boy. And I did enjoy you as Prospero in *The Tempest*."

"At least mother you have some vestige of culture, that's why I am not ashamed of you."

"Oh thank you very much Master Glass."

"Mother! I am in Russia at this moment. I am in the good hands of The People's Will. I have fallen amongst anarchists."

"I'll see if the soup is coming along. That's why you came home. Right?"

"Absolutely! It's also about how we can dispense with my father's ashes."

She smiled a sigh and went into the kitchen. He followed her in there; the elixir of life was bubbling away; the smell was heaven.

"So where were you after making love with Anne Frank?"

"Here; I'm just passing through. So tell me about him, that new man of yours?"

"So, what can I say? I bumped into him at the National Gallery. He came here before. You refused to meet him."

"Did I? Mother, be careful. Who wouldn't want you? You are beautiful and kind and very innocent. How can you trust anyone after dad?"

"Samuel! I feel quite close to David. He's a good man."
He just couldn't keep up the pretence. All his fears were cavorting, pouring into his head.

"You know what this means. It means my father is dead. Forever!"

"Samuel! I'm still quite a young woman. And I cannot bear being all alone. I love you with all my heart. And I want you to live your own life, without me hanging on being a burden."

"What's his name again?"

"I told you! David Simmons!"

"I expect he's some sort of chartered surveyor or a stockbroker."

"That's where you're wrong."

"Well, then, he's your usual Jewish accountant! Right?"

"I never said he was Jewish. But fortunately he is. It helps to be on the same emotional wavelength. And he's not an accountant." Her eyes sought his approval.

"He has to be a lawyer then."

"Sam! You're talking clichés. David studied art at St Martin's, but then, to make a living, he decided to become a picture restorer. If he can restore me I'd be more than grateful. He resurrects Old Masters, actually."

He yawned and stretched. "I'm tired. I need food urgently and maybe a nap."

"I'm sure you two will get on. He's longing to meet you."

Sam sighed. "Please mother! Can you leave me now! I must meditate upon all this."

She was a very brave woman; on her own, lumbered with a son like him.

"I told him all about you. He thinks you're marvellous and he will be absolutely amused by you." He wanted to dash her head against the wall.

"Darling, whatever happens, my love for you can never be diminished."

"Mum! May I ask you a big favour?"

"It depends."

"Serve up the soup. I long for it in Vitebsk."

She laughed. "How terrible and confusing it must be to

be seventeen. One moment you're a monster the next you are my little angel."

"And you are still the best mother in the whole world."

"Sam! Listen! I've an idea. Why don't we, all three of us, go for a Chinese, up West?"

"We'll see."

"How many matzo balls?"

"As many as you can afford. Six!"

Lisa placed the libation before him. "Careful! It's very hot!" She ruffled his hair, and then sat across the kitchen table, lovingly watching him.

"So! You are in Russia. All our family came from Vitebsk."

"Really? Russia is filled with snow. And there is this woman, the image of you; her name was Sarah."

"Did you fall in love with her?"

"Instantly. How did you know?"

Then his dream leapt backwards. He was fourteen at the time. He came home from school in the early afternoon, unexpectedly. The school had given them a half day off; God knows why. There were noises coming from his parents' bedroom. He opened the door slowly. Someone was giggling.

And there they were; they were at it. His mother and father. How could they? Parents don't do that sort of thing, especially in the afternoon. And they didn't jump up and stop, as he gaped at them.

It was the first time he had seen her like this; her breasts of pure ivory. How beautiful she was, chuckling away, waving at him. "Sorry. I didn't know."

He didn't know if he should laugh or cry. And then he felt a wave of happiness; of joy surging over him. Sex was

90

a beautiful thing! It was human; it was Neolithic! It was life. It was the bringer of life. It was religious. His parents were human after all; and that was the most wonderful thing. She was a girl; a woman with golden nipples. How often he had sucked her love milk that had given him such confidence and pride and such a different and crazy mind. She would coo: "Darling baby grow up strong and think for yourself your whole life long." And she also made the most wonderful chicken soup.

This was what it should be.

His dream rolled on.

"Hello dad."

"Hello son. We're just enjoying ourselves. Don't run away."

"I won't. How marvellous you both are."

How beautifully, the man with all his ashes reassembled, moved above her; so lovingly, so soothingly, so gentle; so magnificent. The happenings of that day would go with him always; the love flowing through both his makers.

But did it really happen? He switched to the kitchen, and had never been away.

"Mum! This soup is out of this world. It's wonderful. By the way, I have to go back, soon. We are going to assassinate Tsar Alexander the Second tomorrow."

She looked puzzled.

"You know the anti-Semitic tyrant, who rules in St Petersburg."

"Oh? Good idea!" And she ladled him a second helping. "Sam! I think you're feverish." She hurried to the medicine drawer and returned with a thermometer. Pop this in your mouth."

She glanced at the results. "I simply do not understand. You're dead on normal. Oh! By the way Katie's been looking for you."

And then the pathetic suburban doorbell chimed.

"That must be Katie. Be nice. She likes you a lot." She went to the door. He thought it was time to dash back to the waiting room.

"Wake up! Wake up Shmuel!" The Red Rabbi was shaking him. "You've been having a bad dream."

He yawned. "I've been having a wonderful dream. How long must we wait in this waiting room?"

"We must go to the platform soon. The train leaves in half an hour." The Red Rabbi tugged on him whilst Sarah was pushing a strange comb through the rabbi's matted white hair.

"Thousands of lice, my poor old rabbi."

"Thank you. How kind you are." The old man purred as he laid his head into her lap.

"Murder the lot of them."

"Rely on me; none shall escape. I shall crack every single one of them." She cracked away and Samuel took out the book of his favourite poet. Only books could guide him.

He read the final words of the poem aloud.

We have lingered in the chambers of the sea,
By sea-girls wreathed with seaweed red and brown, till
Human voices wake us, and we drown.

He wanted to cry tears of joy. The others took no notice. And in the distance again he could make out the clanking sound of boxcars on the move. They were running faster, to the devil's schedule. Shunting; moaning far away in the recesses of his brain. "This was the milk of human kindness she poured into me." And he was trying to think up a way of forgiving that very dead Christian poet, Mr Thomas Stearns Eliot who lived and died without ever travelling in a boxcar.

"Come! We must go now. Up you get." Sarah commanded and Sam followed them out, leaving his skateboard behind. He was finished with all that child stuff, forever. He slammed the waiting room door behind him, and they all hurried towards the train. Sarah shouted through the station noise.

"Remember Comrades! Tomorrow, the thirteenth of March, eighteen eighty one is our date with destiny. Onward! Narodnaya Volya."

8

So this was St Petersburg. A surreal and empty world. Salvador Dali might have created this. A city lost in time, built long before the gulags. And Palace Square, pristine, beautiful and freezing cold; a vast open mausoleum built for ghosts, and marching soldiers. This was probably the most beautiful city in the world and it left him cold.

And there was the Alexander Column, and he was with his three comrades, very much alive. Beyond, he could see the Winter Palace soon to be occupied by a new tenant.

"So, what's the next crisis?"

"Shmuel! Be not flippant. This is the big time. Yes! There is always crisis, but solve this one and another and another one will come; and it will be far worse than this impossible crisis. Therefore learn to love your crisis," said the rabbi.

They slowly strolled through the dreamlike square and Sarah hurriedly left her husband briefly and came over and squeezed his arm and kissed his cheek. He was absolutely sure she wanted him. There was magic between Queen Sarah and himself.

Maybe Akiva could be killed tomorrow, a nice, sudden, quick death by the Tsar's bodyguards, beautifully adorned in black and silver and gold. A heroic death, sudden, without pain; his head cut off in one flashing slice and everything would be solved. She would fall into his arms for comfort that very night, and overwhelming, passionate love would inevitably follow.

"Oh Sam! Give it to me, my darling Sam. Give it to me, again and again so that you blot out for a time the terrible image of my darling, dead Akiva. And you can stay with me forever. Just give it to me."

She would pull him so close that he could feel her beating heart. Her breasts were perfect. And he wondered if her nipples were dark brown or pink. But at such a feast either would do. He closed his eyes for a few seconds. They melted together and he was caressing her to assuage her grief.

"Thank you. It's just as well my precious Akiva is dead. The death of a sad, would-be toreador. You cancel him out. You have perfect *deunde*! Fire and spirit. Thank God, I have found proper love in the wild body of a boy from Muswell Hill."

She was pulling away from him. "We must be very careful and circumspect with our secret adoration."

"My lips are sealed." And all his dreaming came to a stop.

They sauntered through the avenues and dead streets and she was sharing a quiet joke with her husband.

"This is early in the morning." She said. "When we reach the busy streets we must separate so that we do not draw too much attention to ourselves. It is dangerous to gather in groups in this country. Russia is a vast suspicious madhouse. Goodbye comrades, Akiva and I will now leave you and we shall meet you both at the Troika Café in one hour. The rabbi knows where it is."

And when they reached the traffic she took her husband's arm. "Goodbye, young man. See you soon." She offered a gentle smile. Those few unemotional words stabbed Sam straight into his balls.

Slowly she walked away. Her grace and beauty were too much of a feast. He smiled back and choked on words that were demanding to be heard. He hated her.

Oh the Corazon! The Corazon.
Oh the song of the heart, bleeding.

Sarah the Queen and Akiva the Nothing crossed the road and disappeared.

The rabbi had been quite silent until now. "In a sense I am sad and would like to apologise to you. I got you into all this. But there is now no turning back."

"*Les jeaux sont fait,*" Sam replied, in his precocious French.

And the Red Rabbi strode ahead as if he knew where he was going.

"I can't wait for breakfast. How far is this café?" Sam said as hungry as ever.

The rabbi, far away in the Land of Always did not reply. Sam was looking forward to imbibing the atmosphere of the café; he loved London's cafés, the ones where artists and intellectuals gathered for coffee and newspapers and chat and argument. And he even liked the cafés around Muswell Hill where they all spoke some kind of arrogant clever crap. You just stayed silent and watched and listened to the human animals, grunting and groaning. He enjoyed it all. He was certain that the Café Troika would be no different.

Sam wondered. Was there a law in any land that forbids sexual passion with your great, great, great grandmother? It would be a first, surely, for the Guinness Book of Records.

The rabbi took his arm and led him away in the opposite direction to the others.

Sometimes he felt guilty for missing school. And times like this made him feel far away and lonely.

The elegance of St Petersburg was another world; its icy wind cut right through him, and its elegant, pristine, empty boulevards moved him. It was like walking through a lonely de Chirico painting.

"Remember Shmuel. We are no longer in our shtetl. We are in *Goyland*. We are close to the heart and soul of Mother Russia."

For a change, the Red Rabbi did not resemble the Grim Reaper. And the people, hurrying along were not wearing rags or faces of despair and took no notice of the strangers. But the side streets were another thing, smelling like stinking, rotten fish.

"Ah Yes! Down here" The rabbi rubbed both hands together. "White Rabbit Lane."

They turned into a narrow, cobbled, side street.

"Our rendezvous!" His talons pointed to the dingy exterior; and the faded blood-red lettering.

Troika Café
Established Eighteen Fifty Five

Some comforting words came to Sam, by way of Ezra Pound. He spoke them to his companion.

What thou lovest well remains, the rest is dross.
What thou lovest well shall not be wrest from thee.

The Red Rabbi grabbed and slobbered over him.

"Shmuel, I love your gibberish."

"Red Rabbi, the man was a madman. He was another great poet who was also an evil anti-Semitic maniac. Why?"

"We have maniacs aplenty in Russia. That's why we are here. So let's go down. Have you never heard of Café Troika? It is famous worldwide. Tomorrow all this will be in the history books."

They entered the plush red and black interior. It was choking and smoky, scorching hot and crammed with customers; enough for another inferno.

"Relax, my son. We are in good company. We are all anarchists down here."

He looked around at each table, where men and women were fervently talking to each other, but it seemed none of them were listening.

"Women anarchists?" Sam was surprised.

"Absolutely! They are mostly refugees from the kitchen where men make the rules, and the women make the tea. But here we are all equal; as long as we live, before we are all picked off and tortured and die. And even there, in death we are all equal."

And there in the corner was Sarah and her toy boy. He walked across to them, smiling.

Akiva was scanning the tables. "Amazing! Not one agent of the Okrhana here."

"I'm not surprised," said Sarah. "They have been very quiet of late. And that worries me. Whenever an action is about to happen they seem to get wind of it and go to ground."

"It's a short life, comrades, but at least it is a terrible one." The Red Rabbi nodded and applauded himself.

Sarah patted the chair beside her. "Samuel. Come! Please

sit next to me." He lost no time taking his place and at once her aroma soaked into him.

A little, bent waiter came with a face as sad as history.

"Gentlemen, and one exceptional lady, what's your poison?"

"Do you serve scrambled eggs on toast?" Sam was a very happy fellow today.

"We serve anyone, your Majesty."

"And some scrumptious blinis with buckets of Bessarabian coffee, please! And excuse me while I scratch my balls." The Red Rabbi enjoyed his busy hands.

"Customers! Shoot the lot of them." The waiter mumbled and then bent over as if tying his shoelaces. And he slipped a note under Sam's plate and waited to watch their reaction. Sam immediately opened the note.

"Careful! The Okrhana are with us." It said.

Sam handed the note to Sarah who tore it into little pieces. The waiter shuffled off, as fast as a pissed tortoise.

Someone started playing the balalaika, and a chorus of customers joined in, adding their deep bass voices.

"Where do we sleep tonight?" Sam asked.

"Don't worry. We have many comrades in this city." She replied. "Now please take note and listen." She produced a scribbled map.

"Now I can divulge the comrades who will join us in this glorious murder feast." She reeled off the names like a litany; "Andrei Zhelyabov. Gesia Gelfman. Nikolai Sablin. Ignatei Grinevitski. Nikolai Kibalchick. Nikolai Rysakov! And Timofei Zhelyabov. Plus myself and one other woman; Sophia Perovskaya. We are a cast of heroes. The People's Will until now has been a joke, we've been disrespected; people laughed at the mention of our name. Tomorrow they will not laugh anymore, our name and our actions will be known and respected and feared by the entire world. Tomorrow we will be in the history books."

"We are all anarchists down here." Akiva remarked.

"Akiva! Please shut up!"

Sam did not cease to be astonished as to why she had married him; a man she obviously disdained.

The Red Rabbi mumbled a few words. "Yes. None of us can think of our next birthday. We will all be picked off and tortured and pickled and then we die. And there, in death, we are all equal. But not me. I would gladly kiss the man who can end my life."

"Can we please return to the map?" She said, sternly.

The three males immediately bent their heads forward to scrutinise the plan on the table.

Princess Sarah continued. "Here we shall be, right where we should be. This street corner. Look! The Catherine Canal. Right on time I shall be moving forward.

"I must drum this into your head, Samuel! You are our reserve. You must only throw your bomb, if God forbid, Akiva and I fail in our task. I must reiterate. Do not throw your bomb unless we fail.

"The Tyrant, Alexander, will be travelling in a closed carriage, from Michaelovsky Palace to the Winter Palace. An armed Cossack will be sitting with the coach driver and another six Cossacks will follow on horseback. Behind them there will be a group of police officers on sledges. If anything goes wrong, and we have to separate we have a perfect place to reassemble. Look! Here! The old Jewish cemetery. Nobody goes there anymore. Draw this map in your head."

"Thank you my love." Akiva murmured, as he nuzzled and kissed his beloved.

Sam intoned a simple prayer. "Please God, if any of us have to die, let it be Akiva. And he will become one of the greatest heroes of all time. And Sarah and I will sing his praises, often, whenever we are not making fantastic love together."

Akiva resembled an Adonis; someone who would seem to be at home in a Wagnerian Valhalla.

"Please listen, everyone," Sarah continued. "We will be successful. But we must then prepare our people; for after the tumultuous death of the tyrant they will suffer the most terrible reprisals. And we must avoid a horrendous legacy."

"Let us go. Much to do!" Akiva stood to call the waiter and pay the bill. Then he turned to Samuel. "You cannot change your mind now."

"Akiva!" She was furious. "Please shut up."

"I have never wanted to change my mind." Sam snapped, not hiding his anger. But he wanted to get away from them, for just a few moments.

"Sarah! Where can I go to be on my own?"

"The cemetery; the old Jewish cemetery, it's a stone's throw from here. We passed it down the road. Remember? It is very peaceful there."

"Jews dead or alive are never peaceful." The Red Rabbi remarked, almost asleep.

"Samuel you do what you must. We understand your trepidation. We will wait for you for one hour."

"Thank you. The old cemetery! Great! Yes."

"Down the end of this street, and turn right. No-one can miss it." She hugged him and he felt happy and reprieved, and he left the Troika Café without looking back.

"WAIT! WAIT!" It was the waiter, running after him, waving, holding something up.

"You left your coat behind."

"Thank you." Sam's eyes filled with tears. "I hope the others give you a good tip. I'm skint myself."

"You must take care. Anarchists are everywhere. May I tell you something personal?"

"Please! Go ahead." Said the young man.

The waiter glanced over his shoulder to see if anyone else was watching them. "I read people. You have something special."

"I know. I read books." Sam smiled. "We are ships that pass in the night. Goodbye."

"Go with God my son and destroy the devil. Toi! Toi! Toi!" He spat seven times through his open fingers. "The Malacha Movis is close. Can't you smell him?" He turned, and walked slowly back into the café.

Sam turned the corner and there were the rusted gates of the old Jewish cemetery. He closed his eyes for some light to guide him. He wanted to run away. But how could he abandon them now? More important; how could he abandon her? He was talking to himself. "It is not my notion to change the world. But is it my nature to follow my love? Going back I may probably die. But if I don't go back I will definitely die. Die in life; of life."

He leaned against the wet railings and recalled being five, tucked up in bed. And his sweet, soft mother Lisa was reading a story to him while he stroked her breast:

"A scorpion wanted to cross a river. But as you know a scorpion cannot swim. But then he chanced to see a frog, hopping around. 'Please take me across the river mister frog' He pleaded. The frog laughed. 'Don't be absurd; if I carry you across you'll sting me and I will die.'

"The scorpion replied. 'Don't be stupid, if I sting you, you will die and so will I; because I cannot swim.'
"The frog nodded. 'Of course! Absolutely! Jump on my back, I'll carry you across.'

"The scorpion thanked the frog profusely and jumped on his back. Halfway across the river the scorpion stung the frog. And soon the frog was dying, downing, and uttering his last words. He looked up at the scorpion.

"'Why? Why?' he said. And the scorpion, also drowning managed his last words. 'Because it's my nature'."

Sam never forgot that story. He had sunk his nose into his mother's long dark hair. And it was the first time he could consciously recall absorbing her wisdom and confidence.

Then he realised it was time to go back and join the others.

9

Sam had no recollection of what followed. He knew it had been a wonderful night in a safe house with oceans of vodka, food, music and black cigarettes, with everyone cuddling and carousing. Then sweet oblivion; falling asleep against Sarah's singing flesh; then waking up ... and there she was, looking out of a window at a white landscape, stretching her arms as if giving birth to this day of days. The falling snow was her confetti. And suddenly he realised they were moving. They were in a droshky.

The droshky was sailing across the silent snow, with a strange figure at the helm. His face was blue, and his fingertips, showing through his threadbare gloves, were bones without flesh. Sam stared at his skeletal face, and stared and stared at him; but now the long night had ended. The dawn was very slow in opening her eyes.

The Princess leaned across and took his hand. "Darling boy! This is our destiny. In a thousand years they will say, 'Those people, The People's Will, were incredibly brave. They took action against all the odds. Without them a great and horrible darkness would have fallen upon the world.' We are the avant-garde, Samuel. Therefore we must expect the first blows of the enemy."

Sam needed to release words into the thin air. A slogan that all young, marching, demonstrating kids knew. He shouted into the blinding flakes:

> *What do we want? Freedom!*
> *Death of the tyrant!*
> *When do we want him dead? Now!*
> *Not tomorrow! Now!*

Just then they slowed as the steam of the horses blew a halo around the conspirators. "We are here. As near as we dare." Then came the first bombshell. "Samuel! In case we are killed or captured, we must make our goodbyes before the event. By the way, Red Rabbi, you will not be coming with us."

He burst into tears. "It's not fair. You promised! You promised!"

"Rabbi! I love you. I feel for you, but you are slightly too old for this game." And she hugged him.

"This might have been my final chance to die, how could you do this to me?"

"Because I do not wish to see you captured and tortured by the Okhrana, and rotting in a deep cell, languishing, tortured in hell, forever. You are too important to us. Rabbi, go back to the old Jewish cemetery and wait for us there."

"So often, in all my lifetimes, have I wanted to vanquish the tyrants, who appear again and again. But God willing, you will carry out the action for me, although without me. Sarah! I understand. I accept. Thank you for your strength and leadership."

The rabbi shouted to the driver. "Peter! Peter the Dead! Stop, on this corner. I am getting off here." He cried. He really cried.

Peter the Dead halted the horses without word of complaint and the Red Rabbi saluted. "Victory for the

People's Will." He croaked, thrusting his clenched fist into the air to hide his sadness as he whistled down the narrow road.

Sarah turned to Sam. "He is too conspicuous; he will be picked off in no time. And we could all fail."

"But he cannot die." Sam was shocked.

"No. But we can; and our mission lost."

Sam had not expected such a ruthless side to her.

"And they will torture him for ever and ever. We cannot rely on him. He's getting worse every day."

"He's as nutty as a fruitcake." Akiva added, with a certain anger in his retort.

"Let us get out now and rest briefly before the last stage of our journey. Quickly now!" Sarah said.

Sam jumped down from the droshky and patted the four gentle horses; giving each creature a democratic whisper into the ear. "Very nice ride my gentlemen!" He nuzzled into the silky coats.

"Come Akiva, my dearest. Into my arms!" She said, very quietly and the couple embraced.

Sam knew he had to put aside his raging jealousy and his wild dreams. He had to survive this day. There was no turning back now.

Peter the Dead, still in the driving seat yawned. The animals stamped and breathed out clouds from their nostrils that in a second changed into droplets of crystal.

"May God, if he is awake today, bless our endeavours and we shall all return to each other." He said.

"Are you ready?" Sarah was reading Sam's raging mind.

"Come back down to earth. We are all afraid. But we are here for a divine purpose. Everything else must be put aside, for now. Come! Time we went."

She looked at her watch. "We must go quickly to our destination. The Tsar is already in his carriage and on his way. Take this." She dipped into her deep bag and handed Sam a polished black ball. "Here's your lovely bomb. Bombs are my true lovers." She held another against her cheek.

"Now don't forget. You are our back-up if things go wrong. And we will after the deed is done, God willing, rendezvous at our safe house, the cellar at Forty One Pushkin Court, off Nevsky Prospect."

The bomb was much larger than a cricket ball. "One little stunning bowl, a perfect googly in the right place and the world will change," Sam thought.

They climbed back into the droshky. There was no turning back. His mind was racing as they hurtled towards their final destination.

"We know the Okhrana has got wind that something spectacular is to happen today; a day that will go down in history; so courage my comrades. We cannot fail, we will not fail."

And time whizzed as a bomb should. And they were right on time and right at the very spot they had planned. The trio emerged from the droshky. And Sam could make out the other comrades, calling to each other, ready for the kill.

"This street corner. Look! See! The Catherine Canal! And right on time! Boys! Kiss me comrades and goodbye. See you in hell, or in heaven, or in the old Jewish cemetery or the Troika café, noshing cake. And now we must go where no-one has gone before."

And Sarah and Akiva went and joined their comrades,

leaving Sam alone. He stood frozen to the place she had ordained for him.

His eyes offered him strange pictures, a series of grainy, scary, moving images in black and white, like in a cinema of the olden days. His only companion was his racing thoughts. Maybe he would never see her again.

His mates, at this time, were probably joking in the playground. His father was an urn of grey crystals on the mantelpiece; but soon he was strolling down Duke's Avenue with Ben on a sunny Sunday, and then suddenly hurrying towards the lakeside cafeteria to beat the queues.

But there was no escape from Russia. Samuel was aware of his fast breathing and his thumping heart that brought him back to the task he had promised to undertake. His eager bomb was clutched in his clenched hand, and he knew he was ready.

Within moments he heard the shouts and screams of crying animals. And the screeching cattle trucks were not to be outdone with the stench of smoke and blood.

His mind was calmer now as he somersaulted in the fairground of death; he was on the high wire, clinging to his life. And he was falling, falling ... ever so slowly, falling. And the crack of pistols and the day had died and the night was waving its flag, turning the sky an apocalyptic black and red. And explosions, like a cackling of witches, echoed their cauldron of hate.

Samuel heard the animals wailing for water. "Water! Water!" A crazy madness possessed them; a jamboree of death brushing past, boxcars into the sidings of nowhere. And logic was a funny clown standing on his head, with a desperate sucking in of air.

And then sudden silence and his brain settled down in a vortex, a fearful vacuum of uncertainty; only to be broken by cheers and a jubilation of shouts.

"We've got the bastard."

"The Tsar is dead!"

"We've got him! We got him! We've got him!"

"All his black blood he bled." And then they fled.

"Run! Away! Away!"

He could hear the fearful onlookers, running, tumbling towards him. Shouting.

"Get away!"

"They're coming. The murderers are coming."

"The People's Will have got their way; have got their will."

Sam knew it was over and it was now his turn to scoot away directly through the warren of side streets.

Over and over again, he began intoning the mantra of remembrance. "To the rendezvous; the safe house! The Cellar! Pushkin Court, by Nevsky Prospect. To the right, past a nest of hovels. Respectable people would not go there."

But first down the steep steps; and the balalaikas were playing as if nothing had changed and the world was exactly where it always was.

The place was crammed with old yellowing men, crammed together, as still as dusty statues in a provincial museum.

How could she have done this to him? Could she be dead? How could she, how dare she be dead? And Akiva and the Red Rabbi also not there. Now he was trapped. He would never get back to England.

He walked upstairs, away, slowly into an empty world, drained of people. One would have thought that the events of the day would have created parties of jubilant people dancing, drunk, carousing, wildly, celebrating the greatest change that had suddenly taken place in almighty Russia.

"The Tsar is dead so where are the revellers?" Not one single human had dared to come out of their hovels and houses and get down on their knees in praise of their long-desired revolution. He quickened his sauntering, and now he was dashing from street to street to catch one hint of impoverished communards partying, intoxicated by the sudden reality and the promise of a new world and a decent, deserved future for all.

Not a sausage. Not even a phalanx of galloping militia; not even a sweep of secret police. From squashed streets to broad boulevards it was all the same. The entire capital had been vacuumed of life.

"If things do not turn out as expected, and we cannot rendezvous in safe houses or the Troika Café; we will meet in the old Jewish Cemetery," she had said. He could hear her words echoing in his head.

"Of course! Of course!" He turned and relieved himself, pissing a torrent of golden rain against a huge grey wall that reached the sky; and he looked again at the memorised map she had shown him earlier. And he knew exactly how to get there.

So he ran all the way and he was there; arriving in that unusual hourglass of time he was enjoyably trapped within. And there were the elongated rusty gates; where the dead were safely sleeping for all eternity.

It was dark. He entered the cemetery with a foreboding

of wind song from the Medusa trees, calling him. "Shmuel! Shmuel! "What took you so long? But why are you here?" They swayed and laughed. It was good to know that Medusa trees did not know everything. And the night seagulls were swooping and screeching. "Help! Help!"

Sam sat on a wonky gravestone. "So, the tyrant is dead. It was dead easy." And now his excursion would soon be ended.

He shivered, and crossed his fingers, his eyes, his legs. "Please God. At least Sarah has got to survive." The thought was a warming consolation; without her he could never have been born. Tired now, he closed his eyes and bowed his nodding head. He was wandering through the symphony of the half awake. Pictures! Snapshots! Juxtaposing, melting into each other.

"I just heard from the rabbis at the Wailing Wall." The Red Rabbi declaimed passionately. "The catastrophe, the cataclysm starts at nine fifteen sharp, tomorrow morning."

What did he mean? There was too much rubbish in his head tonight and dark thoughts started niggling; what if the rabbi finally managed to die on this escapade? How would he get back home? And what then? Home was death. "Keep on the move, Sam, so that Death will not get you in her sights."

This was the prison cell of enigma. Either way, he could not escape. Death was the inescapable chasm, and life was the terrible con; it was like giving you freedom from the everlasting dark, before you were born, then suddenly shoved out into the light of this world and living a life of light and joy. So, for a while you are in a sort of paradise where you fall in love and you dance and sing and have a goddess for a partner and a home of beautiful babies and for a while life is forever and ever. Then they come with white sheets and hover about you. "Come Samuel! It's time you returned to the dark." And here in this cemetery he would, without knowing, join the sleeping forever and ever.

He felt sick and heavy as he climbed to his feet and wandered amongst the community of the dead.

He noticed one small and particular tombstone. It seemed newly planted. So why was it cracked and leaning to one side? The indented words in the marble spoke to him in an unemotional, childlike girl's voice. "Rachel Gurevitch. Born 1867. Died 1880."

"Poor little girl! Without tasting life! Cold, and buried here forever! Where did you come from? St Peterburg?"

"Can't remember! Somewhere far!"

He whispered, in the quiet tone that inhabits cemetery conversations. "What did you die from?"

"From Pogrom!"

"Goodbye Rachel. Go back to sleep."

"Thank you Shmuel! I will! Goodnight."

He sat on the cold grass and could still hear the explosions. Surely it was all over by now? Or were they happening in his head. Now other booming sounds were invading his ears.

These were not bombs, or rifles, but lusty songs of hate invading the night.

Death to the Jewsl Murder the Yids.
Pull out their kishkers! Cut up their kids!
Fried guts for supper, giblets for tea.

Gouge out their eyeballs; feed them to me!
Come on Ye Cossacks. Onward we ride
With swords in our hands and Christ by our side.

The sharp cutting chorus died away and there was his father, jauntily sitting on the edge of a grumbling grave stone.

Hello Sam." He was smiling.

"Hello Dad."

"How are things, my son?"

"Confused."

"Join the club."

"Dad! I was furious with you when you died."

"I know! I wasn't too overjoyed myself. A short life, as they say, but a happy one! Like hell. Nothing compensates for suddenly leaving your family, forever."

Sam felt strangely peaceful, considering what was happening. "What's it like being cremated?"

"How should I know? Endlessness swallows the pain of knowing. Crash! Bang! Wallop! I dissolved. Sort of silver! Exploding like a firework. Then nothing! Until now! Where are we?"

"Russia! 1881."

"Really? Clever boy; takes guts exploring the past. How's your mother?"

"She is wonderful. I give her a hard time. She was devastated when you popped off. She's found a new feller to replace you."

"Really? Good. Is he nice?"

"He seems nice. But is he good? Who knows? I'm meeting him when I get home. I shall hate him. I'm still confused."

113

"She deserves a good man. She is a remarkable loving woman; and so beautiful. I must go now!"

"Why? Wait! Please! There's so much I need to ask you."

"Sorry. I know nothing. Only love remains. I've used up all my words."

"How did you get here? Are you really there? Are you somewhere?"

"Tell her, my lovely wife I always loved her and I will love her for always. I shall now return to Chaos."

"Dad! I think we've killed the Tyrant."

"Good! The tyrant of self?"

"No! The Tsar!"

"Fantastic! Good. There are no concerns in Chaos. There is no chaos in Chaos. The Tsar? Meaningless! I must go now. Vale. Farewell!"

"Wait! Listen! Don't go. I want you to know how I'm growing up dad. I have powerful feelings and longings. I am no longer a boy. I've given up the skateboard, forever."

"Grown up? Is that wise? Sorry! I must go back to sleep."

Sam couldn't hold back the flood of tears as he watched his dead father dissolve.

"Oh yes! And now you reside on the mantelpiece in the living room, in an urn."

"You think I don't know?" The frail voice wailed. "I don't know what I don't know." And he was truly gone.

He was never there, of course. He was never even food for the worms. His ashes were not even scattered in the crematorium garden.

So where were his comrades? Why were they taking so long? They must be dead. And that would be that. Where could he go now? Where could he hide? He was in the silent land of the lost. There were no fiddlers on the tombstones.

Again he heard the trains, rattling; echoing on their usual journey to the land of Gornisht. He covered his ears but it made no difference. The trains were shunting into his head. And the plaintive cry of lowing cattle. Shunting! Singing! Shrill, high sopranos and deep vibrating basses. A choir rehearsing. "Where are they going?" He asked himself. The concert hall of the abattoir? Sam summoned up his whistle. Then ever so slowly, he returned to the small child grave.

"Rachel Gurevitch! I'm lonely. Come out! Come out wherever you are! We can play twenty-twenty. I need company; even the company of ghosts!"

Where were they; the People's Will? Had it all gone wrong? It was chaos. Not his fault.

In the east of St Petersburg, the dawn, on tiptoe, was tentatively creeping across the sky. He could hear the shrill roosters calling for the hens.

His father had been here, and Prince Hamlet was right.

There are more things in heaven and earth, Horatio,
than are dreamt of in your philosophy.

He declaimed to the wild chorus of birds. The sleeping trees were stretching, yawning the dawn. If he ever managed to escape out of this maze of coagulating nights and days, he would settle down with Katie and become an accountant. He lay down on Rachel's grave and closed his eyes; if he ever woke up again that would be too soon.

Then the smell of her. "The Princess!" She pulled him up, to her, against her beautiful, trembling breast.

"Samuel my darling! You know it's over. The tyrant is

dead my lovely boy. The die is cast. We must leave at once this beautiful and cursed city."

He shouted in triumph and danced around Sarah, whooping and hooting. He danced slowly with her to an ascending lark. Then he suddenly froze. Where were the others? And before he could open his lips to ask she answered.

"They are at the gates. Look! Comrade Peter. Peter the Dead; the holy droshky driver has arrived to get us away from here. And look further. There! See! Akiva and the Red Rabbi are alive and kicking, coming towards us. Let's beat them to the droshky."

And they did. Sam high-fived them, they laughed and climbed into the carriage.

But Sam was still looking back to where his father was, and all the dead got out of their coffins and rushed towards the gates, shouting.

Have you heard? He's dead; the tyrant is dead.
He's dead. He's dead. He's gone to dread.

All their faces screamed, pressed against the railings; cheering and laughing. And a Wurlitzer lit up the night and the klezmer jazz band of the lost gathered together, breaking into the making of music. And all the dead rose and jived and hooted and waved. And he waved and waved and wavered back.

"Come Samuel. It's time you switched off your imagination."

"Anything. For you." He sighed. "Sarah! I am so glad we are leaving this theatre of death. And that all the humans of this Land of Once have turned around and are

116

stumbling back to their stone beds."

"Samuel! Your imagination will get you everywhere. But this is not the time."

The Red Rabbi cackled, sending out a withered arm to help him into the droshky. "Let us away, captain, oh my captain. There is no time to lose."

"For fuck's sake! Go!" Akiva screamed. Peter the Dead nodded and cracked his whip and the horses, with their stark, wide-opened, bloodshot eyes shot them into the dark of night.

Sarah whispered to Sam "Amazing! Dead Peter is our trusted and beautiful friend. He is helping us get to Riga. Amazing!" She repeated. "And he's been dead for at least five or fifty years."

10

Peter the Dead looked around furtively. "Come! The coast seems clear." He opened the huge wooden door and waved them into a dank dark hall. "Welcome to my palace."

Sam entered. The rank smells hit him in the face. He immediately noticed the row of empty coffins, piled one on top of the other. Peter turned to him. "I am not just a droshky driver. My proper trade is specialist undertaking. I make the best bespoke coffins in the business."

Sarah shrugged. "Even dead anarchists need to eat."

Peter the Dead continued. "Here you will notice rats, ants, and cockroaches scuttling happily around. It serves my purpose. Who would want to come in here? Not our fastidious, murderous masters."

Statues, ladders, paintings and books were piled high to the ceiling. Clothes! Uniforms! Shoes and boots! All covered with the dust of time. And pots and pans, tables and chairs, saucepans and plates, and mouldy soups in mugs. Shelves upon shelves of hammers and knives, high piles of yellowing newspapers almost reaching the ceiling; most crumbling, like a lost city that had seen a holocaust. And there were glaring masks, spiteful, grinning and crying without sound; and mummified cats.

"You will know I won a top award seventy years ago for making the best coffin in all Mother Russia."

The Red Rabbi went close, to sniff the bespoke coffins. A

sort of ecstasy was covering his face.

"Comrade Rabbi!" Peter the Dead chuckled. "I think this one is for you."

"Just the job! Peter the Dead! You are a genius coffin maker." And he kissed the man.

Sam whispered to the others. "But how can Peter the Dead still be very much alive?"

"He's dead but he won't lie down." Akiva replied.

"We live in very strange times," Sarah responded. "Because we are close to the end of the world as we know it." She turned to the Red Rabbi. "Rabbi! Don't you remember? This is for the funeral we planned for you. We hoped we would tempt you into dying."

"If only. I had forgotten. Of course! I can rehearse my death that surely must come one day. Your coffins are just marvellous. Yes! Yes! Yes! I can use one for our journey to Riga. What a happy boy I am."

Peter the Dead and Akiva the un-dead pulled the coffin out from the shelf and placed it on the floor. And the old man closed his eyes. "This is bliss! This will do nicely. My contentment may even allow me to die this time."

"You see Samuel," Sarah spoke. "Our Red Rabbi will be ever so inconspicuous when he is horizontal. Their eyes will be everywhere. They will be sweeping the city, especially the railway station. But the Russians venerate the dead, far more than the living. A coffin is always sacrosanct and untouchable."

Peter the Dead brought out vodka. "To warm you for your long journey to the dreaded Rigans." He poured the transparent stuff into four huge mugs.

"*L'chaim*! May we all live long and die happy. This is the

stuff that keeps us all alive, in some form, or other." Peter the Dead smiled for the first time.

"This is a laugh." Akiva chimed. "Two old men. One is dead and he won't lie down. The other is alive and can't wait to drown."

Sam snarled inside, imagining Sarah, sharing a bed, naked, alongside a man who was nothing.

"*L'chaim*! To Life!" They all chanted and drained the vodka down.

Sam's throat burned with the poison. "Disgusting and ... woooah ... wonderful." He clutched his gullet. "In for a kopek, in for a rouble." The warm river snaked right down to his toes. "It's a beastly tasting poison. May I have some more?"

Peter The Dead, spoke. "I was in touch with the rest of the committee. And it was agreed that you must proceed to Riga by the night train. From there you will travel on. But going home would be the very worst place to aim for. I assume in Riga they have other plans for your escape. All the others. And if they have survived, like my own good self will stay behind and lie low until the dust settles. If it ever does! The committee have determined that this is the best way to proceed."

"Why is he so bossy?" Sam nudged Akiva.

"Because it so happens he happens to be our boss. That is, if syndicalist anarchists can have a boss. He is the high boss; Sarah is second in command."

"I see." Sam replied. He strolled across to admire the bespoke coffins.

"Death is a booming industry. Live a little longer into the future and we simply will not have enough clients," said

120

Peter the Dead. "Red Rabbi, please do me the honour and try it out for size."

"Absolutely! I thought you would never ask." He clambered into the long box. And coughed and spluttered. He crossed his hands upon his chest in death pose.

"This is remarkably good. Who knows? Maybe I can now achieve my odyssey to find endless death. Nail me down now, if you please. I am so terribly tired."

Then he found a shorter death and went to sleep, accompanied by a fusillade of farts and some deep groans. Then silence.

Akiva looked down on the ridiculous body. "He's very tall. If he stretches right out we might have to saw off his legs. Do you have a saw, Peter?" He looked around for appreciation of his black glee.

The Red Rabbi snored back: blissfully dreaming of death forever. Then they placed some covers on the coffin, and with great gusto did as the Red Rabbi requested. They seemd to be enjoying themselves with hammers and nails.

Peter the Dead pulled down a sack of *schmutters* and handed them around. "Here! Some black garments. Sackcloth! Get into them. We must appear like impoverished supplicants. By travelling thus we too will avoid suspicion," he said.

Sam walked around and admired the long, black boxes. Again his mind led him to Hoop Lane and the mechanics of burning. Collective burning would surely be far more economic? He could see all the naked customers joining the endless queue,

"For the trumpets shall sound and we shall be changed." His song led him to the ravenous flames, and the journey upwards. "And we shall be changed into smoke, all ye six million ...."

And then his jollity did a Dunabunk.

"Holocaust! Get out of my hair." He halted his ridiculous tears. All roads in his mind were turning to smoke, so he turned away and went outside to breathe again.

The horses were grazing; behind Peter's warehouse of death. One brown beauty, Bella, looked down at him.

"Shmuel! Get me out of here. Then go back to Muswell Hill and get on with your life." She seemed to say with her sad eyes pouring out her pure soul.

Horses were lucky, thought Sam. They have no concept of their future. They inherited all the time in the world. They had not yet twigged that they were enslaved by man and eaten by man and await an almighty and horrendous death. They have no concern, no concept of the future.

Then he guessed time was up when Peter the Dead emerged with the others.

"Come Samuel; help us carry the rabbi's coffin to the droshky."

"But," Sam interrupted, "How can we four carry him?"

"Easy! He's just skin and bone and light as a feather."

"Sometimes I think I can just float away." The rabbi hummed from inside the box.

"Oh! I almost forgot." Peter the Dead spat through his fingers, seven times. "Toi! Toi!"Toi! I forgot crucifixes!" He pulled several large, gleaming, red and black crosses from the bottom of the sack.

Peter the Dead, now replete in Christian apparel and adornments led them out of the warehouse and into the cold, gold gleaming day. He mounted into the front of the carriage and gently whispered to his restless horses. "Precious ones! As I always must repeat; I have no favourites and I love every single one of you. Now take us nicely, sedately, slowly to our station."

The others with their bespoke coffin struggled towards the droshky.

Peter the Dead shouted. "You must slip the coffin diagonally into the droshky, so that you will not all be huddled to death. When you alight from the droshky you will walk slowly, with Christian reverence, holding these unholy relics to your holy lips, and chant any deathlike Christian chants you can summon up from the dark dungeons of your immoral minds, and try to think only of buggering your young apprentices; that will give you holy stature; so my dear comrades let us go. Onward to Riga!"

Sam shuddered as he moved. "My mother's grandmother and father came from Riga. They were religious and thought Latvia was their rightful home. Why are we going to Riga?" He asked.

"Shmuel! Riga possesses a wonderful harbour. The best harbour in the Baltic." The Red Rabbi responded from his oblong home, which they were trying to push into the carriage.

"Why do we need a harbour?"

"Every Jew needs a harbour, not too far away. Without a harbour even if only in our minds we would have all been wiped off the face of this earth, long ago. Trust me."

Peter the Dead cracked his whip and they were away.

"The train leaves in one hour." Sarah said. The Tyrant is dead. And we know life will never be the same again. And we do not know what awaits us wherever we go.

123

Comrades! Cover yourselves with blankets to keep the chill off your chests."

They flew through the freezing night.

Akiva brought out a concertina and Sarah sang in Yiddish. And the others joined in.

Tumbala, tumbala, tumbalalaika,
Tumbala, tumbala, tumbalalaika
Tumbalalaika, shpiel balalaika,
Tumbalalaika - freylach zol zayn.

Sarah sighed. "*Tumbalalaika*. May we be happy." And Sam sighed. *Tumbalalaika* was the joyous lullaby of love song that his mother would sing to get him to sleep.

And a sudden light sadness lingered and lasted until they reached the train station. They avoided the main entrance and turned a corner to an empty, quiet cul-de-sac.

The horses were bridled and Sam and the three men carried the long black coffin out and placed it on the pavement.

"Sarah. Please tell me. Why are we off to Riga?" Sam asked, truly puzzled.

"Later." She breathed and kissed his forehead. "Once on the train everything will be explained."

"I am a Nowist! I live for the moment."

"Hush my lovely one." She walked away to share a few last words with Peter the Dead, their true leader.

Akiva, watching, hurried over to Sam. He smiled. "Boychick! You seem to be very fond of my wife. Some could call it desire."

"Absolutely! It is desire. I have fallen in love with Sarah. But who couldn't fail to fall in love with her? But then again Akiva, l fall in love with every woman I meet. I love women. And I shall continue to love them until the day I die."

"Oh! That's very nice, Sam. As long as a wink is never a touch." Akiva walked away, smirking and satisfied.

"Comrades! Gather! Come close. This is my last diatribe." Peter the Dead spoke softly. "Remember my friends; I am going with you to the train and that will be the last you will see of me. I would never in a million years spend more than half an hour in Riga. Now! When we turn this corner we will walk slowly with crucifixes held high, then touch them close to your foreheads. And also remember that the crowds milling in the streets are in a state of bewilderment; scared and dumbfounded by the news of the assassination of their beloved murderer. But they will not dare to question us. They will respect our long journey to the shrines of their wanking saints."

The three men and the Queen lifted the coffin and began their slow walk towards the station hall.

Akiva tapped on the wood. "You alright in there, rabbi?"

"For my sins?" A dark trembling voice responded. "Yes! Of course I'm alright. Get on with it. I could sleep in here forever. Good night."

They entered the concourse of the station in a deliberate slow motion.

"Chant now!" Peter the Dead commanded. Then he spouted in deep bass.

Jesus the Christ; save all our souls.
Kill all the Jews! Chuck them in holes.
Stab them and slice them and burn them in flame.
Jesus, our saviour, we cherish thy name.

And Akiva, his eyes scrambled, high up in his head, took up the torch of chant and mumbled along, joyously, like a true Christian adoring the flagellating of himself.

> *Kill all the Jews! They murdered our Lord.*
> *Oh Christ up in heaven, give me thy sword.*
> *Pull out their guts and pluck out their eyes.*
> *Kill all the Jews! Oh Christians arise.*

Sam had his own litany, a dark, horrible and marvellous song he managed to descant, high above the others. And a wandering soprano emerged; singing a Christian dirge he knew by heart on the perils that the soul encounters on its way from earth to heaven.

> *This ae nighte, this ae nighte.*
> *Every nighte and alle.*
> *Fire and sleet and candle-lighte.*
> *And Christ receive thy saule.*
> *Our saint is holy, our saint is dead.*
> *To Riga we go, to his deathbed.*

Sam thought he could hear applause, and when he looked around he could see the ragged ones, smiling. Approving! Sarah took up the song.

> *Our saint is dead. Our saint of grace! We're off to Riga, his resting place. And Jesus the Christ, his life restore, and kill all the Yids forever more.*

The crowds bowed their heads in reverence as they passed. And some in stark adoration went down on their knees.

When the comrades reached the queue at the ticket office the crowd stumbled away, happy to give preference to the saintly ones.

Sarah stood for a moment with closed eyes, mumbling a gibberish of sounds, hypnotising the goyim with her obvious high church words to the Almighty. They crossed themselves over and over again. But Sam knew she was chanting a true prayer to cancel out the previous blasphemy:

Baruch ata Adonia elohenu melech ha'olam, shehecheyanu, v'kiyimanu, laz'mun hazeh.

Blessed are You Adonai our God, ruler of the Universe who has given us life, sustained us and brought us to this season.

"How long will it take to get to Riga?" Sam asked Akiva. The muffled voice of the Red Rabbi squeaked from within the box. "Shmuel! Fear not! I am with thee."

"Oh no! He now he thinks he's God."

"And when we reach our destination I shall be well refreshed and will have enough juice to send you home to Muswell Hill."

Sarah gently tapped on the wood. "Shut up in there or we are all fodder for the flames." Then silence reigned.

Sarah was about to get the tickets but Peter the Dead pushed her away. "My treat."

"My good man." Peter the Dead spoke with ecclesiastic authority. "Herein this coffin sleeps the High Archdeacon of Nizhni Novgorod. His divine body, his holy relics, within this blissful and celestial coffin, are to be despatched immediately onto the Riga Express that leaves, I believe at ten forty three."

"Yes sir!" Good Sir! I shall see to it myself, right now, sir! Thank you, kind sir! My dear sir."

The purple, blue-faced rat of a man, got down on his knees and prayed to the coffin. Then he groaned himself upright.

"My kind sir; you and your party may now join the Riga Express. My holy ones. Leave everything else to me and follow my men with the trolley. Here are your tickets, and may the divine son of God and our Lady of the Gallows go with you."

There was no joyous or sad goodbye when they shook hands with Peter the Dead.

"My friends. My comrades. I shall now be leaving you. So mazel tov! A safe journey. If we ever meet again it's too soon." He laughed. "Forgive my jokes. You have enough jokes with your joker in the box. Not his fault. All rabbis are jokers. You have covered yourselves with dignity and honour. Long live The People's Will! Long live Narodnaya Volya!"

And he was gone. Not a tear. Not a cheer. He was nowhere in sight.

They climbed into the train and opened the door to their first class and lush compartment. And their narrow beds were waiting for them. The Princess sat opposite, staring out of the windows at endless Russia flashing past.

"Sleep! Sleep! Joyous, undisturbed sleep!" Said Akiva, curled into himself and well away; ready for the embrace of night.

But Sam was not well away. "He's in his coffin. What if he dies in there? What if he achieves his only true ambition? He is the only one, with his bag of tricks, who can save us. I must get back to Muswell Hill. My mother! My mates! Even Katie! I was desperate to get away and now I can't wait to get home."

"Princess! Look at me. I'm scared. What will happen to me? Now you have brought me here and now that the job is done how will you get me home? Do you know the way?"

This time Samuel did not try to hide his tears. They were pouring out of his eyes. "I will never taste my mother's matzo balls ever again." He sobbed.

She went over and hugged him to her breast. Her intoxicating closeness could easily have been turned into an act of love. But now he had to put all that sort of dreaming to one side. He somehow had to stem this sudden and fearful wave of fear. "Princess! Princess! The job is done but the rabbi is useless and I am lost. And he will die in there and that leaves me a lost soul in a century I could well do without."

"My darling boy, it is impossible for the rabbi to die. He is immortal. And his powers can never leave him. And when we get to Riga he will get you home in a wink of an eye."

She kissed him full on his forehead. It was sweet agony. The carriage door opened.

"Sorry. It was stifling in there." The Red Rabbi appeared, as guilty as a child, as he climbed up to his bed.

The Princess smiled.

"But the lid was nailed down," Akiva said joylessly.

"I cannot and will not speculate upon how I did it. I just pushed on the lid and up it went, and out I came."

Sam felt relieved. As long as the Red Rabbi was around there was nothing to fear. He held the key; the road back to Muswell Hill. He might even find a new contentment there. He would see everything with fresh eyes.

The rabbi was already snoring when Sarah called across: "goodnight, sweet prince."

"And may flights of angels sing me to my rest."

"My mind is restless, like yours." She replied. "I was half asleep; we take after each other, Samuel. Look at Akiva. He sleeps like the dead. He's fine. We are all lost in this mystery but you and I are aware of it. I'm sorry. I'm not feeling my best this morning."

Samuel became aware she was unusually nervous. She was not herself.

"What's wrong? What's up?"

But she did not reply. Not at first. Then she looked at him.

"When I leave this land of death and hatred I can see myself in the wonderful future."

"What wonderful future? Where are you going?"

"Samuel, there is something I have been keeping back from you. But I must tell you now. We are going to America, this very morning. We are going to that other Eden; the land of promise!"

"Who will be going?" All three of us?"

"No, my darling. Just Akiva and I."

"What about me?" Then he stuttered into silence, all his words choked within him.

She took out a small piece of parchment and read its contents.

May the children of the stock of Abraham, who dwell in this land, continue to merit and enjoy the good will of the other inhabitants, while everyone shall sit in safety under his own vine and fig tree, and there shall be none to make him afraid.

"George Washington! Isn't that wonderful? I often dreamed I was on my way, escaping from this dark hateful country, dreaming of the future. And I was singing to and suckling my newborn baby daughter. And she was a new beginning for all my descendants, and especially you Samuel, all the way down the tree of tomorrow. I am going to take up that dream and we are on our way to freedom's Holy Land."

She could see his shock, his fear and anger rising within him.

"I am desperately sorry we cannot take you with us."

"Why? Why can't you take me with you?"

"Samuel! I do not make the orders. The ruling was not mine. I begged them to allow us to take you. This was all planned long ago by the powers that be."

"Powers that be? How could you do this to me? I don't understand! Who are these people who call themselves anarchists? Some anarchists! Some joke!"

"We are the People's Will. The Council of Truth. And we must follow the orders of the committee. There is much work to do in America. Samuel, please do not turn away. It was debated, democratically and they decided that it would not be in your interest to leave Europe and that you should be returned to your home as soon as possible."

Inside he was outraged and he laughed bitterly. "I see, so I am left here in this land with a rotting madman."

"The Red Rabbi will get you there; I promise. Naturally, we are all concerned for you. We all love you too much to be uncertain. His psychic strength will come back. I have discussed all this with him. You have been a source of inspiration to us. We will meet again in the future or in the past. Samuel! I know this."

She tried to embrace him but he pushed her away. The thought of losing her was like diving into a boiling, bubbling volcano.

"How dare I find myself born not in New York, but in Muswell Hill, of all places. In New York we could have met and fulfilled ourselves with no-one else in the way."

"Samuel! You are the wonder. The alienated one! Like me. There is always one in every family. We are the restless ones! The Seekers! Don't be afraid. You will achieve something most remarkable. Goodnight. See you in the morning. Sleep tight. Samuel! You must know I love you forever." She said.

"And I love you longer than that." He replied. She kissed him, full on the lips, dimmed the carriage lamps and got into bed, mumbling a Hebrew mantra, and she was gone, drifting into the sea of sleep.

"Go where the love is. Stay away from the lost." And then he turned over, following her into the amazing and brilliant light of nothingness. He had to learn to say goodbye to those he truly loved.

No time had passed, yet he was yawning and everywhere there were people, bustling, busy, emptying carriages.

"Come on darling! Samuel. Wake up. We're here! Riga! Look out of the window."

"Let me gather myself." He was fully clothed. "Oh my greedy God! The port! Look! The ship! SS Ulysses. And you will be gone and I will never find you again."

"Yes," she said, "this is where we must say goodbye. Let's face it; forever."

"Forever is a long time." He replied. "We are the fragments of a dream; a dream that has no dreamer." He dived into his knapsack, pulled out pen and notebook and quickly jotted his words down. She laughed. "Why are you doing that?"

"I don't know. I liked the words. I want to remember. And I am driven. All these things. Words are holy." He said.

"Lucky you!" She said, just a little sad. Her smile manufactured for the last goodbye.

She shook her hair, like a creature walking out of the seas, happy and so beautiful. Then she cuddled him hard.

"You are lucky, my Samuel, rarely can we embrace our future. It looks like you are beginning to know yours."

They walked out of the train and towards the ship.

"Life is a long wank, not to be shared with anyone." He snarled.

The couple walked ahead, and near the gangplank, they turned, waving to him, and the weeping Red Rabbi.

"Goodbye Akiva; if I never see you again that's too soon." Sam shouted.

"Thank you for that, Samuel. I love you too." You could never tell what was going on under the surface of Akiva.

And the waving was finishing and the waves were lapping.

He did not say anything to Sarah. All had been said.

But she did shout back at him for the very last time.

"Never forget to remember the future. The future will embrace you if the past loves you."

And his great, great, great grandmother was gone; forever.

He turned away from the ship; he could not bear to see the tired, impoverished, tempest-tossed masses climb the gangplank. They were silently going to the land of hope, yet there was no hope in their eyes.

"Shmuel! Have a little faith in me. My strength, my powers are returning."

"Rabbi! I love Riga. It's such a beautiful city."

"Do not be bamboozled by its quaint exterior. Within these walls is indescribable horror. The icing on the cake is very thin. Underneath, it is congealed blood. Come!" He did a little mournful caper, then they walked away, without looking back at the SS Ulysses, moaning, enveloped in fog.

11

The fog horns moaned like pre-historic mothers, calling home their children.

Sam wanted to get away as soon as possible. "Red Rabbi, when can you get me home?"

"Home? Home is where we hang our hate. I have never found home. I cannot grieve for something I never knew."

Sam shook his head. But the fear and the anger did not subside. There was no point trying to get through to the rabbi. He was a priceless and useless idiot, now striding ahead with a certainty that made no sense.

"Hey! Wait for me?" Looking back he could see the boat slipping away. "Please! I have to get back to school."

"Shmuel, you are not in a fit state to fly away from us. You are a very tired and worn-out young man. And it is not so easy to zoom across years.

"Now, beware. Down this dark street, Shmuel, we will find Sonia's Cellar. She is not one of us, but she supports us. She will feed us and take care of our needs. Sonia will adore you; an English boy; and a virgin to boot. What could be better? A café, a place of sanctuary where the events going on in the world outside do not impinge."

"I would love to live in a café for the rest of my life." Sam responded.

"Sonia makes the best borsht and latkes you have ever tasted." The rabbi kissed all Sam's fingers, one by one.

"Oh! The sweet touch of youth."

Sam's thoughts raged. Maybe he was a paedophile after all.

"The centuries wear you down, Shmuel. Trust me. When I am fully recovered from something I forget, I shall snap my fingers and your Russian episode will be over. But here we are. Sonia's Cellar! Cellars are our oases. Our water holes. Life would not be worth living without them. Careful Shmuel! These steps are four hundred years old."

Sam followed the rabbi, down and down the twisted stone steps to the entrance.

"Smile! We must not draw too much attention to ourselves. There! Over in that nice cosy corner."

They sat. The rabbi smiled; his teeth gleamed black. He would never belong anywhere, thought Sam.

"My darling boy! A rabbi is only human. Now we are alone I must tell you something."

"Please, not now. I'm starving."

It was useless! The rabbi was always somewhere else.

"We all have needs. Rabbis can be just as ravenous as their congregation. In my long, long life I have loved and buried more than twelve wonderful, but mortal females. The best one in bed was Deborah the Midget. But I'm famished. Let's eat, let's stuff ourselves, for tomorrow we may still be alive and needful of replenishing. Here she cones. You will love Fat Sonia. Everyone loves Fat Sonia, but herself."

Fat Sonia hobbled towards them. She was not just larger than life; she was twice as large. And she stood there, her breasts as generous as her smile. They were beautiful blown up balloons, ready to rise up into the air at any moment. Only her avoirdupois held her down.

Every young nice Jewish boy would give away his precious iPhone for just a naked glimpse of them.

"Rabbi! My darling Red Rabbi! Long time no see. And how are you my pretty, fresh Samuel?"

His thoughts whirled. "She knows my name, already." But Sam, in this particular odyssey had learned to not uncover every mystery as it occurred.

"What can I do you for my big boy? A bed for the night? With pleasure. I have two nice little rooms upstairs! But you will only want one? Bless you both. I love lovers when the young replenish the old. Sexual succour! What a wonderful gift to an innocent lad from Muswell Horn. Look! He looks perplexed! Don't be concerned. We will keep you warm and satisfied. What do you want for your fress? My notorious latkes? My salt beef? My stuffed neck? You couldn't have come to a better place."

"Food. Bring me food. I love everything." Sam cried. "But please, I must inform you. I am not gay."

"You are what you are. Enjoy."

"Borscht! Latkes. Salt beef. The very best," she said, as she wobbled towards the kitchen, but a man with long grey whiskers grabbed her and a piping high voice bellowed. "Give us a song Sonia and make life worthwhile." She giggled and the whole congregation became alive and they got to their feet clapping and stamping.

"A song! A song! Your song!"

Expectant men were dancing with whosoever they could grab.

"If we're all dead tomorrow we may as well sing and dance tonight." A scarlet face shouted.

137

"Okay boys! You've woke up my Wobbles. I'm going to give you all a black eye with them." They banged their glasses on tables.

"A song! A song! Give us one song; your song."

"Right! One song only! My song!"

They clapped, they yelped; then raw expectation made them all go silent.

She strolled around the cellar, flabby and winking. Her low suggestive contralto colouring each word as it slowly popped out of her mouth.

> Sonia! Sonia! The law is at the door!
> Hey the bubble's in the wine!
> Send all the people to the front line.
> Send all the children to the Salt Mines
> Lully,lully. Lully bye bye!

She bowed and wobbled her way to the kitchen.

"Show us your bum. Do what you always do."

Sonia lifted her skirt from behind, revealing the biggest, dirtiest bum in all unholy Russia. And all her regulars cheered. Sam loved it. If only he could export this scene back to England.

The cheering was drowned by the lightning outside, and the belching thunder staggered towards Sonia's Place and shook it like a demented madman.

"Shmuel! I must be honest. Getting you back is not too easy. My *Shekinah*, my feminine side, sleeps. My magic is not working well; if at all. I must shake her. But I must be absolutely honest with you. The fault lies with the singer, not the song. But bear with me my handsome youth. I will do my best to get you back to your mother and your mates.

I promise. Give me a few days."

"What else can I do?" Sam responded, despondent.

"Excellent. Meanwhile enjoy! You are marooned here with me. So smile, and give me your *Rachmunis*! An old washed up wanderer needs a splinter of compassion. And if I have not recharged my batteries in two days, please try to kill me. Maybe in the end it could happen that I am destined for a carving knife hacked into my jugular. I am so homesick for the dead."

Sam nodded. "My pleasure." He didn't know whether to laugh or cry.

"You are a true sport. Thank you Shmuel. You are an Englishman of the top class. Your only fault was merely your desperate desire to get into the knickers of our own precious princess, Sarah, who is now on the ocean with miles of drowning water beneath her.

"I forgive you for your outrageous thoughts. But what else can I expect from a youth who cannot think beyond his burning, yearning weapon. And be not afraid of God's revenge, even if she is your great, great, great grandmother, I do not think you could count that as incest. Therefore I can continue to pray and love you."

"For this relief much thanks." When Sam was lost for words he pinched one from the Bard.

"Excuse me; I need to put a few more words into the slot of my memory. But tell me Shmuel, where is the slot and where are the golden roubles?"

He dived his scrawny hand deep into his interior clothing and pulled out his leather-bound book of Jewish magic, and thumbed through the yellowing, crumbling pages.

"Where was I? Where am I? Where will I be? Take pity

on a poor, broken, useless orphan who may have slaughtered his mother and father in the far off mists of time. Shmuel! After centuries upon centuries of living you tire of yourself and everything. To put it simply, into a can of rotting tomatoes, Death dances with me but He's a teasing old sod."

Sam had not been following his master's words. He was deep into his own dark thoughts. "My father is dead; my mother is being fondled by a David Simmons, an interloper trying to steal and seduce her away from me. And I am lost in nowhere, with a lying, pathetic, farting, old Red Rabbi, stinking of eternity."

Fat Sonia came with the plates of steaming borsht and laid it before them. She twisted Sam's cheek. "Mmm! What a beautiful boy. From what wonderful, sexy stock did you spring from?" But she did not expect an answer. "I could eat you for breakfast, dinner and supper. Eat in good health. Eat while you can."

The cellar was almost empty now. Most of the customers had drifted away. Two staggering sleepwalkers were pissing on the floor as they stumbled up the stairs. One or two lolled, snoring, slobbering over the tablecloths.

Samuel and the rabbi were lost in devouring the borsht before them, whilst Fat Sonia was watching over them, *kvelling* as they slurped each spoonful appreciatively, but even she was tired now, after her all-day performance of coddling and caring for her audience of ravenous beasts.

"I can see you love it! Come to my kitchen. I want to show you around." She winked. "I'll give you seconds, a grasp of your sausage. I'll give you as much as you want, you lucky boy. And if you've got nowhere to go you can stay here tonight. I've got a lovely bed, longing for you."

Sam seemed oblivious. Like the rabbi he was succumbing to the germ of being somewhere else.

"I know just how to serve a strong, starving boy. But take your time; Do it more slowly. I'll bring you the next course, my love, my lover boy." She touched him on the neck and toddled back to her kitchen.

Sam did not move and had not listened. There were other things on his mind. The Red Rabbi, replenished by soup, was *dovenning*, shuffling back and forth, praying for a resurrection of memory. "Work! Work for me! Work this time." Then the oldest man turned to his charge. "Gornisht! I'm afraid." He creaked to his feet and slowly slouched up the stairs.

Sonia came back. "My latkes! My magic latkes! The very best! In the whole of rotten Russia! Or should I say, in this stinking hole called Russia." She snapped.

He got up. "Sorry."

"I made them fresh, just for you."

"I must go."

"Come back. You're tired. Stay tonight. I've got something really special for restless, thrusting virgins. Please. Just once!"

But she was pleading to no-one. He was gone. She spat on the plate. "Go to hell and join me there." She rumbled off.

Sam dashed up the stairs into the darkening sky, and the freezing air whacked him in the face.

The rabbi was hovering in the distance, kissing a lamppost, talking to himself.

Sam shouted at the moon.

141

Ah! Moon of my Delight who know'st no wane!
The Moon of Heaven is rising once again:
How oft hereafter rising shall she look,
Through this same Garden, after me, in vain!

He cried for joy and love, with his mind and soul and flesh and bones, the immortal words of Omar Khayam, his greater master.

The rabbi came to him. "Shmuel! Now I have something to tell you. And I must be honest. My magic is not working well; in fact it is not working at all."

Sam could see the flashing sky through a breathing grille up in the ceiling.

The rabbi came close and spoke softly, for once in his life. "I must be honest with you. I am afraid I cannot get you back to England. You are marooned here with me. I am so desperately sorry. It should not have happened like this. If you could kill me I would be the happiest man no longer alive."

Sam remembered something important. "My skateboard! Where did I leave it? I must have left it on the train, how could I have done that? Damn it! Damn it!"

"You left it in the waiting room in St Petersburg."

"Why did you let me? It was my very best and precious possession."

His father had returned smiling from John Lewis in Brent Cross. "Samuel! Guess what I've got for you?" He was twelve at that time. And now it was gone, lost. And he was lost and his father was lost. Lost in the dead, yellowing pages of time! Now all was lost. All was truly lost. He did not cry. He felt the thin process of age falling upon him.

His childhood was over. He'd chucked it away.

"Shmuel, my son. Can you forgive me?"

"You once said it was God's job to forgive."

"But there is no God."

"Then why are you a rabbi?"

"Why is a tree a tree?"

"Anyway; if there is no God, then it is for man to forgive and therefore I shall have to forgive you. And you me."

The rabbi jutted his face into Samuel's face; and stared into his eyes; eyeball to eyeball. "You are a remarkable young fellow. My Sancho Panza; and life is the windmill I tilt against. Yet it is still such a wonderful place to be."

"Yes. It's nice and serene here."

The sound of the quiet was overwhelming. "Red Rabbi! Where do we go to from here?"

The old man's eyes lit up. "I have had a sudden epiphany. I know where we can go. And we should go. Now!"

Sam looked around the square. All was peaceful.

"Not a uniform in sight. There is no immediate danger here."

"For a Jew there is always danger." The rabbi stood and stretched. "Come! No time to lose."

He walked with amazing speed; his legs pounding. "Come on, Shmuel!"

It was remarkable that an ailing man a few moments ago could now reveal such mad energy. Sam could barely keep up with him.

"Yes! Riga is a beautiful city. It's just a pity it contains Rigans; the greatest murderers of this planet. The city is not yet awake. Oh God, save us from the Latvians."

"What do you mean?"

"The Rumbala Forest! A long bloody story that, God forbid, will happen, but not in this bloody century. God help us."

"For a man who does not believe in God you call upon him more and more often."

"I hedge my bets." Then he got very excited and waved his outstretched arms into the sky. "Shmuel! I know where we can go, and find succour! And safety!"

"You are incredible. You pull me up, you pull me down. Where the hell are you taking me now?"

"Of course! It is obvious! You will like Avram! That mad bastard is perfect. The Greatest Yiddish actor in all Russia! Avram Korngold. Once, when I was dying he tried to help me die. He failed of course; and here I am. He has a company of mad actors touring the entire country with the greatest classics in Yiddish. He will help us without doubt. We will go to him. Now!"

They turned their back on the moon. And walked in the opposite direction. Sam sniffed. "I can smell burning."

"Yes. It lingers. In Russia you can always smell human meat burning. Shmuel! Breathe in your dead and take them with you wherever you go. We have to somehow believe it is not the end of everything."

12

The smell of burning had gone and the aroma from Sonia's latkes was even further away. Being so tired they inhabited a park bench for the night. They could not have gone an inch further.

Sam's nostrils were now well within smelling distance of the rabbi's toes. After a time one could even survive foot stench.

It was almost morning and Sam was freezing. The Red Rabbi stood, licked his finger to find the arctic wind and faced the East. And he started intoning words that were not Hebrew.

"What are you doing?"

"Do any of you ever think with your banal brains that rabbis are cut off from all other believers in this world?"

He seemed drunk with joy when he reached the notes, vibrating high up in his nose. "Sanskrit! The holiest and most secret prayer in the universe. A mantra for the golden glory of the holy everlasting sun.

> *Gayatre Ohm bhuuu Ohm!*
> *Bhuva Ohm.*
> *Tat Savit Devasya Dhvahi.*
> *Divaya Napracha odayat.*
> *Ohm! Ohm! Ohm!"*

Oh ye children of dreams!
Resounding blessing for the upper world;
the middle world and the lower world.

He turned to Sam. If he had been holding a knife he
would have plunged it again and again into the body
of his companion. "Why do you snigger? Can't a rabbi
acknowledge and chant the timeless glory of the second
greatest faith? And furthermore be thankful boy! My
memory is slowly coming back."

"I was not sniggering. I was expressing happiness. Look!
The red sky! It's dawn. It's beautiful."

"That isn't dawn. That's raging fire. That's the mob; it's
a pogrom. Listen! They're coming. We knew it wouldn't
take long. Listen!"

Sam listened and he could hear dreaded slogans carried
on the wind.

The Yids! The Yids! We've gotta get rid of the Yids!

"And they will sing of their beloved country. Russia! The
shithouse of the world; the arsehole of mankind. Shmuel!
We must get away from here."

"But to where? What happens next?"
"Next you won't like. When the killers come with their
crazed faces there will be the burning of our houses, the
rape of our wives and children, and throwing us into the
flames."

A terrible taste of fear clogged Sam's mouth.

But the rabbi was shouting. "They're coming! The mad
mob. The murderers. They will have you up the arse. They
will have you in their mouths; they will have your balls for

146

breakfast." In a strange sort of way the rabbi seemed to be enjoying his threnody.

"Thank you, rabbi. That is very helpful."

"They're coming. They're here." The Red Rabbi cried.

"Nowhere to go! Nowhere to hide. Look! There! To the left! Approaching the square! They're coming! They're coming like the clappers. Take me boy. Grab my arm and take me out of here! My feet are not obeying me."

"Quick, rabbi! Make for the urinal! Quick! We could hide in there." Sam pointed at the little iron cage at the other end of the square. He grabbed the old man with the burning eyes.

"Shmuel! It's the end of everything."

He schlepped the old man along with a strength he never knew he possessed, and they hurtled towards the rusting door and he pushed it open.

"Imagine! A *petit pissoir* may save us. It stinks of centuries of piss. Who would want to come in here? By no means will I eject my fluids into such a shit slippery hole."

The Yids! The Yids! We've got get rid of the Yids.

The chorus of lusty, lusting throats exploded out as the mob thundered into the square.

The Red Rabbi sank down to his knees and mumbled. "I pray to the God of latrines, who, at the moment, is having a little sleep."

And the screaming, filthy mob came rushing past; with their kitchen knives held high, slashing the air, their blades catching the golden flames of the sun; thundering towards the northern part of the city. Their joyous voices gradually disappearing into the distance.

"It's alright, rabbi, they're going! They've gone."

"They'll be back. They're never gone. Oh Riga! A *crenk* on you and your goyim. You will never emerge from the Middle Ages. You are the pyre. Oh Yidden! Oh Virgins! Oh kids! Hide under your beds. Oh mothers! Order your tiny coffins. Oh fathers! Die cursing, as your fat flows from your skeleton. Oh Monsters! Oh Mob! May you all lose more blood than all the waters in the oceans!

"Come Shmuel! Let's get away from here. Let's get to the roadways they have come from. But first, oh cock, I'm bursting. I must have a slash."

"So must I," Sam replied. "Tell me more. Avram! Your actor friend."

"He is the director of the Jericho Players. The best Yiddish acting company in the whole of Russia. They hang out in Raina Vuklvaris. They rehearse and practise there, and they tour the small towns and villages he loves so much. Let's hope they are not touring at this moment in time."

"Let us go then!" Sam replied; desperate to get away from the stench of urine.

"Is Avram a member of the People's Will?"

"Never. Actors always stand outside the fray. They can hardly be members of themselves. That is if they can ever find themselves."

They were walking away from the disappearing chants of the murderers. The Red Rabbi was perusing a map, with one eye that almost touched the page.

"Yes! I know the way! Onward! They were on to us; those would-be saviours of Imperial Russia. And we are alone, left in the lurch by those we love the most, who have escaped to America."

"Sarah and Akiva were just following orders."

"The troubles of this world are always caused by those who follow orders. Think for yourself, Shmuel is my order. But I do apologise. I must not become bitter. It corrodes you heart and soul."

They were striding along the broken road. "We are still in mortal danger. You and I," said the Red Rabbi. "Sarah and her puny pony have escaped into the dark oceans of memory. But can you blame them? The answer is yes and no."

Time and distance flashed past, and now the day was getting itself together. The rabbi was now trotting along, oblivious to everything, humming and singing *niggunim*, his precious little prayer songs. Sam had to hand it to him. The impossible rabbi had not lost his most impossible spirit.

Soon they stopped running. They breathed and panted; their faces tilting towards the charcoal clouds. Then, grabbing water from a bottle thrust from the rabbi, Sam poured some over his head and some down his throat.

Then they started running again, through shtetl after shtetl. Villages came and went, but there was not a human to be seen! Lonely clusters of boarded huts, all as quiet as a discarded film set; withering smoke was still being licked by the flaming tongues of the bastards.

Sam and the Red Rabbi, with pounding hearts, scooted forward. He did not trust the man with a smile fixed to his face who seemed to know where they were going.

"We have made a splendid choice. Avram, with all his myriad faults will shelter and save us."

And night came. Safe night. And they were still running in their marathon. Drinking, gulping, slaking their throats.

And the wild, withering wind became warm and caressed them.

Sam was in and out of his mind, and running and the Red Rabbi sometimes beside him, running and running towards the end of the world.

And night turned towards dawn. Sam stopped, with his head drooping down, and bursting. Someone was laughing hysterically, and he knew it was himself. The rabbi went ahead, relentlessly going on and on, turning his head every so often.

Sam felt he was like an actor about to have a breakdown. "I can't go on." The actor cried. "I can't go on. I go on."

The dawn was up and punching. "Shmuel the Fool! You're not cool. Lay here and die. No-one will come to save you. It's always up to you."

He paused, gasping for breath. "Rabbi! How can it be that you can, you can ... outrun me?"

"Disbelieving youth! Look! We're there!" The rabbi, like Moses, with pointed finger, declaimed. "We're safe! We're safe! Thank God!" He swayed back and forth in prayer.

"Shmuel! Thank your thankless Lord for delivering us safely."

"Rabbi! One minute you curse him; the next you praise him. Did anyone ever tell you are both a wanker and a hypocrite."

"Boychick, I agree with you. But if God is into gratitude, who am I to not suck up to him? Look! Avram's place. Be thankful."

A huge decrepit house stood upon a small field of cinders. The sort of building that seemed about to fall apart, but somehow never quite collapsed, entirely.

And there in the forecourt a huge circus tent was flapping in the wind with a wonky, wooden billboard crying out, in bloody red, smudged lettering:

The Jericho Payers! Hamlet! Performances! Nightly!

"Avram's place! He's not on tour. Marvellous!" The rabbi rubbed his palms together. But for Sam everything looked quite dead.

"There's no-one here! What do we do now?"

"Look boy. Look at the small print. The dates! The plays. This week and the next. They must be here. Anyway, it's almost noon and far too soon for actors. They never get up until the afternoon. How I envy them. They should be counted amongst the angels; they keep our holy language alive. And Avram Korngold, an irritating fellow with a kind heart is the greatest Yiddish actor in the world. So he tells me. He will understand and hide us.

"Shmuel. I command you to believe me. We will rest with them and survive and then I am certain we will find a way to get you home."

The rabbi opened the angry, squeaking, rusty gate and they entered Avram's ground. It was strewn with empty vodka bottles, a rusty broken bed, and several stained pishy mattresses. Cushions lay everywhere. A long table was piled high with unwashed plates; obviously the detritus of last night's dinner. There were coats and armour and swords and sequined dresses draped over armchairs and stacked on a rostrum that had seen better centuries.

Sam wandered over towards the huge tent.

"Not in there, dear boy; some of his underlings will be flat out, sleeping off a heavy night's flagons of booze."

They wandered around, and then their eyes lit up. There were two living, unbearably thin, chestnut horses attempting to graze a few meagre tufts of grass. The horses lifted their inquisitive heads perusing the strangers for a moment, before returning to their gentle nibbling.

Then Sam saw a third horse, lying on its side with its belly bloated. Its hide was as shiny black as a raven of the tower. It was most certainly very dead. "Goodnight sweet prince." Sam uttered and walked away.

"I'm starving! When will somebody wake and give us breakfast?"

And, as if commanded by Sam's desire, the doors of two caravans squeaked open and sleepwalking bodies started to emerge, squinting in the sunrise. The Red Rabbi rose from his tree stump to greet them. "Good morning, my good friends. It's been a long time."

One or two nodded, out of courtesy, but they didn't really seem to remember the bedraggled stranger. He stood straightened to his full height. "Surely you remember me. I am the notorious Red Rabbi of fury and fame; an old friend of your dear boss, Avram, and his dear wife, Carola. Are they awake? If not, surely one of you will have the kindness to call him."

They yawned but they did not move.

"I don't understand. We have come to escape the terrible things going on out there in the real world. Surely even actors would have heard the news." The Red Rabbi's invective caused him to go even redder in the face. But there was no response whatsoever.

"Why are you actors so cut off from the real world?"

One of the group, a gawking boy with a funny moon

face came to life to prove that even actors were born with tongues, even off the stage.

"Sorry sir. We had a rough night. I'm Shlomo; known as Shlomo the Schmock. Apprentice actor and dogsbody. If I wake Mr Korngold he will have my balls for table tennis, but I can see you are in a quandary so I'll call him." He loped off to the least battered caravan, knocked on the door and dared to creep inside. And Shlomo the Schmock rushed out again and hid behind the indolent others. One young male, with a sweet soft face, smelling like lilies of the valley came to life.

"Please, my good sir, we are still in the arms of Morpheus. Can we get you some coffee? My name's Osip." He sounded very sweet.

"Ah! A rather pleasant, wide awake young man, a *feygele*, who likes other men. Wonderful! Thank you, Osip, for acknowledging that we are here having just escaped from a terrible pogrom out there in the world."

"And we are starving." Sam added. "And maybe you just happen to have some black bread and a morsel of goat's cheese? And possibly some honey on toast? And is a cup of coffee too much to ask for?"

A small bonfire, fed by sticks of wood was smoking away and the shivering actors were watching, waiting for the huge black kettle to boil.

An older man approached Sam and the rabbi.

"How do you do; I am Max, known as Max the Elder; the oldest artiste in this den of thieves. I have wasted all my life, trapped by this madness called acting. I hope you will not join us, for your own sake. Get a proper job; a proper future; not this pathetic substitution for living."

153

The old man was uttering his own private soliloquy; honed to perfection.

"Don't ever aspire to the arms of Hecuba, I beg you. Live while you're alive. I'm afraid, as you can see, I am getting on in my dwindling years, trapped in my lousy profession..."

The Red Rabbi interrupted him,

"Remember me, the famous and notorious Red Rabbi of Vitebsk. And meet my apprentice Shmuel Glass from Muswell Hill, North London. You must have heard of me? I am legend."

Total silence was the loud response.

Max exhaled a long sigh that said everything an old Jew needed to speak in this world. "It's been years. Yes! It is coming back. The Red Rabbi. Of course! You are on the tip of my brain. Yes! I do remember you, rabbi, from those old days; we once had a very short chat about longevity, and a very long chat about this very short life. You were once revered, were you not? As for me, I remember nothing." Max nodded, like he knew everything in this mysterious existence.

A deep bass voice boomed. It could belong to no-one else. "Is this a dagger I see before me? No! 'tis my old rascal chum; the Red Rabbi, who I have not seen since the beginning of the world."

The rabbi turned. "Avram! My darling!" The two men embraced and hugged like lovers. And they danced a quick merry jig together, whilst the others looked on, not bemused, not amused. Not smirking, not anything.

The two old men were oblivious to anything as they smothered and slobbered each other with Russian kisses.

Chortling and pinching cheeks, and scratching each other's hair.

"You old rascal! You stinky old fellow! Rabbi! Marvellous. You're still alive! How did that happen?"

"If you remember Avram, I am not the dying sort." The Red Rabbi replied. "How are things with you, dear boy? Broke as usual?"

"You can always rely on poverty. Why did you leave us for so long? I have deeply missed your stink of garlic, and my health suffered, but now you have made an old man very, very happy."

"Are you still a sex fiend of legend, my dear friend? Are your balls busy?"

"Worse than ever. I am human." Avram laughed. "The longer I live, the more desirable I become. Carola my darling wife enjoys my dalliances. I am, as I always was very generous at spilling my magnificent seed. I do it for her of course. She will be delighted to see you; you old reprobate. She will be up and singing like a plump lark. She was always one for a lark. A very naughty lark."

Then Avram turned to Sam. "Nice build. Good for an actor. Tell me; who is this handsome youth I see before me? No doubt you have purloined him for reprehensible practices.

"So, rabbi, we are all only human. And who cares if you have found your true vocation at last. But whoever thought you were an ancient feygele? Anyway, who cares any more. Each to his own poison."

Avram laughed right down to his very pregnant belly, a laugh like Falstaff as he pinched and pummelled his long lost friend's long dead erogenous zone.

155

The Red Rabbi's tone changed at once to urgent gravity. "We have been running for our lives."

"How terrible. Pogroms! Pogroms everywhere! Therefore, do not ask for whom the bell tolls; It tolls for thee. But what the hell. I am the great Avram Korngold, I am an actor. Politics is not my *gesheft*. It is not my business. I do not wish to know. Ignorance is bliss. Let us change the subject. What do you want? Nobody suddenly turns up without wanting something."

They both sighed together the music of despair; and then they laughed.

Sam was amazed by the actor's face. You could call it a well-lived in face. It was a face of extremes; an old, yellowing map of a survivor who still believed in buried treasure; a face of defeat and deceit and debacle, a face not to be trusted.

He had learned how to read faces from his beloved grandfather Maurice. "Samuel! Come here; you are not too young at thirteen to study people's movements. I must teach you how to read the signs and the movements of the body. It is called the language of Semiotics." Maurice knew everything and loved to use impressive words. And now he was dead and knew nothing.

Avram turned to Sam again and squinted. "And who is this rather elegant young fellow who seems so clinical in his stare?"

"I am Samuel Glass from Muswell Hill."

"That explains everything. And nothing!"

"He is my apprentice." The old man stroked Sam's hair. Sam grinned to hide his anger.

"Since when did rabbis have apprentices? Nevertheless

he is a handsome boy. I trust you are circumcised young fellow. Good! Running away from home, are you? Nothing ventured, nothing gained. Don't worry, we know the story. All actors are sort of runaways from home. Rabbi, I'm amazed that you are still with us on this blessed globe."

"Avram! We are in trouble. We're on the run."

"Moishe! You reprobate, who isn't? But please, whatever your news, please keep it to yourself. Up to your old tricks, no doubt, the old, useless politics again. What a vocation for a rabbi. Will you never grow up? Anarchism! Useless crap! Without Government? What a senseless dream." Always the entertainer, Avram broke into song.

> *The Tsar is dead. He's gone to dread.*
> *We'll feel the chill. It's the People's Will.*
> *So when you go, to get no pay,*
> *Remember why you'll rue this day.*

The other actors gathered and applauded their boss. "Just as well they approve. Their wage packets would be rather invisible, come next *Shabbes*. What a way to waste a lifetime, and in your case several lifetimes. Sometimes your name comes up and sometimes I hear about you; sometimes I even read about you. You old gonif."

"Hark, whose talking!" The rabbi laughed, and Avram turned to his employees. "Only art and artists, music, drama and actors can change this world? Come Moishe, walk with me and tell me everything."

He turned to Sam. "You seem a very different sort of boy. Don't run away; I might have something in mind for you." Then he put his arm around the rabbi's waist and they wandered from the others.

"What an amazing fellow." Sam said.

Shlomo came close. "My horse, Pipik is dead."

"I know! I saw him. I feel for you."

"And I feel for you; trusting those two old bastards."

"Why do you want to be an actor?" Sam felt close and sorry for the kid.

"Who knows? I fell into it. We were starving at home. I envy those who can live a normal life. Please don't tell on me."

"Never! I won't. I always thought actors were very special and loved their work. What about the others?"

"We're the same. We all think the same. We're all in the same boat and it's sinking; fast."

"I would just love to be an actor." Sam said.

"You must be hungry. Come, I'll scrape up some *zavtrak*, a perfect Russian breakfast."

Sam quickly followed the sallow youth into the tent.

All the others were already there feeding their faces. The intense ceremony of fressing caused a minimal amount of conversation.

"What's your name, young man?" A large, buxom woman fixed Samuel in a voracious smile.

"My name is Sam." He replied. The scent wafting across and gassing him in the face did not exactly come from the perfume department of John Lewis of Brent Cross.

"Zelda. Zelda, the willowy zephyr." All the other laughed. She joined in. Zelda was approaching the galloping years of middle age. She was somewhere between chubby and sensationally sexually obese. She twinkled at him, expressing something sizzling, overwhelming.

"You are a very beautiful youth. Surely you know

158

that? Have you come to join us?" She cooed like a bird of paradise. She would have his guts for garters. He would have to avoid her. It would be curtains down before it was curtain up.

"Hello everyone." Another woman strolled in, her eyes opening wide as she noticed Sam. "Ah! A lovely newcomer in our midst." She was a carbon copy of Zelda of the lost years. The only difference was the singing, dazzling colour of her hair. She was a peroxide blonde0 with a slow wiggle. She shoved herself between two young men too busy staring into their empty plates to acknowledge her. "Sorry I'm late. I was having a terrible dream and I could not tear myself away. How do you do young man? With whom am I having the pleasure?"

"I'm Sam. Sam I am."

"And I am Leah! Some of our exalted company call me Leah the Lost. Actors! What can you expect of us? I am not lost. I am merely waiting to be found. Ooh! What a gorgeous boy you are. You make me quiver."

It seemed the whole gang of actors were around the table. Sam was impressed by the high priests of drama but not by the two ageing sirens.

The Red Rabbi and Avram entered, lost in intense conversation; and they all clapped and yelped as the harassed Shlomo came running with a crammed tray. "Come and get it. The whole *gunz*. Shi! Borsht! Kasha! Hot buckwheat porridge! Milk! Sugar! Butter! Tea! Blinis! And honey."

Max the Morose nudged the newcomer. "I am cursed to hide in these changing garbs, and to living other people's lives."

But it was the rabbi responded "Max Levine! You belittle yourself. You were fantastic." He gave his new companion a slobbering kiss on his cheek.

Max the Morose nodded, his watery eyes staring back into the magnificent and inspiring past. "Ever since I could crawl I hid in the garb of others. I never fell in love; except with myself. I never felt the joy of having a beautiful bride and a child. I was my own child. Goodbye then, my friends. Very nice talking with you! Lovely day. Enjoy the repast. You seem a nice sensible boy, Sam, I beg you once again, leave while the going's good."

He wandered away to the flap of the tent. "Enjoy! Enjoy."

Max seemed such a nice man, Sam thought. But nice people were so vulnerable. He had to beware that he would not catch the virus of niceness.

Silence fell upon the slurpers; each lost in their own dish. "I must go and awake my adored and adoring, passionate lady wife, Carola," said Avram.

"Wait! Listen! All of you!" It was Shlomo. "I was down the village earlier, getting milk, when I heard disturbing news. And all the villagers were crowding around."

"Out with it boy! Forget the subtext! Give me the meat! Out with it! What news?"

"Someone's gone and killed the tyrant."

"What? Are you joking boy? The Tsar? You are sure?"

"I heard with my own ears. It happened a few days ago."

A cheer went up amongst the Hecubians.

"Oh my godfathers." Avram said. "The fat's in the fire."

All the frozen around the table, sprang to sudden life.

"Are you kidding? Are you telling us that? Alexander the Second is no longer Alexander the Second?"

"That's what I heard; honest. That's what I saw. Why would I joke?"

Sam could see Avram Korngold staring straight at the Red Rabbi who was grinning away and could not hide his delight.

Avram knew. It was obvious. "Who was it? Who killed him? You, rabbi? Do you know who killed our beloved shit-bag? Was it you?"

"Me? Are you crazy? Was it you, Samuel? Or was it me? All by myself? If only. Sadly I cannot subscribe to the great honour of assassinating even a monster."

"Listen! All of you." Shlomo was really enjoying himself. "In the village people were jabbering away. Joyous! Singing! Dancing!"

"You'll laugh soon enough, when a hot poker is shoved up your *tuchas*." Shrieked Zelda.

Avram's eyes froze. He knew the score alright. He stared at the rabbi.

"Please!" The Red Rabbi placed his finger against his top lip. "Keep shtum, and let's get on with our lives."

"You mean, let's get on with our fast approaching and terrible death."

"Something like that!" The rabbi gulped down a thick strand of herring. "The universal delight! Don't you just love a large slither of shmaltz?" He rubbed his belly and burped, and farted. "Sorry! Excuse me for that."

Avram nodded and scowled. He was not overjoyed.

13

The rabbi hurriedly left the tent. Sam quickly followed. "Why are you smiling, Sam? You haven't smiled since Sarah escaped."

"Red Rabbi! I suddenly feel happier, heartened. Being here, with these travelling Jewish gypsies, has made me see things differently. I feel I could live their sort of life. I might have found my future."

"Marvellous!" Said the man who could not die. "Be patient. I too don't feel so desperate. I feel I may be close to the source of my energy."

The rabbi's talons were rapidly turning the pages of the book. "I will try again and again. It is so close; on the tip of my brain. Here is a black pencil. Scrawl these words on my forehead. Emet! Emet! Do it please! Work! Work for me! Emet! *Emet*! It means truth. Do it! Do it for the both of us."

Sam obliged and wrote the words as commanded.

"Nothing! *Gornisht*! But I don't give up. You will be home long before you will want to say 'to hell with the rabbi'."

They both laughed.

"Rabbi! Listen to the words that haunt and save me.
Home, sweet honeycomb."

But the rabbi's indifferent eyes flickered fast.

"We are too close to Riga. If the rotters are on the rampage we are right in their line of butchery."

Avram approached and Sam walked away and picked up a script of Macbeth. It was useless, he was far too aware of what was going on to read it.

"My livelihood! My whole world! Gone; forever. How will I survive? My poor company?"

"We did what he had to do, for the sake of mankind."

"Fuck mankind." Avram shouted and the whole company gathered around.

"There is no turning back. We will all be dancing with a noose round our necks. Because of you lot." Cried Leah.

"Avram, if you go, will you take me and the boy with you?"

"We have no other choice. We can't leave you here."

"Thank you. They are all wrong; you have a heart after all." The Red Rabbi said and they kissed.

"Where is my bloody wife?" Avram shouted. "We have so much to discuss and she avoids me." He joined the anxious group now sitting around the smoky fire; deep in their coven of gossip.

"My friends, my babies, you know I love you all. We, the actors, are the dreamers, the leaders of mankind. We will ignore this rumour for now. Russia is replete with rumours. We shall run through our schedule of where we shall be going, and when we shall be going and what we shall be performing there. And I shall have some special notes for every one of you."

They all hid their yawns and Avram got off the rostrum of his seniority. "Oh! One thing more! We may have to leave here in a hurry if all the riffraff, the gonifs, the goyim, the mob, are really on the rampage.

"We are the Jericho Payers, and even if all the walls of

the world fall down, we shall still bring drama and act upon the debris. Thank you all for being so patient. Now I must consult my lovely wife, Carola."

He swanned over to his caravan.

The Red Rabbi stood on a box and declaimed. "And thank you all for your kindness, to me and my handsome youth. And now I must go to where no one can go for me." He turned to Sam. "Carry on eating. It is incumbent upon the living." Then he thrust his moth-eaten cloak around one shoulder and left.

Most of them laughed at his exit. But when the laughing blew itself out, the gathering broke up and they all went their own ways into the day.

Sam was alone, feeling quite contented. Something had happened to him. The fear he had been carrying since he had arrived had lifted. The concerns of an impending crisis were gone. There was now the possibility that he would join the company for a time. What could be more exciting? He could put the return journey to the sanitised world of North Ten aside for a while. He was free of the burden he had been carrying; there was no more an urgent need to return to the three M's. Mother! Mates! And Muswell on the Hill!

But something was sending golden waves of warmth into his back. It was not the sun; it was a beautiful, slim and pale girl, her piercing blue eyes and black raven hair staring into him. She was a young actress he had not noticed before.

Their eyes met. She smiled. Sam was fixed. He could hear the thumping of his own heart.

She had all the right equipment, from her silver aura

to her toes. He wanted her like an astronaut wanted the moon.

"Hello Samuel. You have such beautiful curly hair." She said.

He was quite puzzled. "How do you know my name?"

She shrugged. "My name is Sylvia. That much I do know."

> *Who is Sylvia, what is she,*
> *That all our swains commend her?*

Sam noticed her smile with delight. Shakespeare never let him down when he was desperate to impress. So he continued.

> *Holy, fair, and wise is she;*
> *The heaven such grace did lend her,*
> *That she might admirèd be.*
> *Is she kind as she is fair?*
> *For beauty lives with kindness.*

"I love you!" She said.

"I want to be a troubadour; or a poet; or an actor. My mind is not quite made up. This is my odyssey, where I hope to find myself. And what is your journey?"

"Being somewhere else. Acting is life."

"What role is your most favourite?"

"The sad ones! The mad ones! The glad ones and the bad ones. Jessica! Ophelia! Cordelia! Katherine! I must go soon. Goodbye."

"Wait! I am Samuel Glass! And I am from London. I came to Russia with consummate ease, but now I don't seem to want to go back." He said.

She shrugged. "I want to be brought alive, before we

all truly die. We are all grains of sand on the shores of eternity."

He gazed before he could speak again. Her beautiful lips were calling to be kissed.

"You must be a wonderful actress." He finally said.

"Yes! I am. I love you hair. Come to me. But not now."

"I must see you act." He replied.

"I love your hair." She said again.

"Thank you. Yes. It is rather beautiful." He knew that intelligent girls love conceited boys.

She closed her eyes, touched his hand; and swallowed.

"I really must leave you now."

"Wait! May I walk you back to where you're going?"

"You can do anything you like with me, but not now! Later!"

Her eyes twinkled, brighter than the last morning star; and she gave him the Mona Lisa gaze, and wandered off. She was gliding through the beautiful pink morning that sometimes happens in Northern Russia. He wanted her with all his heart.

The Red Rabbi had been watching from a distance, but now he approached: "Have Ithaca always in your mind."

"How could you know that, rabbi? That poem will be written years into the future, after all this?"

"What is time to a timeless man?"

"Rabbi! You are a patient fiddler and I don't have faith in you anymore. Yet you have done me much good. And I believe in you."

"That's interesting. If only I could believe in myself." He sighed his long Jewish scythe of a sigh. "Time maybe running out for mere mortals, but sadly time never runs out for me." He walked away.

Sam noticed that Shlomo was down on his knees, staring at the dead horse. He was crying. "Poor Pipik! Poor old man." Tears were streaming down his face. Leah went over to him. "He had a good life; as horses go." She kicked the carcass several times and wandered off.

"He's very dead." Shlomo cried. Chaim was juggling with three beetroots. "Remember when we were performing *Yiddle Mit his Fiddle* in Slutsck, and our chestnut mare, Persephone, dropped dead on the road. We had to pull that bloody caravan ourselves and we sold her carcass to a goyisher butcher... Acting? What a profession!"

"Is there a heaven for horses?" Shlomo called.

"Fool, there's not even a heaven for people," Chaim replied.

"I'm looking forward to a nice drop of horse soup," chimed Leah.

"He wouldn't even make a decent pot of glue." Zelda giggled.

Shlomo kissed the carcass. And rain began to gently fall. He turned to Sam. "Come Samuel. Come with me. And we'll find you somewhere to sleep."

But Sam was still looking around desperate for a glimpse of Sylvia. "I'll come later." He said.

Avram climbed onto the rostrum.

"Listen babies! This is the schedule. Write it down, Please! Diobele! Tukums! Jaunpils! Jelgava! Avoci! Ozolnieki! Kandava! Augtiene! Snepele! We are booked into these villages where people will spend their last kopeks on the classics rather than food. We will be doing Hamlet and King Lear. Study the two texts again and again. And do remember Yiddish is the holy tongue.

167

"And tomorrow morning we must find a horse to replace our irreplaceable Pipik."

The rain was now pissing down and the actors scurried towards the exit flaps.

"Wait! Wait!" Avram shouted. "We shall start rehearsing this afternoon. The call is for two o'clock." And he departed.

The handsome young Osip approached Sam. "Any time you feel lonely and need someone to confide in, please come to me. You are so pretty." He thrust his soft hand forward. Sam was sad. He liked this young and gentle man but he was not of the same ilk.

Max came over. Sam immediately felt comfortable and sympathetic with the oldest actor in the company.

"Were you fortunate to be born of rich parents?" He asked.

"There is only my mother. My father died young."

"How remiss of him. Did he leave your mother any money?"

"We're quite comfortable, I suppose like everyone else in Muswell Hill."

"What do you mean by 'comfortable'?"

"We are not exactly on our uppers." Sam smiled. He loved the directness of the man. Maybe he could learn from him.

"Sad! How did he die?"

"I don't wish to talk about it."

"Sorry. But may I say something?"

Samuel nodded.

"I feel sorry for you, Samuel. The rabbi is a wonderful man, but he is totally insane. Don't trust him."

"Thank you! I don't even trust myself. Please, mind your

own business. I know he seems ridiculous to some, but he has opened up my life."

"I'm only trying to be helpful. I think you seem a very interesting youth. You have great depth." Max rubbed his two hands together. "So? Life goes on. You seem tired. The afternoon meeting is not for you. Why not have a nice little *schluff*. A sleep will do you good"

"Yes. Doing nothing is very tiring. And worry makes me want to jump off the world." They were now strolling outside the tent.

"There is my caravan; I share it with the other males. It stinks a little, but after a time you will not notice it too much. I suggest you take advantage of your needs. We are busy today. My bed is yours. I offer this as a true friend."

"How kind you are. For this relief much thanks."

"I love the way you constantly quote. That separates you from the banality of almost everyone. You'll recognise my bed; it is surrounded and assailed by a tower of books. Go Samuel You are already sleeping on your feet. Go now."

"Thank you Max, I'm on my way."

The old man pointed and watched, nodding benignly as Sam opened the door and went inside.

He lay on the bed, and his hand stretched out to get a frail book on top of the pile. It was a book on stamp collecting with sweet images of Alexander the Second as a child in a sailor suit. He looked intently for a moment and put it back.

He felt good. A curtain had lifted. He couldn't put his finger on exactly why he had metamorphosed into a new, contented creature. He was not too concerned about home or anything.

"Could I become an actor if I survive this journey?"

His eyes became heavy. He thought he could smell the scent of his mother. He breathed her in and felt safe. And the world dissolved, and he went down into the dark; into the far end of real life! He was swimming in the dark green river, towards the horizon; the precipice.

"Samuel! Samuel!" His father was trying to wake him.

Overjoyed he swam towards his waving merman.

"Oh my father; father of my life and love! Wait for me. I'll bring you back. At last I see my future. I want to be an actor."

Ben waved back.

"Goodbye my love, my life! I am on my way to nowhere. I am gone. I am gone. Gone!" He dived beneath the waves ... and was gone.

"I am not yet ready for the world without you." Sam was singing the ocean.

> *I have heard the Mermaids singing each to each.*
> *I do not think they will sing to me.*

The waves were sighing a chorus.

> *We come and go. We come and go. We go. We go.*
> *But if there is only nowhere, where is nowhere?*
> *Where do we go?*

And God, the bastard hovering over the whole universe of never-ending time, took out his false teeth and sucked and sucked up everything you could call life. Shattering dreams were feeding the young man, reaching up for the urn on the mantelpiece.

He woke with a start; stretching to salvage his life; his

wild sleep; his odyssey of dream and nightmare.

He was totally back inside his own daytime body and realised he was not in such a hurry to return home. Being there, in eighteen eighty one, with so much happening had distanced him and made him consider what he really didn't want to do in life. His mother would be livid.

How could he face her with the good news? He had put aside his fear and his fast-beating heart by entering the whirlwind. At last he was living in the now. This juggernaut journey had helped him. He could never survive joining the human race of mediocrity.

He sat up. Someone was hovering before him. It was the beautiful Sylvia.

"What do you want? I was dreaming."

"I know." She replied, smiling, lowering her head towards him. "Sam! You are incredibly beautiful and I want you."

"Thank you very much." It was not possible to respond without some banality.

"Over there! That other bed has more room. It will be very good there." She slowly slipped off all her clothes

"This is my very lucky day." He stammered. "Sorry! I'm being truthful."

"All the more urgent, all the more desirable. There is no time for prevarication in this world."

He loved women. The way they were not the same as men.

"Sorry. I don't exactly know how to do this."

She took his hand. "Come. I will be your teacher."

The bed was on the far side of the caravan and she floated backwards, a few inches above the ground, silently, like a ghost princess in a Japanese film.

"I will show you. We will do everything. Come to me."
She whispered and fell backwards on the bed, in slow
motion. Time was in slow motion.

"You have come to the sacred forest of ultimate joy."

He also fell, but ever so slowly upon her.

"Please! First may I smell your hair?"

"My darling! Do what you want with me. All that I have
is yours."

"You are so generous and lovely." He buried his face in
her raven forest. It was the same fragrance that Lisa and
Sarah possessed.

His body pressed to hers. He entered the synagogue of
desire and her body was a flowing river. He was falling,
falling, into golden space.

"The odyssey is the orgasm within you." She whispered
as he entered her. "If you come quickly that is alright.
That is in the cards for first time youth."

"I love you. I love you." He said, trying to hold back the
dam of silvery sperm. She nodded and laughed. And he
laughed.

Did my heart love till now?
Forswear its sight!
For I ne'er saw true beauty
Till this night.

"Samuel! Thank you."

She was stroking his forehead with one finger. "Fantastic!
I became Juliet. My Romeo. Did you enjoy me?"

"It was marvellous; far better than bagels and cream
cheese. But I want a happy ending."

She burst into tears. And he licked them off her cheek. It

172

was strange; they tasted not of salt but pomegranate juice.

"Ah well! Life goes on. And death." He spoke softly.

"My mother told me that when I was about three years old, she heard me screaming in the bath. She rushed to find me dipping my head into and out of the water, trying to drown myself. She lifted me out and I said. I hate God, because now that I am alive I have to die."

"That takes a very special person, Samuel. Have you ambitions to join the company?"

"Yes or no? I am not sure. But what a terrifying but marvellous life it would be. Like a child you can always dress up and be someone else."

She went to the door and leaned her back against it.

"Funny." He said. "I am so full of joy and you seem full of sorrow. Don't cry. Don't go."

"I always cry when something wonderful happens to me. Life is not for me. Listen! If you have any intention of becoming an actor you will acquire the two faces. Comedy and Tragedy. One is wonderful and creative; knowing so much about the joys and perils of life. But the other? Actors are ghosts; lost souls, never in their own skin. I do not know who I am until I enter the stage."

"You become another person," said Sam

"It is an actor's fate to inhabit others; because we cannot inhabit our own selves. Sorry for the lecture. Now come over to me. Kiss me goodbye."

Puzzled, he went and they kissed and he slid his hand down onto her lilywhite breast and clutched it, like picking an apple off a tree.

"You are the most beautiful woman in the world. And I will love thee forever and ever."

"Goodbye Sam, I hope I did not disturb your sleep too much. You are the best of all the grown men who ever tried to possess me. Go back to your world and love your life. You are too wonderful to be lost. I could have loved you forever if ever there was such a condition called love."

She opened the door and re-entered her world. And the chill wind sweeping in from Siberia turned right and blew her away.

14

He wandered back to where the others were deep in the craft of drama, being torn to shreds by Avram, the Terrible. "NO! NO! NO! Chaim! Do you call yourself an actor? Where was the magic? Where was the belief? You made a turd out of one of the most beautiful passages in the whole of drama. Where was your compassion? I cannot believe in you. You are not a prince; you are a stinking toe-rag. Listen well, or I shall expunge you from our precious presence.

"And I have another bone to pick with you. You dared to say 'Alas, poor Yorick! I knew him well, Horatio.' Well? WELL? There is no 'well' in the text. Where did you pinch it from? Get out of my sight. Are you a villain or just a *klutz?*"

Sam was trying hard to hide his glee at the outrageous ego of the man. If only he could be so sure of himself. "Listen! All of you! It should go like this.

> *Alas, poor Yorick! I knew him, Horatio:*
> *a fellow of infinite jest, of most excellent fancy:*
> *he hath borne me on his back a thousand times.*

"And this speech should finish with Hamlet sighing wistfully:

> *Where be your gibes now? Your gambols?*
> *Your songs? Your flashes of merriment.*

Sam savoured every single word. He was touched by the rendering from a man who was truly a great actor and a remarkable magician, who pulled out chilling words from the top hat of nowhere. But he was also a monster.

All was silent and as still as the coffin, but Carola, their headmistress, strode out of her caravan, striding towards them; smiling from her haughty height.

"Good morning all! And hello my dearest darling Avram. I wondered where you were."

"Ah! My darling; welcome to a bright new day."

"I missed you in bed last night. Still alive I see."

"I love you too."

"I thought you might have had a stroke in the night." She replied.

"No such luck."

"How charming! You bastard!"

"Just joking! I love you my darling, Carola."

"Good. Now go to hell."

"Certainly, dear heart! But first I must hang around to applaud your final exit."

They grinned at each other. None of the others seemed discomforted by their duologue. She did not have a whip in her hand; she carried it in her tongue.

"Carry on!" She demanded. Chaim was about to start spouting again.

"No! No! Stop! Forget it!" Avram was not in a merry mood. He rasped at pathetic Chaim. "You are all so banal, so terrible. You are the worst of amateurs. I could pull off a better one from any stinking street. You should become a tailor or a shoemaker. All of you; this call is cancelled. We will have another one later. Meanwhile get all your knickknacks together for our departure tomorrow."

Sam and the rabbi were in conclave. "Shmuel! The whole world is before you. So you must try. It would seem the perfect solution for your future." He danced around the young man. "Hey diddledee! An actor's life for me."

"Then you have given up getting me back home?"

"No! But for the moment you need to be busy." Then the rabbi saw his friend slinking away behind the tent.

"Avram! Wait for me. We have business to discuss."

"My pleasure. Life is not complex, it's bloody interminable."

They disappeared. Sam wandered, perplexed. .

"Lost something? Looking for someone?" It was Osip.

"Yes! The girl Sylvia! The actress. One of your company."

"Sylvia? You are sure that was her name?"

"Definitely! I sang Shakespeare's song to her; you know. Who is Sylvia?"

"Sorry!" He made a hasty retreat into his text.

Sam was puzzled. Lost was his life. Everything was lost.

He could see Carola watching him in the distance. He was a scared rabbit caught in her blazing headlights. She walked towards him and he wanted to run, but his legs refused to let him move.

"So, you are Samuel and you are beautiful. And we are so fortunate that such a handsome prince has entered our lives."

Her perfume encircled him. She was vividly intoxicating. He could see her gaze was fixed on his nether regions.

"I just love strong young men who are scared. They are always more hungry than others."

"Actually I'm looking for someone," He said.

She was outrageous in her dress; a vivid crimson and a black, arrogant lily pinned to her skinny frame.

"Tell me all about it."

"It's very strange. She was here minutes ago but she seems to have disappeared. Her name is Sylvia."

"And wise is she to have such an enticing youth looking for her. I am Carola and wicked fate has brought me to fall amongst this nest of garbage. And where does my handsome prince come from?"

"Muswell Hill. London. North Ten!"

"Be happy Samuel. If you are not just passing through, I promise we shall become good friends. You desire to be an actor, of course. Otherwise why should you be here? Once cursed with this condition there is no escape. We are all her victims."

"I have not yet made up my mind of where I am going and who I want to be." Sam stammered.

She laughed, and her two long fingernails twisted his cheek. It hurt. He was somewhat relieved when she departed back into her den.

The gathered actors were looking at him, amused. Yet another youth was soon about to enter the petals of the flower. And be devoured.

The Red Rabbi and Avram returned; both quite red in the face and clearly pissed.

Avram barked loudly. "Boy! I saw you with my old witch. Beautiful! Enjoy! But beware! She has macerated too many. And now she has you in her sights. Thank God! She will leave me alone at last. Take her, take her. I am desperate to unload her. Remember, what doesn't destroy you makes you stronger. A great actor needs the wild juice of courage. So cheer up. You have nothing to lose except the wastelands of suburbia."

"Sorry. I am totally innocent and I have no intention of doing anything. And I shall avoid her. I am so nervous of her."

"Great! Nervous is good. Nervous is truth. Truth is the main ingredient in an actor's bag of tricks. Read. Speak the speech I pray you as I pronounced it to you, trippingly, on the tongue. Be Hamlet, or what you will. Up on the rostrum boy!"

"I don't understand."

"Let's see what you're made of. Up on the rostrum and find yourself."

The others stared at him with expectant and wicked smiles, watching as he slowly stepped forward and climbed up on to the gallows like the doomed Sydney Carton at the end of *A Tale of Two Cities*, waiting for the guillotine.

And the words haltingly began to flow.

> *It is a far, far better thing that I do,*
> *than I have ever done;*
> *it is a far, far better rest that I go to*
> *than I have ever known.*

He felt he was mumbling. Dirk Bogarde never did that in the film. This was scary. He wanted to howl and thought of Allen Ginsberg's *Howl*. He took a deep breath and his voice took on a strange power. A mishmash of words, memories and dreams began pouring through him.

"Oh you comrades of the dust, rise up. I am your Mussolini of Muswell Hill. And this is our home. Antlanta. Hitler and God are dead, and I don't feel so well myself.

Tomorrow I shall bring you uniforms. Reassemble your ashes on the dark shores of everlasting eternity. We are the strong; the survivors; we are the mighty. And we shall exist forever."

Was this rubbish? No! He could see by their faces they were all held, transfixed. He plucked up the courage and dredged up, from the deep caverns of love and nightmare, words he had written, snatches of thoughts, verses and poems. He would dedicate this to the wonderful, short life of his father.

"Oh my father! Now ashes in that urn on my mantelpiece. Will I never see you again? I breathed you in when you slid into the fire in Hoop Lane, not too far from Temple Fortune where Manny's bagel bakery stood as holy as the Second Temple.

"Oh! The sad and pathetic chutzpah of those who are left behind, who dare to breathe fresh air. Top quality medium, smoked salmon with cream cheese is only for the brave. Oh you who survive the furnace. We are the lost memories of dreams; dreams that have no dreamer."

He stopped there. Gosh! He thought. Even the actors are applauding this improvised shit.

Avram was clapping hard, with praying hands. "Dear boy. From what drama were you reading?"

"I don't know. I found a crumbling manuscript in a charity shop on the Broadway. There was no title and no author's name. I bought it for one pound fifty. The words have haunted me ever since. It inspired me today. I was also thinking about my lovely dad."

"Avram! Buy the boy at once." Max said. "He has a natural and remarkable talent."

"I'm not buying. The Red Rabbi is virtually giving him away."

Carola turned to Sam. "Tell me, have I misunderstood your sexual needs. You're not a feygele, are you?"

"Feygele? Sorry. A feygele is a bird, surely."

"Oh my dearest, forgive me. Of course you are not one of those who have gone over to the other side. A feygele is a boy who wants a man. Or a man who wants a boy. Sad!"

"You mean a gay."

"Nothing gay about poor feygeles. I am so happy. Boys like you do not grow on trees. Forgive me. You will give me heartache. We will talk later. Now I must go and tend to my needs. For what Carola wants Carola gets."

Snakelike, she slowly slid away.

Avram smirked. And Carola shouted across: "Avram! Take care. Don't fall asleep. Or I'll bite off your balls and pickle them."

"Thank you darling." He shouted back. She slammed the door hard behind her.

The Red Rabbi beckoned his charge. "Come boy. Come. It's done. We have just agreed terms for your apprenticeship."

Sam felt a zigzag of fear running through him. "But what about my journey home?"

"Don't be concerned." Avram added. "This is a temporary measure. You will have the choice to stay or to leave us. Samuel you have reached a major crossroads of your life."

"You have a beautiful future in the past." The rabbi beamed.

"How much did you pay Mr Korngold for this transaction?"

"My darling boy, money does not come into this. We are prepared to take you on as an apprentice and teach you the tricks of the trade."

"How much money did you give him? I feel like a slave." Sam raised his voice.

"Money!" Avram grunted. "Let's not talk of money. Who cares about money?"

"Only those with it, and those without it!" The rabbi laughted. "Shmuel! I didn't give him actual money, as collateral. I have none. I paid him a few golden roubles. Unique and precious coins that I had secreted on my person centuries ago. I was saving them for a rainy day. And look, look up at the heavens! It's chucking it down." The two decrepit old men, *alter cuckers,* hugged and giggled. But Sam did not share their merriment.

"Samuel! Let's get down to the sheer bollocks of this deal. There is a possibility that we have not yet mentioned. It's a perfect solution for you. The Jericho Players may be performing in London. And soon. The way things are it will soon be our thrilling and fantastic bolthole."

"Truly? In London!" His anxiety subsided for a moment. "But how do we get there?"

"We'll get there. There is no reason for you to be concerned. This is my job to sort out."

Sam was persistent. "I don't understand. Have you received an invitation from London?"

Avram patted his new charge. "Samuel! You must trust people. To cut a long story sideways, the Chief Rabbi of England, the world famous Rabbi Korngold, happens to be my cousin. We have been corresponding for months now. He understands the dreadful situation we have to tolerate.

"He informs me that he has found the perfect premises for a Yiddish Theatre in the heart of Jewish London, somewhere along the Commercial Road, a few streets from Whitechapel where most of our brethren have settled. He wants to help us flee this murderous land should things get even worse."

Sam's mind was put at rest. He put aside his confusion with past, present and future.

"Terrific! I shall become an actor in the past. And maybe I shall never want to return to Muswell Hill. If you teach me the tricks of the trade I shall be famous. And fame will help me forget my family. I have had enough of them, especially my dead father and my mother and her new boyfriend."

The Red Rabbi was most content. "Be brave. Families can be hell. Stand on your own two feet, Shmuel, and welcome to manhood."

Sam breathed deeper and deeper and felt a miraculous lightening of spirit. He had been carrying around the paradox, the heavy burden of almost everything. Being seventeen was to be endured, not something to be enjoyed.

"Thank you, rabbi, I have turned the page."

Avram was still at it as he jingled his few gold roubles in his pocket.

"The entire Jewish world outside this dark country will be only too delighted to give us employment and succour. We are the beating heart; keeping Yiddish, our mother language. We are the carriers of the torch. We are the singers and the song.

"Max! Bring out some of your delicious cherry brandy and let us drink to this exceptional lad who is joining us. We must celebrate this event, for God knows there is so little to celebrate these days."

The grumpy actors did as they were told. They applauded and raised a pathetic cheer, with faint hearts and forced smiles. They had been on the road for far too long to be enthusiastic about anything. Only Sad Shlomo got carried away and complied; kissing his new companion. And the two old actors toddled to their respected caravans and quickly returned.

Max was beaming. "I bring cherry brandy and cheese-cake. The very best in the world. My dying mother sent them to me only last week. Bring me a knife someone. For cutting cake, not throats."

"And I bring you Advocaat," said Avram, "the very best libation direct from Holland, so come to the table and I command you all to be happy. And we shall all have a Bunny Hug and love each other."

They all gathered around and noshed away and Carola joined them, and the bottles were emptying fast; and even actors, on a very dark day, started singing. Chaim was playing his accordion and Zelda and Leah were dancing with concentrated abandon, unaware of the others; and not caring one jot for the usual contempt of the others. Osip danced with himself. And they all were singing.

Max had tears in his eyes and he leaned over and whispered into Sam's ear. "I believe there is a ship leaving for London in a week's time. I would love to be on it, but how can I leave my ailing mother in Kiev? There was such a terrible pogrom there a few weeks back. What can I do? I am the only child she has left."

It was just approaching noon and red fingers were poking through the black clouds. The horses seemed wildly restless and Sam looked for the rabbi to explain the sudden change of atmosphere. He could smell burning.

"Take no notice Shmuel. The Cossacks are nowhere near us. They do not come as far as Latvia. They leave it to the mob; our filthy Christian neighbours to murder us."

"I'm sure I can smell burning. Sam repeated.

"So? You're a Yid. Yids can always smell burning."

Leah, she who was born for sorrow, was unusually calm. "We may be lucky. We may be alright. We're all a little worked up. These actions blow up and often die down again. And, even if this is our very last day on this earth, be happy. It was, sometimes, quite nice knowing you all."

Avram took Shlomo aside and whispered something in his ear. The boy ran off. Everyone else seemed to be in deep conversation. Sam moved away and followed the boy and caught up with him.

"Shlomo! Tell me, what did Avram whisper?"

"Oh! He just told me to get the horses ready and to start loading up, just in case."

"In case of what?"

"Sniff! There is smoke! But it might be nothing. Peasants have much to burn these days. They give birth to so many babies and they can't afford burials." He then turned to his horses, stroking and cooing to them in turn.

Sam returned to the others. Hilarity had replaced concern. Avram, the rabbi and Max were squatting down on their haunches and trying to dance the Kazatsky.

"Who's going to join us?"

But no other one dared. The rabbi beckoned Sam. "Shmuel! Poke out your tongue at the man with the sighing scythe. You hearing pogroms? You're a Jew; what else can you expect? Come! Dance with us. Life is a joke

185

and the joke is on us, so enjoy, be jolly."

Sam retreated behind the two plump ladies, Zelda and Leah. He was mystified. Where was the young actress Sylvia? And who was there to play Hermia? Or Jessica, or Rosalind, Ophelia or Juliet? Where on earth was the young actress who played those crucial roles?

Surely not these two blubbery females, cracking dirty jokes, collapsing in paroxysms of laughter before him?

The three creaking old men, down on their knees, laughing like clowns, were torturing themselves and determined to continue their dance: "Enjoy! Enjoy!" They shouted. "We may not be here tomorrow."

"Don't worry my darlings. One door closes another door closes."

Sam laughed, realising that Jewish people survived on black humour.

15

He quietly buttonholed Shlomo. "By the way, have you seen Sylvia anywhere?"

Shlomo looked puzzled. "Sorry! Don't know anyone by that name. Sorry."

Sam crunched his teeth. It was obvious. The boy was backward and not quite all there.

"She's the young actress. She's in the company. I was with her an hour ago."

"Must go! I'm dashing down to the village to try and buy a horse; a nice chestnut mare, hopefully, and I shall name her Natasha, after my mother. Bye!" And he was off.

Am I going mad?" He stood pondering. Then he approached the two ladies, who were deep into a game of chess and gossip."

"Can I help you, darling?" Zelda pouted a sweet kiss. "Isn't he lovely?"

"Excuse me? Have you seen Sylvia?"

"Who? Sylvia? Sorry. I don't know who you mean. There are no Sylvias round here."

"This is ridiculous. She's the young actress of the company, right? You must know her. I was with her not an hour ago."

They looked at each other and shook their heads.

"Sorry darling. You can't get blood out of a stone, but if you need nice company for tonight we might be able to oblige."

He went over to where Osip and Chaim were working together, hearing each other's lines."

"What play are you doing?"

"Foreplay!" Osip replied.

"Sorry to disturb you, but have you seen ...?"

Chaim did not let him finish. "We have not heard or seen a girl called Sylvia." But Osip was less sharp. "You are a very sweet young man, even if you are a pain in the arse."

Sam sat alone under the giant oak. He was puzzled, unable to continue his search for Sylvia; and was now totally lost in his head. How could he solve such a mystery? How could she do this to him? How could she come and go just like that?

He knew exactly what his dad would have said. "All young men carry their first true encounter, their Sylvia throughout their lives."

Sam wondered. If he were to die in this country, would they hold a memorial morning for him in school? Would he be cremated and his ashes sprinkled into his father's urn on the mantelpiece?

The wind howled around him. He could hear singing from a choir, far off. Sam knew the prayer. He quietly joined in.

Ani ma'amin be'emuna shlema B'viat amashiach.
V'af al pi sheyitmahemeia.

Even though he is a little late I still believe that the
Messiah will come.

He shook his head. He did not believe.

"You're deep in *shtooch* my boy," Grandpa Maurice would have said. "How are you going to get out of it? Get on with your life. We are all flesh and blood. We all come from nowhere and we all go nowhere. But one day, in the glorious future, we will all love one another. We must move into the future." Two days later he was moved into his coffin. His beloved Grandfather! And here he was again, falling deep within his family's warming embrace.

Wonderful days peeked through the dark curtain and the sun was blazing down on the amazing, deep blue, dazzling Aegean. They were all kids again and life was full and forever. They were laughing, all three of them. Lisa, his incredibly young and girlish mother, was being dunked into the ocean by her husband; his handsome, powerful father. They were all enraptured and living in the moment.

A few days later Lisa received from her son the best grades in the school. All life was meant to be as happy as then. Those last days in Greece were the happiest times he could remember.

But a week later, in a quiet street of North Ten, where the sleepwalkers live, his dad dived onto the carpet; his lovely father, now smoky grey grit, in the once living room, now forever to be known as the dying room.

Sam could hear himself shouting, echoing through the Tunnel of Return. "Come back! Come back Anne! Granddad! Dad! Dad! Come back. Ah love that came and never went. Ah love that went flying through the air. Come back. Come back! Come back. Sarah! Ben Glass, my father. Come back! Come back!"

"What about you Samuel? When will you come back? Are you on your way home?" He spoke aloud to himself.

"Yes. But by a circuitous route. Can anyone direct me to where I am?"

His wandering mind came back to where he was; under the oak tree, somewhere in Russia and the frozen world of rehearsing actors.

"The years crumble, Samuel. Aeons! Good luck! Who would have thought that luck would become the definitive issue? Ben, your old dad, is off now. Be happy and I shall always love you and my fondest undying love to your mother!"

Sam shot up. Max was coming towards him. "What's the time?"

"Six o'clock, in the evening." Max replied. "I saw you all lonely by yourself, and I wonder why you are so disturbed, my son."

"I'm looking for Sylvia. Have you seen her? I've looked everywhere."

"Sylvia! Let me see. Hang on." Max clenched his eyes. Something was stirring in the old actor's head. "I think I remember. It's on the tip of my brain ... wait! Be patient. Yes! Of course! Of course!"

"Sylvia! Her name is Sylvia. You must remember."

"The cogs turn slowly in my head. An actor lives by his memory; if I were to lose my memory I will have lost my past and my future. Without memory I have no job. I am finished. There can be no more drama for me."

"Stop torturing me and let me know what you know about Sylvia."

"Yes! Fair enough. Young man! I do not wish to hurt you but you insist, so I have no choice." Max put his arm around the new apprentice.

"Of course! I remember Sylvia. She was amazing. Her Juliet unsurpassed! Her fabulous, haunting Jessica. Her heartrending Ophelia! She was an actress of exceptional perfection. She was not a tactical actress. She was emotional, incredible."

"What do you mean? 'Was'."

"Oh! You are of the sort who needs to hear it all. Young Samuel, please shut up, and listen."

"Max! I saw her. She was here today."

"Sylvia could not have been here today. She took her own life three or four years ago. She hanged herself on that tree, over there." He pointed to a small, leafless willow tree.

"My love is dead? I had a love that went and never came!" He was wretched.

"Sorry, my son. You insisted. Kick open the door of memory and it all comes flooding back. You are not the only person who has seen her. But I for one never encountered her ghost. It's puzzling and sad why the seemingly happy and most talented ones so often take their own lives. The further we go in life the more we are confronted by the enigma. The longer I live, the less I understand. Samuel. She was only a ghost. Listen! Be careful! I conjured up an aphorism this very morning. What doesn't destroy me makes me stronger."

"Thank you so much Mister Nietzsche. I must go."

Max, the old fashioned gentleman, stiffened and shook the young man's hand. "You are a very clever boy. You'll survive this. We humans seem to survive everything. Go in good health."

Sam felt the chill of his own impending death. It was possible he could achieve another sixty or seventy years, but that did not fill him with hope. All those years could collide and fade in a blink. He was on his own. No-one would come with the answer. Because there was no answer. This was the dark true terror of existence. Life was all about loneliness! It was a journey into nothingness. He had seen a vision and loved her. Just once! Dante's Beatrice had also died.

> *I stood in Venice, on the Bridge of Sighs*
> *A palace and a prison on each hand:*
> *Saw from out the wave her structures rise.*
> *As from the stroke of the enchanter's wand.*

And he was comforted by the words. Poetry was the panacea. A poultice covering the cold cauldron of death.

He had seen Sylvia on the Bridge of Sighs and desired her and loved her and would love her, forever. But she was a mirage; she was not there, and she would never be there. And the people he loved were mere fading shadows. He had reached the bottom and he was glad.

"I had to go all the way down, in order to kick myself up to the surface again." He comforted himself.

"Listen everyone!" It was Avram booming. "I have just changed the schedule. Tomorrow we will not be playing Hamlet in Ozolnieki! Instead I have decided we will do King Lear. Thank you. Now I must have my rest."

Sam wondered why Avram's remark could produce a snigger from the male actors but Avram ignored them and continued.

"Zelda! Come into my office please. I have some notes for you on your Regan."

Zelda dragged herself up and lifted her eyes to heaven, whereupon cometh no help, and she slowly followed Avram into his caravan. The rest of the crew laughed out loud.

"What's going on?" Sam could not read the runes.

"Bastard!" Leah muttered to herself.

"Can't you guess, ducky? Your turn next." Osip piped with amusement. But Sam could not guess.

"Why is everyone so amused? What's happening in there?" He asked.

"Let's put it this way. They're not playing ping pong. It happens twice a week, come heaven, come apocalypse." Osip responded.

Carola appeared and flew over to the piss-takers and slapped Osip hard, six times across his face. "You miserable little feygele. What do you know about love?" She strolled back towards her own little caravan, smiling with anger.

"Isn't there a law for battered actors in this enlightened land?" Max said. He kissed Osip's cheek. "Cheer up dear boy. It's called life." He whispered to Sam. "Poor little feygeles! They're so vulnerable."

Osip snarled. "And what does Carola do, while the bastard is swallowing his oats? She thrives on it. It's quid pro quo. Let's hope you are not her 'quo'. She also fine tunes anyone she desires. When I started here she didn't know how queer and sensitive I was, and she tried so hard to have her wicked way with me. Me! Of all people! How dare she not recognise that I am immune from any horrible female practices?"

"We do not behave like this and persecute homosexuals any more in England." Sam responded.

Chaim nudged Sam. "Each to his own poison."

It seemed like just a few minutes had past when Zelda emerged from Avram's caravan, looking dazed, flushed and bedraggled.

"That was quick! How was it?" Leah called over to Zelda who was trying to regain her balance.

"How many times?"

"Twice!"

"Twice? Fast or slow?"

"Slow. Very slow."

"Slow is better!"

Max nodded. "When the prick stands the brain dies. In this life some remain beasts and will never ascend from primeval depravity."

Avram poked his head out of the window, not at all mindful of the others. "Leah! You turn! Come. I owe you a tutorial. Please hurry."

"Oh master of the goats' herd. I'm coming."

"Many times I hope." Avram replied and he opened the door for her."

"In she goes, to the boring scaffold of his bed." Max sneered.

And Sam was full of delight, as the others went into conclave over Leah's fate. Gossip and argument was the cement that kept the company together.

"Smoke! I smell smoke. Pogrom smoke. Can't you?" The Red Rabbi stood there, sniffing, transfixed with wild eyes; an Old Testament prophet, pointing at the sky, seeking apocalypse.

"I smell nothing, just the rancid smell of travelling actors." Chaim added.

"Wait! Listen! All of you! Shtum." Max commanded. Avram ran out of his door in his *gutkers*. "Smoke! Can you smell smoke?" He started to sniff around like a hungry dog. "I can smell smoke. I can smell burning. I can smell flesh."

Carola emerged in her Japanese kimono. "I can hear screaming. far off."

"THE MOB! THE RABBLE!"

"They're coming! The hoards."

"The pogrom is coming!"

"Can't you hear them! Quick! They'll murder us."

"Shlomo! Are the horses ready? Hurry! Get us away from here."

Max tried to steady the ship of wild creatures, running around in circles. "In my humble estimation they are just about one hour away. Time and sound are always at odds in this accursed country."

Leah came out of the caravan, quickly getting into her pyjamas. "They'll kill us all. I am not ready for death."

The whole company was scooting around like bedbugs, looking at the sky, looking at each other; fearful. Suddenly it was night.

"Where's Shlomo?"

"Here!" The boy came running in from the road.

"Everyone is running around in the village. People are crying; screaming."

"The sky! Look! Flames!"

Sam grabbed the rabbi's cloak. "You must get me out of this. My mother will never survive my death. Neither will I."

"Shmuel! Your mother is not yet born. Besides, it is not so terrible to die. It is life that is terrible." The Red Rabbi shivered as he morphed into sermonising mode. "It's God's joke."

"But there is no God, you keep saying."

"That's the joke." The rabbi replied.

"The bastards are looking for us because you and Shmuel

killed the Tsar, leaving us to face the fire." Chaim was wild with rage.

Avram jumped on the rostrom. "Babies! Silence! All of you. And stand still. Listen! Everyone! We must leave at once. They are still miles off. We must pack, but not panic. We will go to where we are going. Only sooner. A small town; one they are sure to avoid with not enough Jews there for the killing. We must get moving. Now! You know the drill, so do it. And if anyone gets lost we will reassemble at the harbour, just beyond Riga. It's not too far."

"Away! Away! No time for gossip you lousy low lives. Get cracking. Get moving!" Carola's seemed to be enjoying this total chaos. Her voice was a circus whip, cracking at her animals.

"Rabbi! Don't stare at the sky or the hills from where your help doth not come."

Zelda came rushing out of her caravan, a little late. Fire! Fire! The Cossacks are coming! They'll rape us." She cried.

"Nincompoop! There are no Cossacks in Latvia. Get cracking. Anyway, we know the local mob is far more frightful."

Leah whimpered. "I was born for sorrow. That's the meaning of my name." Then she rushed off to gather her things.

"Go! Go my feygeles, or your tuchases won't be there for passion anymore." Avram stood in the centre, pointing at all the objects they had to take with them. "We have time to spare but no time to waste. Make haste."

He sniffed the air and jumped on the sofa to see beyond his domain. "Yes! They are definitely coming closer. But we still have time. Trust me babies. Have I not saved us all

196

from disaster, time and time again?"

"No!" Snapped Carola. "You bloody, pathetic fool. Don't gabble. Just get on with it."

"Thank you darling, I do so adore you in crisis, and even between the sheets. Remember I am the conductor keeping my musicians together in this bloody serenade."

"Dolt!" She responded and walked sharply away.

Shlomo had brought a third horse. "Her name is Antigone, she's so beautiful I want to cry. Load up everyone. The horses are fed and watered and ready." Then he went to each horse and whispered words of love into their twitching ears.

"We are the Jericho players. We will thrive. We live on hope and madness. Help me. Good. Good girl! Antigone!" He spoke softly and directly into the new black horse's ear. "Antigone! You join us in crisis, but fear not. You will enjoy a wonderful life with us."

The Red Rabbi laughed at the touching scene of Shlomo and his four-legged friend. "So what's new? The Jews are on their way once more. Move yourself boy, if you ever want to see your nice safe home again; hurry! We have not much time, yet all the time in the world, if you include the immensity of the universe."

"We are a long, long way away from my home," Sam replied.

"We're getting there, my babies. We will not succumb to having our throats sliced open in this filthy, desperate land."

Far away the bells were tolling. Everything was packed and they were now ready to leave. Sam mumbled a prayer. "The Lord is our shepherd and it serves him right." All the others nodded.

Out of the charcoal sky came bolts of jagged lightning and rumbling thunder.

Avram could not let this crisis pass without a curtain speech. "If only your acting was as sharp as your exodus. We shall be gone in less than five minutes; and God willing we shall unload in a small Jewish town, a place forgotten by time, a quiet and peaceful place. Surely the pogrom and wild mob with their bread knives will not greet us there? The Jericho Players will endure. Of this I am certain. So now, onward! Onward to Ozolnieki!"

16

Samuel and the Red Rabbi sat in the synagogue hall crammed in the front row, surrounded by a restless, vociferous audience of peasants. It seemed that the whole population of Ozolnieki was there; and not a Christian in sight. It was amazing! All these were Jews, and wildly dissimilar to those he witnessed in the synagogue on Saturday mornings in Muswell Hill.

Some were knitting, some, clapping, some singing, some arguing, some were cracking nuts; some were eating, some arguing and some of the young women, looking like old ladies, their faces smudged with dirt, were suckling their babies. Most were alive and noisy and expectant. But a few had nodded off and were snoring. And they had brought their own chairs.

Then there came a happy chorus, shouting and a stamping of feet. "Why are we waiting? WE CAME TO SEE A PLAY! WHEN WILL IT START! WHEN WILL IT START?"

The Red Rabbi peeped through the curtain and pinched his nostrils." They all stink down there!"

"Just like you. What can you expect from peasants?" Max shouted through the cacophony.

Sam closed his eyes, thinking about something else. She was on the dark sea; the mouth of oblivion. Sarah, on her way to her Promised Land. He would never see her again. "God Bless America." He sighed.

The rabbi giggled. "We outrun the murderous mob. They went the wrong way. They are probably pillaging and murdering somewhere else. Who would come here? Except pathetic actors. Who would want to?"

"Where will we be sleeping tonight?" Sam was unsettled.

"Shush! Here! On this floor, when the show is over and these pathetic peasants take their chairs home. Do not worry; there will be blankets for all."

The oblivious peasants were getting louder and louder. But in good humour; still stamping their feet and laughing and whistling.

Avram was ready, in his tattered, fading, gold crown and Shlomo opened the curtains and, in one instant, silence reigned when Avram walked forward and addressed the audience.

"Ladies and Gentlemen! Mazel tov. We are here. And I greet you, This may well be our last time to perform in this shtetl, speaking our *mama loshen*, our blessed, holy language. Yiddish. You may thank our beloved Tsar for this tragic ending."

Avram was getting into his stride.

"God help us. He never stops. This will be longer than the play," Zelda whispered to Sam, offstage.

"Therefore sit back and enjoy our play. And you will hear and see the tragic story of King Lear and his three daughters."

The audience clapped like thunder.

"So enjoy. This may well be the last Jewish play this tyrannical country will ever experience to the last syllable of recorded time."

Avram's words multiplied in his mouth, and poured out

without any sign of drying up.

"We are the Jericho Players and tonight we are performing King Lear; a masterpiece written three hundred years ago by the famous Jacob Spiro, a mere genius; a shoemaker from Smolensk. I, Avram Korngold will play the King."

As he spoke the curtain opened, revealing all the cast.

"And these are my two evil daughters, performed by our two lovely ladies, Leah as Goneril. And the insidious Regan, played by Zelda. And of course, our beautiful leading lady, Carola, who will play the King's precious and truthful daughter, Cordelia.

"The play is set in Minsk, in an unspecified period in the past. Act One! Lear, King of all the Russias, declares his intention to abdicate and divide his kingdom between all three of his daughters. Enjoy! Enjoy! And place your hands together to show your appreciation." This brought ear-splitting applause.

"It is possible you have not witnessed live drama before. Tonight you are fortunate enough to witness the perfect story of the deep differences of siblings; their cocktail of love and hated; and an old man's fear of old age, and needing love and reassurance. It is the story of life. Thank you for all your kindness." He stepped backwards and bowed. The gas lights were dimmed.

"Thank God. Let's face it. Avram is not the best player in the world, but then again even mediocre actors cannot destroy this play, entirely." Osip remarked.

And as the actors moved through the actions of their make-believe world, Sam watched with wonder.

The three daughters entered the palace throne room and took their places. Avram the King came into the arena, ready for action. There was static silence throughout the hall. The actors on stage were struck dumb, as if time itself had frozen them to a standstill.

Sam could not curtail his need to carry out an inner autopsy. The question was, had Lear gone mad before the play started or would he go mad now, when he confronts his daughters? Are all families destroyed by the curse of guilt, jealousy and greed? Why do we all tear ourselves and our loved ones to pieces? Home was the last possible cage of safety; and despair! One could never truly escape the family where you found yourself having emerged from endlessness.

"Sam!" He said to himself. "This play is fucking marvellous. I am going to sit on this impossible chair and enjoy."

"Meanwhile we shall express our darker purpose." Spake King Avram. "Give me the map there."

All the eyes of village were wide open, staring, amazed, drinking in Avram's throbbing words and gravelly voice.

"Know that we have three in our kingdom to shake all cares and business from our age, conferring them on younger strengths while we unburdened crawl towards death." The King took out a rather stained and overused handkerchief, and improvised.

"Excuse me ladies and gentlemen. It is very dank and fearsomely hot in this magnificent hall. I must awhile wipe my moistened brow, for we are all mere groundlings and foundlings."

The audience were not perturbed by all these asides; indeed they thought it was all part of the play, except Sam, who was amused by the collaboration between William Shakespeare and Avram Korngold.

Zelda, before it was her turn to be questioned by her father, the king, caught Sam's eye and blew him a kiss. Then she re-entered the drama again.

The audience, munching furiously on crusts of bread and cheese and apples and liquorice were also devouring every single word. Drama was their beneficial friend; freeing them for a moment in time from their endless, harsh and monotonous lives.

Now Lear's daughters were gathered around the feeble king. Avram, the Great Kosher ham, suited the role entirely.

"Which of you shall we say doth love us most." The King demandeth. "Goneril! Our eldest born, speak first."

There was a long drawn out silence. The Princess gasped; she had forgotten her lines. "Goneril! Leah! *Meshuggener*! Daft, silly bitch of a pregnant cow! Make with the words."

The audience roared with overwhelming enjoyment.

"I love you more than words can weld the matter. Dearer than eyesight; space and liberty ...." She gasped. "No less than life, with grace, health, beauty, honour. A love that makes breath poor and speech unable! Beyond all manner of so much I love you."

"Good girl!" Then he drew her close and muttered and hissed quietly. "You found your bloody words at last. I'm docking your next payment. You stupid bitch." Sam couldn't fail to hear his anger, but for the hungry audience it was all added gold dust.

Avram sweetly smiled when he returned back to the drama. "Dear darling girl. I thank thee."

Then Zelda, as Regan said in a syrupy voice: "Only I truly love thee your highness," And Avram kissed her forehead with a satisfied, regal air.

Carola stepped forward; talking aside, to herself. "What shall Cordelia do? Love and be silent?" She hissed. She was looking as young as Methuselah in her immortal sarcophagus of black silk.

"Then Poor Cordelia! To thee I speak. What can you say to draw a third more opulent than your sister?"

"Nothing my lord!"

"Nothing! He roared back. The whole audience, with two hands to mouth, gasped.

"Nothing." Cordelia said again.

Avram's face turned red and belched out anger. "Nothing will come of nothing. Get out of my sight! You bitch."

A matchstick woman stood up in the middle of the astonished audience. She was clutching her baby with one hand, and waving a clenched fist at the astonished Avram, "You bastard! You monster! How could you do that to your beautiful daughter?"

"Good for you, Miriam Shapiro," someone else chimed in. The audience were now in uproar; enjoying, living it all immensely. Carola scowled and Avram screamed down at the groundlings. "Stupid bitch! This is not real. This is meant to be a play. Sit down and shut up."

"Why don't you shut up yourself?" Snapped Carola. Then she turned to the cast "Let's get on with the bleeding play you idiots." Now the entire audience were standing up and clapping. But up on the stage the cast were astonished, transfixed, frozen in their appointed roles.

Sam's hearing changed. Cattle! Boxcars! Again the Boxcars! The trains were clanging, clattering, crossing through the dark junction of his mind; backwards and forwards, echoing, reverberating. And shouting peasants, assassins and murderers came close. He covered his ears, afraid the noise would pierce his eardrums. And the suckling woman stood clutching her baby and shouted a stab of that one terrifying word. "Pogrom!"

"The mob. They'll cut our throats, they'll burn us alive."

The audience was in a dream state, coagulating, some rushing for the way out. This was not the play; this was for real.

Chaos was smiling on his rostrum, conducting the scene. The hall was alight and the crowds from outside rushed in with burning torches. The cast huddled together on stage. The audience was a tangled, screaming, unbelieving crowd.

And the mob went in amongst them. "Death to the Yids. Pogrom! Pogrom! You bastard Jews. You're finished in this country." And daggers and breadknives were doing their job, a flashing flood; and blood was fountaining, pouring down and hammers were crashing, and smashing and nightmare was king.

The hall ignited and the slavering flames licked at the bundle of actors upon the stage. And down in the hall, peasants cried and fought each other and tore at each other desperate to get outside.

"Death to the Yids! Death to the Yids." The chorus continued outside.

"We're finished. We're finished. God help us. They are burning us. They are turning us into smoke." They cried and a vacuum of silence rushed in from the world; and the woman with her baby was sliding in the blood where the dead lay, gushing in their innards.

The baby was still sucking the breast, and as she sang softly a lullaby. "Sleep my baby sleep. *Rozhinkers mit*

Mandlen, almonds and raisins, sweet and bitter, sleep my baby sleep."

And then there was utter silence. The mob had gone to continue their pogrom in the next village.

"Come Samuel! We are untouched up here." The actors seemed to melt into each other. "We're all alive. Thank God the mob did not look upwards. But then mobs never do. Come now! Shmuel, jump up here. Now! If you ever want to return to Muswell Hill."

"Quick!" Avram shouted. "The back door to the synagogue has a burial ground behind it. Come now! Now! Follow me."

Avram the King was trying to take full command. There are times when most people reveal their true nature.

"Come! I will lead you out of Sodom."

Sam rushed up the stairs to the stage and the rabbi put a consoling arm around him.

Leah cried. "Thank God we're all alive!"

"God had nothing to do with it. He abandoned us long ago." Zelda had reached her lowest.

They came out of the burning hall and into the deep, refreshing air outside. Sam's teeth chattered from the sudden cold. Reality and chaos were dancing a tango. Someone was screaming a prayer. "*Baruch ata Adonai-Elohanou ....*"

Sam's thoughts were racing. "How will my mother ever know if I died in a madhouse? For the rest of her life my unknown death will haunt her." He laid still on the frosty grass.

Shakespeare appears in impossible times,
but in my soul my courage climbs.

And more words came.

> Look! Jessica. See how the floor of heaven
> is thick inlaid with patterns of bright gold."

He was going mad.

> Golden girls and lads all must
> like chimney sweepers come to dust.

He changed his mind, because he was free – an apprentice poet was allowed to be free. He was going sane.

> The things you run away from you run right into.

The chaos of his father's death had led him to this. And where would this lead him if he couldn't get home?

Outside, far away and disappearing in the dark, he could hear the pogrom mob carousing, with songs of death and destruction for all the Jews in the world. And he imagined he could hear Hitler screaming, long before he or anyone was even born.

> Sieg Heil! Seig Heil!

"Oh! It is not just the mad murderer we should fear. We should fear the acquiescent mass of the darkening kingdom!" The Red Rabbi was shouting, his face raging with blood.

Sam knew no-one would come with the answer. He was on his own, in a fast pinch of disappearing days and the books were burning.

The Red Rabbi was stretching his creaking bones. "Come quickly Shmuel; I know the perfect place. Look! The ancient cemetery! See! It's adjoining the synagogue, just behind those oak trees. Let us go and breathe in its loving sanctuary; quick."

Sam came back down to earth and followed the crazed Red Rabbi.

"Shmuel! I'm trying to remember those words that brought you through the Tunnel of Return. But don't despair. They are on the tip of my brain."

"I also forget them. My mind is all over the place." Sam responded.

They were now in the enfolding arms of the cemetery, standing silent, to slow their breath. The rabbi pulled him towards a diagonal tombstone that boasted that three hundred years had passed for its interred resident.

"Against all the odds we survive, Shmuel! Do not despair if I have to lose you here. I have already passed on to Max those key words that will get you to the Tunnel of Return, and home."

Sam murmured his thanks and surveyed his new hiding place. Another graveyard with unpredictable residents.

"You will be safe here. No-one comes here. The goyim cringe away from the Jewish dead, but not the dying. Their main purpose is to see us die. Our tombstones are the only places left for sanctuary. Those mobs will depart, eventually; those harbingers of death. And then we will get on with our lives."

The others now appeared; like apparitions between two worlds. They were silent; too busy catching their breath and gasping, thankful. Locked in the miracle of their narrow escape. Avram, with closed eyes, leaned against a collapsing holy wall, totally shagged out for words. But his loving wife, Carola was as pristine, as if she had just walked out of a window display.

The Red Rabbi whispered, almost licking into Sam's ear. "Shmuel, you will go with the others. And you will go home as soon as possible. You have a whole life ahead and your exams will be pending. Later, you can re-join them in the Commercial Road, in the East End of London and serve out your apprenticeship.

"As for me, I shall be coming in my own time; if there is any time left for humans on this little world. But first I have to enter the synagogue to rescue my lovers. The Scrolls of the Law! The Torah! Shmuel! There is no time left. Pray for me that this day will be my last."

He clicked his fingers and the sky went black. "You see? I am returning to myself. Please wait outside for me before you re-join the others."

The Red Rabbi rushed towards the back door of the synagogue, which was being devoured by the raging appetite of the roaring flames. And he was singing as he was swallowed up by the ravenous monster.

Before Sam could go to the others, the blackened, naked apparition returned, cuddling and kissing two golden scrolls. His hair and his beard were gone and his parchment skin was peeling off; singed by the roaring fire.

"These are my lovers. My scrolls! My lovers! My Torah! The Law! Without the Law where are we? Shmuel! Look! My lovers."

He thrust the two scrolls into Sam's arms. "Take them Shmuel, embrace and bury them, here in this cemetery and they shall never be defiled. And make the mourner's *Kaddish* over them. And pray for me and all mankind."

Sam cried, pulling the two scrolls close to his chest. "Are

you not coming with us?"

"There is no time left. Today is the day of days. Today is the day of return. And this is my day, at last. If one can applaud the miracle of birth then surely one must also be able to achieve the miracle of everlasting death.

"At last! Shmuel, these are my last words. Do not forget to remember the future! Goodnight, my lovely young man. It was a pleasure meeting you. Goodbye!"

He started to hum a little prayer, a fervent *niggun*, and he dashed back into the gaping mouth of the synagogue. His last words never seemed to trail off.

"Goodbye! Goodbye!"

The words cascaded on and on and on, trailing through the smoke cloud of sky.

"He's gone." Max came to Sam. He seemed unusually happy.

"A little poem just came to me. Listen! 'He lost his magic; this tragic *Tsaddik*'." He laughed. "Yes! And it seems he is never coming back. But who knows? The older I get the less I know. But I shall be your foster father now."

He put his arms around his charge.

"Come! The burial. I shall sing him a song of jubilation. And after us there will be no Jews left in this accursed country. And in their torment they will fly straight to Moloch and Gehenna."

The hole was dug in the earth and Sam watched the Jericho Players praying in a circle around the gaping earth.

The local rabbi came running; he gabbled through the eulogy for the dead and the burying of the scrolls. It was exactly as if he was burying a person he wanted out of the way.

Yit'gadal v'yit'kadash sh'mei raba!

May His great name grow exalted and sanctified.

He swallowed all his words. And then continued. "Oh Lord, what is man that you regard him, or the son of man, that you take account of him? Man is like a breath; his days are like a passing shadow. You sweep away all men. They are like a dream; like grass which is renewed in the morning. In the morning it flourishes and grows, but in the evening it fades and withers."

For a moment there was utter silence. The kind you could stick a knife into. And the beautiful wooden building behind them screamed and was devoured. And it was now no more.

"Maybe this time, at last, our Red Rabbi has finally achieved his heart's desire."

Avram, overwhelmed, took the stage. "Where's Shlomo? Where is that Shlomo! Is that you? Are you pissing in the dark? It's sacrilege in a Jewish cemetery."

"No! How can you even think that?" said Shlomo who had come dashing through the gates. "I've been to see the caravans. They are untouched. Like virgins. But...."

"Lobbos, Gonif. You are a rascal and a thief. I didn't even see you go." Avram shook the boy. "Tell me! You make me sick! What are you trying to say? Speak! Or I'll give you the boot."

Shlomo managed to spit out his message. "I saw it on a tree, end of the village. A proclamation! Yiddish can no longer be spoken in Russia. It is now a criminal language. If you even speak one word of Yiddish you are committing a capital offence against the State. And it merits certain death. One word of our holy tongue and you're hanged by a rope and your tongue sticks out and you go a bluish mauve in the face and you are fucked." Then Shlomo ran out of words.

"We will not go to the caravans yet," Avram declared. "They are too much in the open and the mob may well return. These pogroms have no precise definition. They are the sudden nightmares of humans whose brains have been infested but worms. But a few of you can go now to the caravans to bring back blankets and food. Anything that will suffice for one night. And we shall sleep here, huddled on this grass.

"Go on! Go! Go! For God's sake! Bring fruit! Water! And tomorrow, please God, if we survive this night, we will go straight for the harbour of Libua and board our ship for merry England."

Two actors ran to his command, but Sam sidled away, amongst the dangerously leaning tombstones.

One opened, like Tower Bridge, and Ben Glass came out and waved, beckoning his son to come closer.

"What's wrong? Don't you want to speak to me anymore?"

"I have nothing much to say. Seems I've used up all my words."

"You? Lost for words? That'll be the day. So Samuel, what was this journey all about?"

"Dad! I don't know! I am not the me that I was. I told you My skateboard days are over. I left it in a waiting room, in Vitebsk. The boxcars follow me, wherever I go. I feel they will never leave me. I wanted to make love to Anne when I found her, to make love before the cataclysm. But I didn't, because that would have spoiled everything.

"If life is about anything it's about the fears and the sorrows and the joys. And being cool. You have no choice. You don't have to find and chase life. Things come to you. It's called living. Is that enough Dad?

"Sorry dad. I'm crying and I'm happy and just making with the words. Today I really think I am a man. For what that's worth. Life is glorious when you get over all the shit it throws at you. Sorry! I don't make sense. Neither does life."

Ben's hand reached towards him and he disintegrated into a shimmering silver dust that sprinkled down into the sodden earth. And he was gone.

Carola approached. "I've been looking for you. Everywhere! Please! We are turning our back on this wonderful country."

"I know. But you vilify it," said Sam.

"The die is cast. We are leaving for the ship and freedom when it is light. We are ditching this country forever; our past, our costumes, our darling horses; everything. But I must retrieve certain things from my caravan. Please help me. I'm scared. Take me there."

They reached the caravans, none of them touched by the pogrom.

Carola yawned. "I am so tired. How wonderful to feel your body heat so close to me. I want to sleep forever; or at least a few hours before we leave this obnoxious land."

She opened the door. "Please come inside. I have something to warm you up."

"Sorry!" He stammered. I must get back to the others. Maybe another time."

213

She tried to pull him inside.

"You will experience such joy. I promise."

"Carola! No!" He tore himself away. And then dashed to join the others, who had promised to wait for him outside the cemetery gates. But they were not there.

17

The Jericho Players were not anywhere. He wandered the deserted streets but could not find his way to the harbour. The day was creeping tentatively along the narrow alleyways, not sure if it should turn over and go back to sleep. The chilling wind from the east, had a voice of its own. "You're lost Sam. You're very lost." Sam was on the verge of tears, but too frozen to cry.

The morning inevitably advanced and a cacophony of foghorns from the ships in the harbour started playing *La Marseillaise*.

> *Allons enfants de la Patrie*
> *Le Jour de gloire est arrivé.*

It gave him fresh hope. He had been running in the wrong direction, away from the harbour. He turned around just as Shlomo appeared, breathless and rushing towards him.

"Where have you been? Come quick. I've been sent out to find you. Our ship leaves in half an hour. This way!" They ran together without a word and then there she was.

"SS Victoria! Fantastic! England here we come!"

He looked up and they looked down at him, waving. And it was a relief to see Carola also up there, waving down at him.

"Where have you been? We've all been worried!"

"We thought you wanted to stay here, amongst the cave

dwellers. I'm so relieved we found you. Come on, up the gangplank."

"Shlomo. You go. I'll follow. I want to say goodbye first, to this terrible and wonderful land."

But when he turned away from the boat he stopped suddenly. There was Sylvia, walking in a circle. He catapulted towards her.

"SYLVIA!"

It was impossible. How could the ghost girl be there?

"Sylvia! Sylvia!" He called. "I'm over here! What joy!"

She turned around but she was not smiling. Vacancy was her face. "Ghosts are like that." He told himself.

"Don't you know me? Don't you recognise me?" He went close, slowly, to not scare her off. She was so frail and beautiful that he wanted to cry.

"Sylvia! Wait! Don't you remember? We loved. We loved."

"We loved? What the fuck does that mean? Goodbye. I must join with the others. That is where I must go."

He felt sick. Angry. As she rushed away from him and faded towards the gangplank. He was stuck there; his mind a maze. Then Max came down "You look as if you've seen a ghost? Come! Quick! You are coming with us. We must hurry; you are the last to board."

"It was Sylvia. Max, I believe I am going quite mad."

He put his arm round the young man as they slowly climbed onto the deck.

"Sylvia doesn't exist. Your brain has been troubled by the flames." At that moment the ship's bell sounded and the vessel began to move.

"She must be here. Didn't you see her?"

"I've told you, she no longer exists. I saw her hanging

216

body years ago, and she was very dead. Her face all blue and her tongue purple, hanging out of her mouth. You must get her out of your mind. Hallucinations enter when the mind is lost."

"Do you remember the magic words the Red Rabbi told you to get me home?"

"Magic is a lost boy with a bag of tricks." Max replied.

"Come, everyone was worried about you."

Sam was feverishly shouting. "Did anyone see Sylvia, the young actress? Tell me where she is. She came on board a few minutes ago. I saw her."

Getting a head shake from Max they all shook their heads, and melted away. Forlorn, Sam sat down on the deck.

"Max! How will I get to the Tunnel of Return? How will I get home? Tell me. There is no tunnel is there? I was minding my own business, getting on with my life when the rabbi appeared. So how did I get here in the first place? There is just me, lost, stranded in nowhere." He stood and went to the rail, and there she was, on the deck, gliding away into the distance. He was glad. He would never see her again. He was finished with ghosts.

"The problem, Sam is not getting you back to England. That will happen. We will arrive there tomorrow, or the day after. The problem is we are stuck in the world of eighteen eighty one. Your parents are not yet born. Your house is not there. I do not have the answer."

Sam laughed ironically. He couldn't wait to get away from home; now all he wanted was to get back. He stared into the dark ocean.

"So how will I get back to my own world? My mother is

falling for a conman who can't wait to get into her knickers. And my mates? Also not yet born! I miss them all Horatio. But I am a young man with infinite jest. I must get there somehow. And find them there, where I left them. That's my problem Max. It falls on me. Things I shall have to confront when I finally get to Victorian London."

"See you at supper." Max retreated, happy to slip away from the boy.

And Carola appeared and touched him gently. "Your cheek is so soft. Like a new-born baby. Actors do not make good parents. But the need is always there."

"I thought you would command Avram to not let me go to England with you."

"You think I hate you? Never. You are my lost child. I just want you close." The harridan had morphed into a sweet and gentle girl. "Wishes are fishes; some you catch, some you are sadly glad when they get away." She pecked him on the cheek and hurried away. "See you at supper. Don't get lost again. We all love you!"

Shlomo was the only other one on deck. He was staring out into the ocean. He called across. "They're all downstairs in the large lounge. Isn't it great! I longed for this all my fifteen years, to get away; to travel on a great big ship and now that I am here I am full of sorrow. They wouldn't allow the horses to come with us. So we had to sell them for horsemeat. I'll never get over it."

But then he lightened. "But the thing is that we are safe from pogroms and I love my new mother, the SS Victoria." Thick, dazzling snowflakes were now bedazzling, obliterating the tossing, sloping world. It was goodbye to Riga and that monster called Russia.

The seagulls were shrieking, as they whirled in a vortex above the ship. But Sam was tingling warm with joy. What a journey he was on. He had seen and escaped Latvia, the land where his forebears lived for centuries. Through the dark he could hear them. The seagulls were screeching ancestors. "Why? Why?" They cried. "Why did they hate us? Why did they murder us?" Imagine Jewish seagulls. Sam giggled.

He went down to join he others but they were busy, deep in their texts, and Sam's eyes were heavy. He slid down into a large leather chair. It was so inviting. He could have slept within it forever.

Avram banged a spoon and climbed onto the table.

"Oh God! Here we go again. Zelda muttered. "The Tsar is dead but Avram lives on, God help us."

Avram looked down on his children beneath him. There was a touch of Moses in him. "Listen, my darlings. I have a few words to say. We are on our way to England. There are no Cossacks there. So what is new, my friends? We are the double Jews. Outsiders! Yiddish actors, condemned forever to travel through a world of chaos. We belong nowhere; therefore everywhere is home. Towns, villages, cities, faces may coalesce, yet we are the most fortunate. We bring Yiddish, the holy tongue. We are the holy magicians. We bring the classics of the world and act the history of our people. The bitter-sweet matrix of our lives. We bring transformation. We bring the universality of theatre. Out of nothing we create something. We are the Nomads of nowhere. One last word. As we move across these dangerous waters, always remember we travel with hope. For hope is our metier. Now go to bed. And wake up with hope."

"Avram! Please don't burden me with hope." Max shouted and everyone laughed. Even Avram! And they wound down the stairs into the belly of the ship, to find their cabins and a little sleep.

"Come my darling Avram," Carola took her husband's hand. "You've been a good boy. You will fully deserve my whip tonight."

They were gone but Max hung back, watching the new apprentice, bending dangerously over the rail, hypnotised by the pounding waves.

Max approached gingerly. Sam did not turn around. "It's alright Max. I'm not going to commit suicide. Go to bed."

"Certainly. I too am pondering this ocean; this world. And who I am and why? And where I came from and where am I going? Tell me, seriously, what profession will you go for?"

Sam dived into his many desires. "I think I might become a sculptor; or an archaeologist or perhaps a poet, or a troubadour; or maybe a philosopher."

"Nice! In that case you could open a philosophy shop. And starve for the rest of your life." Max went into paroxysms of laugher.

Sam climbed onto the rail of the ship and threw both his arms outwards, to balance.

Max startled, stood there gasping. "Come down! You silly boy! Come! Come! Help me someone." No-one was there, only the mist.

Sam was like a two year old. And he undid his flies and let loose a long golden flow. "One solitary little ant, pissing into the endless ocean. Every little helps," He said.

Max cleared his throat. "Come down, please. Or you'll

give me a stroke. Come down for your mother's sake."

Sam obliged.

"You're totally barmy. Your mother must have been glad when you disappeared. My heart is desperately trying to survive your antics."

"Sorry! In the end you have to grow up, I suppose. In the end you have to laugh."

And Sam dreamed and chuckled and cried at of the ones he had lost. The Red Rabbi, Sarah, Sylvia, his mother and Katie; and his father and Maurice.

"If I didn't laugh I'd cry, just one tiny tear, in the mighty ocean of time." Max responded. "A boy of seventeen should be allowed his imagination. Remember we must live with hope."

Sam threw Max's words back at him. "Mr Levine, please don't burden me with hope."

18

SS Victoria ploughed on through the endless waves. And they finally emerged into the early morning of an English dawn. No-one kissed the pavements of Tilbury. England might have been a free country but it was not the Holy Land.

The crowd of actors shuffled onward towards the Commercial Road and the East End. All were staring, startled; astonished by the cacophony of noise and the crowds of people walking in all directions.

"London! At last! We're in London." Carola stared.

"London! What a filthy hole. Where is the beauty?"

"The beauty is in freedom." Chaim replied. "A country where we can get on with our acting and our lives."

"God help us. God help us." Zelda was shaking.

"God can't even help himself." Leah replied.

"It's a long way from Riga!" Said Max, bemused.

Avram was perusing a map and he pointed to the right. "That way is where the goyim exist, but the other way, to our left is Whitechapel – our new home! One hundred thousand *Yidden* live here, maybe. All hungry and thirst for their culture and us. We will flourish here. So forget the greyness; forget the fog. We will light up this world. We, The Jericho Players, will have our own Yiddish theatre The Paragon Theatre. Within weeks, within days. No more touring."

The traffic was an endless flow of horse-drawn carts all hurtling past.

"Come Sam. Aren't you excited? What's wrong?"

Sam hesitated. The others were already darting through the traffic, taking their lives in their hands to get to the other side of the road.

"What's wrong? Aren't you coming?" Shlomo was tugging at him.

And Sam started to cross over. There was something he had to say as he gingerly walked the tightrope, while carts upon carts came, thundering, crowded with produce; vegetables, boxes, furniture.

And the deep dark fog was swirling in. And he realised everything was black and white. He had landed in a black and white world. It was definitely London, but not the London he knew. He looked at his fingers. They were no longer pink. It was very all very peculiar.

"Come on slowcoach!" Someone shouted.

Sam and Shlomo negotiated their way through the mass of traffic and joined the others, to great applause.

"Wait! Sorry, there's something I must tell you."

All noise seemed to disappear. "I am not going with you. I'm going home. Sorry. Home is special."

They all stayed silent, bamboozled.

"I'm not going to become an actor. I've decided. I'm going another way. I'll be alright. I'll be able to find myself there."

They were all silent and static. Only Carola managed to find her voice. "But Sam, we all love you."

"Thank you. But I'm going now to Aldgate East. Goodbye."

"Sam! Please, come with us. Please come and settle with

223

us and we will try to help you. You belong to us."

"Avram! I belong to me."

"Avram! Leave the boy alone. He must follow his own star." Carola shouted.

"Thank you very much for having me. It was fun. Goodbye."

"I understand. You still need your mother." Avram had to make a little dig.

Sam laughed. "Avram! I am not a poor little puppy dog who needs mother's milk." He offered his hand.

Avram grasped the young man's hand. He seemed sad and plaintive.

"We lost you. My lovely apprentice, if you ever change your mind you know where to come. You will never get over us."

Avram went away, bemused, shaking his head. He joined the others and they all stared as Sam turned and briskly walked off.

He did not look back.

As he passed along the Commercial Road he noticed one horse and cart standing static in the kerb. The costermonger was rolling himself up a fag.

"You alright mate? Wanna fag?"

"No! Thank you. I'm fine."

"You seem troubled. Life's a bastard. Don't I know it. Here! Take a bite." He chucked down a rosy apple.

"Cox's Orange Pippin. The best. Take care." He took up the reins, laughed, waved and rattled off on his cart.

"Many thanks." Sam took a huge bite into the sweetness and goodness of the fruit. He felt warmth flowing through him. Humans could be quite beautiful. He walked more quickly and breathed more easily. He didn't stand out amongst the crowds. His clothes had seen far better days.

He had come through the endless main road and was now approaching a huge junction. He darted into the mass of back streets where people were scurrying, and where the shops and houses huddled together. Snotty nose kids were dawdling and were being dragged to school.

And he knew his only ambition was to find a way out of eighteen eighty one and to get home. But he had a pain in his belly. He could almost smell the vision of a bowl of steaming chicken soup and matzo balls, and this spurred him onward.

He saw a man ahead in a uniform holding a batch of letters. He had to be a postman.

"Excuse me." .

"Can I help you my old son?"

"Yeah! What year is this?"

"Eighteen eighty one! Eight thirty in the morning. November the twenty eighth."

"Can you please direct me to Muswell Hill?"

"You want to go to the horseracing at Alexandra Palace?"

"Near there."

"Sorry. Never been there myself. Don't look so down-hearted. If you smile, good fortune will be attracted to you. Meanwhile, take a halfpenny, just for luck." He flipped the coin in the air and Sam grabbed and caught it. The dour profile of Queen Victoria went straight into his pocket.

"How can I possibly thank you?

"Cor! You're posh, so what are you doing in these stinking streets?"

"I'm on my way home. If I am lucky."

"You're lost ain't ya? I've been lost all my life." Sam smiled and quickly walked away. It wasn't all dark in this Cockney London. He just wished some colour would pour into the streets of the famous East End.

Grandfather Maurice once took him on a nostalgic visit to the streets of his childhood and he'd loved it. Maurice needed company to hear his tale of how he struggled to escape from Whitechapel, but only made it as far as Stamford Hill. Most of the others managed to go onward, through the North West passage to settle in Finchley, Totteridge, Harrow and Muswell Hill where the air was sweeter and the homes were palaces set in paradise.

Oh, those endless stories of survival. Those marvellous, terrible stories of these teeming streets. That daily grind of trying to make a living.

"You should have experienced such days Samuel. Oy! The bugs scuttling up and down the walls! And when you crushed them, oh God; the worst smell in the world. It made you retch and vomit. And the fleas! Oy! The fleas! Those hopping little bastards, sucking out blood from every part of every sleeping body. No-one was spared. And the characters? The thieves and the low-lives. The *schmoosers*. The *schmerrels*. The *schmocks*. The unemployed. Everyone stank to high heaven. Hanging around, haranguing each other on street corners. Spouting politics, revolution; and the price of chopped liver and smoked salmon. Anything to pass the endless waste of listless time; flying past.

"Samuel, I was a marvellous bespoke tailor. With nothing to bespoke. Once. My cutter, Morry was a lovely man, but my presser? A *momser*! A bastard. A *gonif*! A fresh *shikse* to sleep with every night."

And now Maurice was dead; a skeleton in his box; in the equal world of crumbling bones. How he missed that lovely man.

Sam was walking towards the hub of the Jewish world: Whitechapel, huddling close to the docks, from where the tired and persecuted poured in. Now his grandson was reclaiming these same streets.

The shrill Christian bells of Whitechapel Church were declaring nine o'clock. And the stallholders along the Mile End Waste were setting out their goods. And all the gossiping old *yuchners,* were at it already, pressing the vegetables and smelling the arseholes of the hanging fowls. "This stinks. This is rotten!" This is not a fresh cut chicken. This is not fit to eat. How much? What? Do me a favour. You must be *meshuggah*! Think I'm mad?"

It was all part of the daily ritual. Then he came to breathe in the best stall of all. The Delicatessen! And being close to starvation he could not resist the temptation of self-flagellation and he breathed in the heavenly aroma of pickled herrings. He was starving. He was cold. He was skint and his stomach was churning.

"You alright son?" One jolly woman said. He noticed her fat fingers. They should have been blood red but were black from all the years of dipping them into the pickling liquid.

"You're very pale. Want a taster? Come on son! You need a taster. Come on open your mouth and Aunt Sadie will give you what you want; and what you need. Open your cake 'ole." He obeyed and she took out a fat prime fish. This she cut into little chunks and she slowly slipped, piece after piece, into his mouth and down they went, happily into his welcoming gullet.

227

"You need nourishment. That's what you need. You need a nice lady to satisfy your appetites." She chortled and giggled; she seemed a little in need a different kind of nourishment herself. Her fat wobbled all over her body. And her frail silent husband, beside her, did not enjoying his generous wife feeding the penniless.

She twisted Sam's cheek. "Here son, take a fried gefilte fish ball with you. Go in good health. But be careful. These streets hide some dirty rotten low lives. Here take a bagel and some best quality cream cheese, and some nice smoked salmon. Take! Enjoy! And go; before I eat you all up myself."

He grabbed. "Thank you very much. You saved my life." Sam moved on, slowly nibbling his fish ball. Then he sat down on some steep stone steps and bit into his bagel, and looked around at the other down-and-outs, suspiciously clocking him.

"Also on yer uppers, are you?" Said a man with black teeth who looked like a proper Yid; but why was he wearing a dangling cross around his neck?

"You're a nice yiddisher boy, *sholem aleichem*, peace be with you, down on your luck, come with me son and find the Lord. And you will become resurrected. Come, come and be changed. And our Lord, our Jesus Christ will look kindly on you, and you will not hurtle down into the fiery pit. Trust me and come with me. There is food and clean clothing inside and clean beds in there. I was a nefarious bugger. But now my son, I am pure. As pure as honey."

He licked his lips. And Sam thought this was the best time to scram. First, he gave the man a piece of his mind.

"A Jew who pretends he is not a Jew, deserves to be a

lousy Goy forever. As for me, I am Jewish to the end of time. Sorry! I must go now." And he quickly scarpered.

And the angry cold wind, coming down from the Arctic, turned right at Leytonstone and hit him in the face. How could he possibly get to his precious mother? How could he have been so rude to her, of all people since his dad copped it?

Sam didn't look back. He did not relish the idea of being turned into a pillar of salt; not just yet.

He heard someone singing along the Mile End Waste. He sang so sweetly. He had a cap in his hand. Sam slowly approached. He was a real tramp of a boy, of around fourteen years, with a well-lived-in face, without shoes or socks, and standing in the gutter, proffering the cap in his hands.

The boy sang so plaintively

There was a ship come from the North Country
And the name of our ship was the Golden Vanity,
And we feared she might be taken by the Turkish enemy
That sailed long the Lowlands, low

A lady, all in Victorian black dropped a coin into the cap and hurried on. The boy continued:

Then up stepped our cabin boy and boldly outspoke he And
he said to our captain "what would you give to me if I would
swim alongside of the Turkish enemy
And sink her in the Lowlands low."
"Oh, I will give you silver and I will give you gold..."

The boy stopped singing and picked out the coin. "Wot! A lousy farving! He shouted at Sam. "Wot can you 'spect from a Jew-lady?"

Anti-Semitism was everywhere. Even in the heart of Whitechapel, where poverty stricken Jews were trying to scrape a living, this cancer thrived. Even here the black curse of endless, mindless racism was following Sam.

Sam reproached the urchin. "You were born into another time and you couldn't know what happened to the world. So I suppose I must forgive you."

"Don't understand a fing you're saying. You were staring at me when I was singing. Did ya hate my song? Was I that bad?"

"On the contrary, I loved it. Would you like a bit of my bagel?"

"Bagels – best fings you Jews ever invented. You're a Yid, ain't ya?"

"Yes! I am a Yid." Sam started to walk away.

"Wait!" You promised me a bit of your bagel."

Sam nodded, and tore his bagel in half. "Here! Best quality smoked salmon."

The street urchin grabbed and chewed the offering. "Did you also invent smoked salmon? Marvellous. Fanks! You're not too bad for a Yid. All Yids are rich! Ain't they?"

"Rich in many ways, but not in money. Not down here in the East End. But I'm lost and broke, right now. So long!"

"Wait! What's your name?"

"Sam! Samuel Glass. What's yours?"

"I'm Joe. Joseph Christie. And proud. London Irish I am. My dad built the Metropolitan Line here, down in the East End."

"What? All by himself!"

"Yeah. Don't be daft. Oy, where you are going? Wait for me! Don't go. Gonna sing another song now. Soon as I swallow my bagel."

He took off his cap and put on a pathetic face and bellowed forth his new song.

A doe eyed girl from Dublin was found in Camden Town.
Strangled out at seventeen; they never found the man.
She was always such a good girl her mother told the press
So please piss off you rotten sods and leave us all in peace.

Widows gathered and applauded, and some dropped a few coins into his cap. He rushed over to his new found friend.

"Did you like my song?"

"I loved it. You moved me."

"My dad died down here, building the railway line. Something fell on his head and he was a goner. And me mum took to the booze and went barmy. The family was ripped apart. Me young bruvvers and sisters were taken away. Only my sister, Gladys, stayed and loved me. But she died too young and I cried and cried. So here I am. Though I was good wiv my songs, weren't I?"

"Joe! You were tremendous."

"Fanks, Sam." He dived into his cap and brought out a few silver coins. "Cor! You brought me luck. One silver sixpence! One thruppeny bit! Two pennies; and four farvings. I owe you breakfast."

"Sorry! I've got to go."

"Wait! We could be mates. Hey! Why don't you try and have a go?

"Me? Leave it out. I can't sing."

"You're skint! You'll need a few coppers if you're on your way."

Sam did not feel like disappointing someone with such

231

enthusiasm. "Can I sing a very old song that refuses to die?"

"You can spout anyfing, as long as you don't pour shit on the queen. God bless her."

"What can I lose? I'm lost enough already. You're right! I could do with a few bob to help me get home."

"There you go Mister Samuel Glass. Have a go."

Sam closed his eyes, breathed deep and opened his heart.

> *It was a lover and his lass, with a hey and a ho*
> *And a hey nonny no, that o'er the green cornfields did*
> *Pass in springtime; the only pretty ring time,*
> *When birds do sing hey ding a ding a ding*
> *Sweet lovers love the spring.*

It was far from the blessed season; the cold was burning his bollocks off.

A few down-and-outs, and old widows rummaging through greens, potatoes and rhubarb, and a giggle of girls, stopped and laughed.

"Ain't he posh? Where does he come from? Eton College?"

Some jeered as they passed; but two comely young women whispered and jingled some coins into Joe's cap.

Sam stopped singing his folderols.

"Thanks! You on your way to school?"

"Na! We're felling hands. Improvers! And we're late for work. Lovely voice! Fanks! You nearly made me cry. Bye!" And they hurried on.

And time passed as it was apt to do. The strangest people you would never believe took a quick gander and chucked coins into the hat. Compassion and caring was still alive in the shtetl that was the old East End.

Joe picked up his cap and tapped a little pavement hornpipe and slapped his new friend hard on the back. "My lovely, posh, Jew boy friend. This is smashing. This is bleeding good! We've got some lovely stuff going on here. Shake hands. It's called mates. We're partners from now on."

He sat down on the kerb and slowly counted the booty, and whooped with delight. "Who cares about money? Only those with it, and those without it! We're rich! Sam, me old tosser! Count wiv me. One beautiful shilling; five pence, two ha'pennies and four farthings. And you've got a lovely girl voice. You're not one of those bummers are you? Na! Course not. I saw the way you clocked those two luscious Jew girls with beautiful tits! Cor! What pleasure for a lost lad. You'd have to be the luckiest sod in London if you could get into their bloomers. Dreams are nice, ain't they? Wet dreams are even better."

"Where do you live Joe?"

"Here! On these streets. I snuggle up in empty barrows; my mattress is a pile of rotten vegetables that have seen better days. I cover myself with old sacks and fings. But it could be worse. Sometimes I go to the Tuppenny Lean, if I've got the spondoolicks. I've done skippers from everywhere and I can't wait to be dead."

"You'll be alright. You'll come through. Redemption is surely waiting in the wings."

"Wot's that? Can you eat it?"

Sam replied. "Do you know, Joe, you've got a kind heart. And you deserve better."

"Will you stay with me then? We could be best mates."

"We'll see! I've got a lot of gefilte fish to catch. We'll see how it pans out." Sam churned inside. He had to be on

233

his way and soon. Nothing was going to stop him from his inevitable journey homeward. But for the moment he could afford a few hours with this bright shining lad; just another lost soul he had found on his quest; this frightening journey in this idyll called life.

"Come on. I'm starving! You must be also; let's mosey down to the pie shop for some lovely jellied eels and mash."

"Eels are not kosher." Sam joked.

"What's kosher?" Joe asked.

"Life is kosher. Maybe I'll kosher the eels myself. Good job the Red Rabbi isn't around. He'd scoff the lot and tell me off for not being kosher."

"What's this Red Rabbit? Where is he?"

"He is dancing in the garden of paradise with the golden trumpets of Abraham blaring loud; achieving the other side of the Euphrates."

"If this is a sane world, thank God you're mad. But anyways, what you doing in these streets? A posh geezer like you. Never 'eard of a Jew boy down on 'is luck."

"What's today?"

"Friday! All day I believe."

"Impoverished Friday with no fishwives and no chicken soup, therefore no matzo balls. And, no Sarah, my queen who has gone forever. He burst into gratuitous song.

One enchanting shabbos. You will meet a lobos.

Oh Joe. You live in a small world, called the East End. Be thankful for that. In Russia you would have been dead, long before you were born."

"Sam, you speak such funny fings. Where do you come from? Where are you going?"

Sam shrugged. "You've just spoken the most important question in this dreaming existence."

"Come on mate; finking ain't good for you. Let's go." Joe grabbed Sam's his arm and pulled him away from his conundrums.

19

They were in Cambridge Heath Road and they dived into Harry's Pie Shop.

The eels and mash were bunged down before them. Sam wanted to vomit. "Not a very salubrious dish to set before the king." He said. The plate was filled to the brim with black and white jelly and pieces of dead eel were swimming around; as is their wont.

"If you don't fancy it, shove it to me." Joe's plate was now almost empty. Sam closed his eyes, his stomach heaving, revolting, but he wanted to please the lad. So he plucked up the courage and stabbed at a piece of eel and gingerly nibbled at the meat.

But it was no good. "I'm giving it a miss. Not feeling well this morning." All those centuries of being a Jew had not deserted him on this foggy nowhere. And he was glad.

"Give it me." Joe grabbed the plate. "Pie, mash and liquor! Good for yer. The best in the world!" He sloshed it all down with noisy abandon.

Sam turned his eyes away and looked out of the window; trying to concentrate and figure out ways of getting home. All the money he had earned was being blown away by this disgusting feast.

"No cardboard box tonight, mate! Can't sleep out on the streets anyway. It's winter wot freezes your bollocks off. But worry not, my old mate. We've just got enough for the

Tuppenny Lean."

"Tuppenny Lean? What's that?"

"It's a doss house for tuppence. You and me! You're homeless yeah? Like me. Obvious!"

"Not exactly homeless. My home's somewhere on the other side of London. But how do I get there? That's the question without answers. My mother and my father are not yet born."

"Blimey! And I fought I was lost. But I s'pose I was lost before I was born. But now fings are changing. You and me, like teaming up. No-one's done it before on The Waste. No more skippers down Rothschild Buildings.

"Sometimes I fink I never had a home. Been on the streets half my life. The early days was good. But one day in the middle of the night, a bit of metal casing fell on my old man's head and smashed his skull to smithereens. That was the end of it. When I was eight or nine I was buggered by some Methy drinkers; passed from one to the other."

Sam was staring across at the lost boy. Funny. He was part of the black and white world, but his eyes were a piercing cornflower blue. Things were looking up. Maybe soon all the colour would come pouring back.

"Let's get back to the pitch for the afternoon performance. Funny! Teeming up with a Jew boy."

"Yes!" Sam sighed, far away in his head. They walked back into the Jewish world.

When they were back at the pitch, Joe sang for all he was worth.

The minstrel boy to the war is gone,
In the ranks of death ye will find him;

237

His father's sword he hath girded on,
And his wild harp slung behind him;
Land of Song!" said the warrior bard,
Tho' all the world betray thee,
One sword, at least, thy rights shall guard,
One faithful harp shall praise thee!

Sam went round the crowd with a cap. But rain came hurling down angry nails. And the shivering audience of three melted away and Joe's eyes were now black and white, and they were getting soaked to the skin. Joe spat as he counted their fortune. "Eight and a half blinking pennies! Still, better than nuffing." And The London winter sky belched and poured black rain on them.

"Let's go! Tuppenny Lean! Vallance Road, before it gets too crowded. Life's bloody marvellous, ain't it?"

They ran all the way.

"It's still Friday. Perhaps I should go and find the Soup Kitchen for the Jewish Poor. My granddad told me about it. They would understand my plight and place a plate of chicken soup before me, with five matzo balls, and after they would find a way of getting me back to Muswell Hill."

Sam was dreaming more and more. Reality seemed to have deserted him. He was just feeling like the end of the world.

"'Ere we are! Tuppenny Lean." Joe shouted. "In we go."
The Whitechapel Mission. The poster declared, and the two lads joined the long queue of shivering, stinking, blokes. Someone had scrawled on the wall: "This is no place to stand and wonder. This is the place to fart like thunder." The message had certainly been taken to heart; and

arse. The whole place stank of old man's fart. The line of slouching skeletons slowly shuffled towards the ticket kiosk.

"Another bloody day gorn! Another shitty night in this hellhole. One ticket please," groaned the bedraggled human in front of Sam. He muttered to himself. "Gateway to the coffin, if you're lucky." And he laughed, a cauldron of scorn. "Death would be more merciful; but she's a deaf old whore."

Sam handed over two coins and grabbed his ticket from the impoverished clerk in his cubbyhole.

"Glad we came early." Joe muttered. "At least it's a place to pull your old pudding. You'll hear them in the night, Sam, pulling their wrinkled, stinking old pricks. Still, it's better than trying to bum you when you're out like a light."

The soft shoe shuffle at last brought them to the payment window.

"Two tonight, mate. Me and my old chum Samuel." The man poked out his snaky head to evaluate the newcomer.

"No alcohol! No bedbugs crawling up your back? Give us four pence! I know you of old, don't I? You kids always bring trouble. No larking or any other funny stuff, either. In you go. Don't like young lads. I need kids like I need another hole in my arse. Keep quiet. And No offering your bums to no-one. Understand? Or you're out in the cold."

But then the gravelly voice switched to a sort of whispered kindness. "Get inside lads and have a cosy kip." He even managed a smile.

"Careful! Sam! Don't take off any clothes. Sleep in your overcoat; too many rotten geezers in here. Come."

They entered the hall. The stench of a hundred old men

was overwhelming.

"Oh! Our nice little Joey brought us a nice new mate. Nice! Welcome to Hades you sweet little fucker. But careful! Don't sleep or we'll all be trying to get up yer." He grinned, revealing a mouth full of no teeth.

"He looks like a Jew boy." Someone shouted. "No Jew boy has ever been here before." Hooted another.

"Dante never came to a place as rotten as this." Sam trembled; his flesh creeping.

"Take no notice. They won't try nothing; not with me around."

"Where are the beds?" Sam tugged Joe's jacket. "There seems to be a dearth of beds."

Everyone close roared with laughter. "Did you hear that? This little Jew boy wants a bed in the Tuppenny Lean? Fresh meat! Nice fresh meat. Where you bin kid, all your life?"

"I've been in Russia."

That brought another torrent of laughter. "Welcome to hell you little lying thief."

"Sam! There are no beds down here, mate." Joe said. "Look!"

Sam noticed the long thick rope, tied from one end of the hall to the other. Most of the inmates in the dark hall were already leaning on the rope, all with one arm hanging over, and all their bodies limp and far away in deep doze, the stepbrother of death.

Sam was appalled. "I can't do that. I can't sleep here."

"It's easy my old mate. Nuffin to it. Just put your right arm over the rope and lean over it and you're away. Sleep does the rest."

And all the while more and more old men came shuffling in.

"See that door in the corner? It's for them who don't wake up in the morning. They say, in there is a chute that sends you all the way to hell."

Sam put his right arm over and hung on the rope and did the hokey cokey, like a very sleepy marionette; slumping and falling. And the very last vision he saw were the battalions of bed bugs, scuttling up and down the wall. And everything mashed together in the black, insatiable night.

He hurtled down and down to where his dad was in repose. And the coffin slowly moved across his clenched eyes, into the furnace of Hoop Lane. "Rabbi! Help me! Help me!" He could hear someone shouting. But the rabbi who could never die was dead; forever. No-one would come with the answer. He could hear himself sobbing in his sleep. And no sooner done than undone. Day and night were in collusion.

It was morning already and he shook himself back into the world. He was still leaning on the thick, coarse rope and his arm was dead. They could lop it off and he wouldn't feel a thing, but life slowly came back to him.

"Get up you lousy tykes! You shitty toe rags! Up! Up! And out. Up and out. Get out! You lazy, shithouse toe rags."

Two men, the harbingers, untied the rope at the other end and the bodies all fell to the floor. Sam sprang to his feet and prepared to defend himself. If he was to be a child sacrifice, poking his tongue out at the Great Moloch was the last and the least thing he could do under the circumstances. But most of the old men, bleary and sloth-like were crawling around, like blind sticks, trying to get back into their bodies.

The two caretakers began kicking and punching the pathetic old bastards, all over the concrete floor. The stinker men just moaned and groaned, trying to hide their bodies, their collection of bones, under their sheltering arms. All this was done quietly, without anger or aggravation. The daily ritual was known and accepted. If you were impoverished you had no status.

Out of the window that had not been cleaned since the beginning of time, Sam noticed the world outside. Through the detritus of years he saw a freezing morning and a terrible pea-soup fog covering East London. It had to be the end of the world and everything, and he had to get home to thank his mother for giving him life and a last supper of chicken soup. "And Mum, don't forget! Four matzo balls if you please."

He looked around for Joe.

"Joe? Where you hiding? Joe! Joe!" He called. No-one took any notice. They were hardly aware that they were there. One old geezer was killing body lice, cracking them with two filthy fingernails.

It was alright. Joe was probably having a long slash. Sam was sure none of these gorgons had swallowed him. He walked backwards and forward along the black mass of the tangled old men, not one of them could possibly remember what a bed was like. For them there were only two things left in their world. The rope at night, and being kicked out into the death of the morning.

Sam darted to the entrance, now an exit, as the old tramps and the young tramps stumbled out into the gutter.

"I'm looking for my mate, Joe." His stomach was churning fear. "Please! Has anyone seen Joe him, anywhere?"

No-one bothered to answer. All were locked inside theselves with troubles of their own, trying to face the day.

Sam hurried out of the stink palace into the pelting, freezing, streets. Zombies were inhabiting the pavements, on their way to yet another lousy day of the daily grind, called work.

He rushed the length of Vallance Road, shouting for his lost friend.

"Joe! Joe! Stop playing silly buggers."

Not a sausage! A few people stared and walked on. He dashed back towards the main thoroughfare. He was always trapped in the ever-present now. The future and the past were not feeling too well, and the present had troubles of its own.

He turned into the Whitechapel Road. His mind was rushing towards momentous extremes. Joe had probably got up early and simply had gone back to his pitch. But when he reached the Mile End Waste there was still no sign of his new friend. Sam sat on the kerb, wondering, waiting.

Costermongers were now arriving, and setting out their stalls and the market started coming back to life. The cruel wind coming from Siberia, swept along Bow Road and was veering towards Aldgate. He laughed. The Russian Arctic wind didn't care a toss and laughed back. "Samuel! This is our revenge for killing our beloved Tsar."

The wind swooped. It was on its way to Mare Street, passing St Joseph's Hospice where the kind Jesus girls, called nuns, helped his lovely grandfather Maurice to die peacefully.

He wandered among the stalls, smiling, interrupting the busy stallholders, who were serving intense customers.

"Have you seen Joe? You know, the young kid, the busker, the boy who sings for his supper?"

Silence and shaking heads replied. They were too busy trying to survive yet another day. Sam sat on a kerbstone, stony broke, starving. The smell of frying bacon wafted across from a Greasy Spoon, a caff on wheels.

At that moment, the elixir of bacon, that rejected and delicious food of the goyim, was a sin he would gladly die for. But first he would have to earn a few coppers. He grabbed an empty orange box, clambered aboard and started his sad madrigal.

> *When that I was and a little tiny boy,*
> *With hey,ho, the wind and the rain,*
> *A foolish thing was but a toy,*

But everyone was rushing past to get out of the persistent rain; not one single face stopped to listen. Sam continued. If he seemed pathetic enough someone would surely reward him.

> *For the rain it raineth every day.*
> *But that's all one, our play is done.*
> *And we'll strive to please you every day.*

It was a deluge. It raineth cats and dogs alright. It was the end of the world. And kids were crying and muking and puking as they were viciously dragged towards school.
And on the ground there was not one coin; not one penny, not a single sausage!

A dark chocolate voice cut into Sam's sorrow.

"My darling. Why are you weeping?"

"I'm not. I just peeled an opinion." He replied.

And there was a beautiful, slim young woman with dark eyes under an umbrella, smiling down on him.

"My God. You poor boy; you look like a drowned fish." She seemed alarmed.

"I'm a gefilte fish; How do you do? I'm Samuel Glass on my way to Muswell Hill." He proffered his hand. She took it, gladly.

"Oooh! You're freezing; you're dying of cold."

"What's your name?" He knew that knowing names brought you closer. He would not mind being closer to this apparition.

"You're not a ghost girl, are you?"

She was puzzled but grinned. "I'm Phoebe. Come under my umbrella. You'll be drowned otherwise."

He did as he was told. He fancied her rotten, but she was a treasure beyond reach. He wanted to show off, so he did. "I love quoting poetry in the morning; it gets you through the day." He dived straight into words that were beautiful and mournful.

> *What can ail thee knight-at-arms,*
> *Alone and palely loitering?*
> *The sedge is wither'd on the lake*
> *And no birds sing.*

He paused and to his utter amazement and surprise she continued the poem:

> *I see a lily on thy brow*
> *With anguish moist and fever dew.*

245

And on thy cheeks a fading rose
Fast witherest too.

"La Belle Dame Sans Merci. John Keats. He died in Rome, too young." She said.

"From terminal blood." He replied. "February the twenty fourth. Eighteen twenty one. He was twenty five years old."

"I love anyone who loves Keats." She replied. "But what are you doing here, amongst down and outs, drenched with rain, and your amazing knowledge of poetry."

"Long story," he replied. "I'm on the last legs of a journey to find myself."

"How long will it take? Tell me your story? Tell me everything."

"Everything is too much, not here, please. It's too damp. I'm trying to get to Muswell Hill by way of St Petersburg and Latvia. Such tales I could tell, but it would take several weeks."

"I love young men with tales to tell. They're dying out. Come with me, Samuel. I'll get you warm."

He looped the loop in his head. He was in with more than a chance. But he tried to be cool and not show his obvious hunger. Even though it was obvious she wanted what he wanted. The other! How lucky. How lucky he was. Life turns on a stroke of luck.

"You're Jewish?"

"What else? I'm a nice kosher Jewish girl." But her sad expression spoke of something else.

"So why is a nice Jewish girl inviting lost boys to her tent in the wilderness?"

"Long story, just like yours." She replied. "Come."

246

They walked away from the Mile End Waste. Both were silent. But not for long. Silence was not a state he usually inhabited.

"I slept last night in a Tuppenny Lean, and lost my only friend."

"Samuel! You and me and everyone else."

"But I'm very lost. I don't understand why everything is in black and white."

"Nice pretty Jewish boys should never get lost. We're nearly there."

She had that wonderful fragrance; that smell of female sweat, melding in with cheap perfume. Everything else faded. The resurrection of arousal was exciting him; killing him. He hoped he could perform like a proper man. Boys were pathetic. He hoped he had finally left his boyhood behind, like his skateboard.

"I'm starving." He uttered.

She giggled. "Samuel Glass! I've got something in the cupboard to please you."

"You're very comely. You're quite sure you are not a ghost girl?"

She slowly shook her head. "I'm very much alive. You'll see."

He wanted to quote from *The Song of Solomon*, but bravely held back. He was not into words at this moment. He was into the beautiful action of deepest needs.

20

Sam sang quietly too himself.

Who is Syvia, what is she
That all our swains commend her?
Holy fair and wise is she
The heavens such grace did lend her.
That she might admired be.
Is she wise as she is fair?
For beauty lives with kindness.

He felt guilty. The dead girl he loved was gone forever. And the girl beside him was fast asleep. And as he put on his clothes he realised he was becoming a man.

She stirred. "Lovely song. Samuel. You've got a lovely voice. Are you going? Come over here and kiss me goodbye before you go."

He obeyed her soft command willingly. He wanted to kiss and smell her jet black hair and carry with him forever the kindness of her mouth, her breasts and the generosity of her body.

"I heard you crying in the night. For your mother." She said, still on the precipice of sleep. "Normally I charge. But instead I think I owe you something. You are so beautiful and have given me something."

She reached out and slipped a silver coin into his hand.

"Anyway, giving is getting. Half a crown, I owe you, for me thinking we were in love, when you were inside me. I am a night worker and I need my beauty sleep. Go now!"

"Goodbye Phoebe. Thanks for the gift of your passion."

"Goodbye Samuel." Her words still slurred from sleep.

"Go in good health, said the Scorpion to the Frog."

"Giving is getting." She whispered on the parapet of sleep. She was definitely not a ghost girl.

Outside the sun glared down and this was definitely the day to seek and find Muswell Hill. He ran down the tenement steps two at a time; a seven year old again. And he strode into the black and white huddled streets of Whitechapel. At last he had truly passed his baptism of fire.

He knew he would never see her again as he clutched the silver coin in his pocket.

He sauntered through the early crowds of Wentworth Street market.

Anxious yuchners were squeezing and smelling fruit at the stalls. Others were grabbing at fresh chickens, no longer in this world, newly cut and killed by a sharp razor knife. And opposite had to be the kosher poultry abattoir, with three bearded executioners, standing outside, taking a rest and a quick drag from a fag; their white aprons smothered with black blood; and breathing in the putrid air before returning inside for another bloody day.

This Wentworth Street was the Holocaust of helpless chickens. Sam thought he could hear the screeching, the last chorus of the birds within, as they met the knife; the savage, gleaming honed blades, slicing and then the fountain of black blood.

Sam had no compassion for chickens. Without them there would be no chicken soup.

Then it dawned. "Of course." It was Friday. Everyone was crowding into the Wentworth Street shtetl, preparing for tonight, when the Sabbath Queen would arrive. This was his heritage.

He found himself outside The Soup Kitchen for the Jewish Poor. The wealthy ladies from beyond the North West passage were handing out thick green pea soup and black bread. It helped to keep them alive.

Maurice and Granma Rosie used to talk of their childhood, the terrible grind of day after day; the desperation of the hungry, and death slinking in the corner of the so-called living room.

None of the kids of his time had known poverty. Poverty of the mind, most certainly!

"We didn't want to be chucked into an early pauper's grave." Maurice had said. "If you were poor, in them days, life was on the other side of nowhere. It was about nothing."

Sam knew that his people resided deep in his bones. He could not escape the destiny of the tribe. It was all so ironic. Existence was a short stay in a world that had no meaning.

But he had to get to his home tonight; before *shabbat* somehow. He would shower, and then go straight to the table where his mother would smile as she placed her steaming elixir of life before him. He just had to find a way of getting there.

Then, standing outside the library at Aldgate East, someone with a rasping voice was shouting.

"Rags! Old clothes and rags! Bring out your rags! Cash for old clothes! Give a kick! Inspect your old cupboards where you chuck away your shmutters, and bottles and bones! Old Clothes! Old Rags! Rags for instant cash!"

The man on the cart stopped whipping his poor, old, tired horse and looked down at the youth.

"Hey! Son! Your muvver got any old rags to dispose of in yer house?"

"If only I had a mum. She's in another century."

The rag and bone man sneered. "Buzz off, you lousy, clever, big mouth. Can't abide street urchins. You're all rotten little tykes." He whipped his shagged-out horse to get going again.

"Wait! Please wait! I have a proposition" Sam held up the coin. "Half a crown. It's all yours if you take me to Muswell Hill!"

"Don't kid me you little so and so. Where would you get half a crown?"

Sam held the coin forward, towards the geezer. And the man's eyes lit up and he did not hesitate, his face suddenly acquired a benevolent smile. "Show us it proper."

Sam obliged and the man grabbed the half a crown.

"Where did you get this? Stole it, did ya? Anyways, it's not my business. Give us it. You're a bit different from the thieving little gonifs who crowd our gutters."

He bit the coin and nodded. "It's kosher alright. Where do you wanna go, son?"

"Muswell Hill! I told you."

"Never worked outside the old East End. Muswell Hill is where posh bastards live, right? Never been there, meself! Never trust the rich. That's my motto. Hop aboard then.

Anyways, I might try and work some streets up there, among those bleedin' rich and squeeze a few bob out of them."

Sam climbed up, beside him. And the rag and bone man whipped the poor old creature. He whipped and he whipped and growled and whipped, and they slowly moved away from the teeming streets.

"Good boy! Good boy!" The Rag and Bone cooed. "You're a lovely old horse. Salt of the earth! But I'm sorry Ursula, me old mate, it's the knackers for you in a fortnight. She understands. She can do with a rest. She's a lovely old girl who gives out great manure; the best shit in London. It's got a lovely fragrance. Doing her a favour really."

Sam nodded, but his mind was somewhere else.

"You're running away from home, aint ya?"

"No. Running to it, if I can."

The costermonger cleared his throat, and coughed up a ball of black and white phlegm, perused it, and hurled it away and again whipped the poor old creature. And they scooted all along the Whitechapel Road, turned left into Cambridge Heath Road and it was goodbye to the East End.

The man scratched his head. "I fink I know the truth 'bout you. You've escaped from Colney Hatch! The looney bin. Right? Okay! Now you want to go back! Your affair; seems to me you're no more mad than the rest of the world. I won't let you down."

Sam did not respond. Then the rag and bone man burst into song:

In Scarlet Town where I was born
There lived a fair maid dwelling.
Made every youth cry well a day
Her name was Barbara Allen.
All in the merry month of May
When flowers were a-bloomin',
Sweet William on his deathbed lay
For love of Barbara Allen.

"I love a sad song. Don't you?" He continued.

He sent his servant to the town,
To the place where she was dwellin',
"My Master dear has sent me here
If your name be Barbara Allen."
Then slowly slowly she got up,
And slowly went she nigh him,
And all she said when she got there,
"Young man, I think you're dyin'."

"I love songs. They take you out of yourself." He slapped his traveller, broke into raucous laughter and returned to his calling.

"Any old rags! Any old bones! Any old clothes! Get rid of your bug-bitten crap."

He turned to Sam. "I love words; I'm a wordsmith meself. Every night I try to learn a new one."

But Sam wasn't quite there. And here they were again. They seemed to warn him seconds before they got there. The piercing noises. Those boxcar sounds high up in his head. What filters of the brain had he blown through the dreaded tunnel of darkness, deep in his inner self; following him for the rest of his life, until his dying day?

Sam realised he had dozed off. The man was still whipping his horse. "We're well on our way, mate. We're way past Holloway and far away from the West End where those rich Jews live. Good luck to them. They work hard, don't they? I've got nuffink against them Jews; the children of the Book, ain't they? I love books. Wish I was born Jewish. I would be stinking rich by now. You awake now? Didn't want to disturb ya."

Sam nodded. He had been asleep for most of the journey.

"Here we are then! Among the great mansions of Muswell Hill, where the chosen rest from the slavery called work. God bless 'em and all who sail in them. So off you get. And tell your dad to give you a good hiding for getting lost."

"I wish I could. Goodbye."

"So long mate!"

"Incidentally, my name is Sam. Samuel Glass."

They shook hands. "And I'm Steve. A fierce friend of the People of the Book! And may your tribe flourish, Samuel Glass."

Sam jumped down onto the familiar streets. "And don't forget to tell your mum and dad that Steve, the rag and bone man rescued you from the thieving dens of Whitechapel. So long Sam and don't pull your pudding too much. It'll make hair grow on your hands and people will fink you're a monkey. Farewell!" And off he went.

"Old bones! Any old bones! And old clothes! Any old rags! Instant cash if you have a bash!"

Soon his voice and the creaking cart faded into the distance. And just round the corner had to be home, but he did not dash to get there in case it wasn't there. And no-one, not one single soul was about. Maybe all had been sucked up by oblivion. "Nonsense! You suffer from too much imagination. Life has to be there and working," he told himself. It was before the mad time of the morning, when everyone rushed towards their separate prisons.

He walked towards the old Green Man Inn near the top of Muswell Hill and then he opened his mouth wide as the monochrome streets were washed away and colour started returning, pouring gently down into the day. The green trees, the blue sky and the clouds all silver as they slowly passed overhead. He was absolutely back inside the twenty first century.

He quickened his step and his beating heart was going hell for leather as he turned the corner. And he prayed to all the deaf, dumb and blind gods of his father. "Please be there." His house had to be there, with his parents born and his father dead.

And there it was, the house he knew, with those mauve curtains in the Edwardian windows. The Saab was still there, in the front garden, tangled by weeds and snoring away in steel oblivion. And his mother had to be inside. And if she was not there he would throw himself off Suicide Bridge.

He closed his eyes and opened them again and slowly walked the tightrope, crossing the road to the door that was slightly opened.

"Hello! Anyone there?" He called as he entered and there she was. The Lisa he loved, his mother, pink and beautiful, standing before him, smiling, shaking her head.

"Where the hell have you been?"

"Out!"

"What have you been doing?"

"Nothing."

"I've been looking for you everywhere. You've been a hell of a long time." She glanced at her watch. "At least half an hour. And look at you! You're absolutely filthy. How did you get into such a state?"

"Long story."

"You were in your room, taking to yourself, deep in a book as usual. Sam my darling, as you get older I understand you less and less. It's Friday night. Remember? Shabbat! And I'm very busy."

"What's for dinner?"

"What else? Chicken soup with matzo balls."

"Ah! the profligate smells heaven."

"You smell. You stink to high heaven. Take a bath. Now!"

"I cannot tell you where I've been. You would be amazed."

"Nothing will surprise me, precious, precocious, impossible child of my loins. Looks like you've been rolling in the mud in Alexandra Park? I'll run the bath."

"No! I'll do it myself, thank you very much."

"I always run your bath."

"Sorry! Those days are over."

"Let me feel your forehead." She did. "As I thought; feverish, as usual. I'll lay out some nice, clean Shabbat clothes."

"Mother; please don't fuss. Mum, actually I've been in Russia. Everyone stinks there."

"Russia? That's nice."

"I've been assisting in the assassination of Alexander the Second. It was eighteen eighty one."

"The doctor's surgery opens at nine. Book an appointment."

"By the way, I missed you terribly."

"That's nice. Go! Get clean. Quick!"

"I also must tell you something even more important, I lost my virginity. To a young and beautiful actress. Sylvia!"

She gritted her teeth. "That's nice. Well, it had to happen, I suppose." She mumbled.

"Then I discovered she was a ghost. However she gave me the present of her body, and therefore the rites of passage."

"Samuel. I think maybe just a little brain operation will do the trick."

He ignored her quips and continued. "I've passed through that passage of death, otherwise known as childhood. There was Queen Sarah, the image of you; as a matter of fact she was your great, great, great grandmother. She was so beautiful; actually I wanted to cross over the morality line and make love to her, after all, as Grandpa Maurice once said. "Incest is fine if you keep it in the family."

Lisa gaped; she was aghast and silent.

"But it didn't happen. She was as beautiful as you."

"What can you do when you have such an impossible and lovable son like you?"

"Mum! I am now to be treated as a grown-up adult. And oh yes! On my way back to England I met a Jewish prostitute in the East End called Phoebe. And she wasn't a ghost; one sexual lesson with her was like transubstantiation; she was fantastic. She was a lovely, Jewish girl."

"Nice! Jewish? That's very nice Samuel!" She sighed and smiled. "What can you do with such a child? Go! Get into the bath and you'll feel better. Now!"

His eyes turned to the urn of his father's ashes on the mantelpiece.

"Mother! We must get rid of father."

She screamed at him. "You horrible, nasty boy. Into the bathroom! Go drown yourself."

"I'm having a shower. Where's the bathroom?"

"It's where it always was. And always will be." She pushed him towards it.

"You really are the very best mother in the world."

"And while you're about it wash your brain and clean your mouth."

"I love you very much."

"Thank you!"

Then the doorbell rang.

"Oh! Sorry! I forgot to tell you! We have a guest for Shabbat dinner."

"Who?"

"David Simmons! Remember? I told you all about him."

"That's nice. That's very nice! Thank you. It's your life."

"You wicked, wicked boy. What's happened to you? You used to be nice."

"Never! I was never nice." Sam strode to the bathroom, both hands holding his head tight to make sure it didn't fall off. "How could she do that to me?" He entered the pristine throne room of hell.

There was another ring on the bell. Sam pressed his ears hard against the door. The hateful guest entered and Sam could pick out the conversation between victim and predator.

"David! How nice of you! What wonderful lilies!"

"My pleasure. Lisa! You seem upset."

258

"He's getting worse. He was such a lovely, uncomplicated child. And he was always so funny. Whenever he entered the room, it lit up with joy and laughter."

"He's a teenager. What can you expect?" The man spoke banal platitudes. How could he possibly be nice to a man who obviously desired to slide into bed with his mother?

Sam stood naked, ready for the shower. But he needed to throw some more shit at her; so he opened the door, slightly.

"Mrs Glass! May I speak to you for a moment?" He conjured up a nice sotto voce voice. She came to the crack, furious behind her smiling mask, as if she knew that a flood of invective was about to cascade upon her.

"Yes darling? What is it?"

"How could you? And your beloved husband's ashes, staring down at you. You never loved him." He hissed.

"Thank you, darling. Have a nice shower."

"I hate you. I hate you forever." He cried. And he cried. And he would cry forever.

21

He entered the living room and offered his polite hand to Mr David Simmons. "How do you do, I'm ever so pleased to meet you!"

The man gleamed. "Ah! Sam! May I call you Sam? I see they teach you good manners in your school. I've been so looking forward to meeting you."

David Simmons seemed pathetically normal. He was definitely trying to hook the most beautiful woman in the world, and who could blame him?

Yes you could! Who wouldn't want to devour such a beautiful and passionate woman? Mr David Simmons was a ravenous fox on the rampage.

"Mother! You look so beautiful tonight."

"Thank you." She replied.

"I must concur." The man added.

She hadn't lost her precious smell. She was not a duplicate doppelganger. She was Lisa, a first class lady, the genuine article.

She smiled back at her son, but her eyes flashing from inner turmoil, were speaking. "Who would want to be the mother of Samuel Glass?"

"Oh Sam! I clean forgot. Katie's in your room! She slipped in while you were taking your shower. She was desperate to see you. I'm serving dinner in fifteen minutes. Please don't be long!"

"I'll be quick as Ariel, my mother darling." He immediately shot into his den.

Katie stood before him. She seemed a little different; a little more mature, and lovely. He was seeing her through new eyes. Her breasts were fuller, not just pretty bumps; only a few days ago they were flat as a waffle dripping with honey. He simply could not take his eyes away from her silky, diaphanous dress. He would just love to smell and kiss her pubic hair.

> *A damsel with a dulcimer*
> *In a vision once I saw:*
> *It was an Abyssinian maid,*
> *And on her dulcimer she played.*

Her scent wafted and wound around him, and he closed his eyes, inhaling her. "You've changed since I've been away." He spoke softly, flatly.

He would have it away with her soon. Very soon. He would give her the gift of the rites of passage. She needed it; she was longing for it. She deserved it. Better him than all the other pathetic wankers. He would transport her to sexual paradise. He was experienced now, what with the generosity of Anne, Sylvia and Phoebe. He was past his baptism of fire. He would have to offer her paradise. Not today, nor tomorrow, but maybe the day after.

"You've changed since I've been away in St Petersburg, killing the Tsar."

"Sam! You have not been away anywhere, except in your head. And that's nothing new."

She was a crazy girl. Maybe that was the magnetic attraction. She had always been besotted; obsessed by him.

She was such a pushover and soon, tomorrow maybe he would push her onto the bed.

"You're very beautiful, Katie. You've changed, overnight! In a flash! I really, really like you. You're no longer a child but a beautiful young woman, with everything coming into shape. How did it happen?"

Her response was a cynical laugh that surprised him.

"I've always respected you; liked you." He said. "And sort of loved you, in a way."

"In a way?"

She almost spat in his face. "I've said it all. You emotionally possessed me and played with me and I wanted you. I wanted to give you my heart; my mind, my body, my soul; but now all that is over and dead. I've come to say goodbye."

"Goodbye? What are you talking about? Why?"

"We are moving away, next Wednesday. We're leaving England forever. You know my father works for a bank. He's a bigwig. He's moving to another bank, in Auckland, New Zealand. We are leaving on Wednesday and I will never see you again. Goodbye Samuel, I hope you have a lovely life." She wiped her tears, opened the door, and ran out, crying.

Sam was stunned as he joined his mother and the interloper at the table.

Whether you were a believer in the Red Rabbi, or God or Satan or anything; like a Nihilist, Fascist, Atheist or Nowist, Shabbat was a very special occasion. Silence reigned as Lisa ladled the holy soup into the special John Lewis Friday night bowls.

"So what was wrong with Katie? She left sobbing. How

many matzo balls? Sam?"

"As many as you can spare. Four or five. Katie was very upset about leaving. And who could blame her? Did you know they're moving next Wednesday to New Zealand, Auckland of all places! Pity. We were very good friends. Sometimes."

"It must be terrible being uprooted and transferred to the other side of the world. And to Auckland, of all places." The pristine David said in sympathy, trying to conceal his lasciviousness.

"And at her age!" Said Lisa, the compassionate. "Sad! Very, very sad! Sam, you can have two more matzo balls and that's your lot."

"How kind you are, mother."

David Simmons continued with some more humane detritus. "Moving away is always so horrendous. It must be a sort of death."

"Mr Simmons. You are absolutely right." Sam said. He was up to the man's pathetic tricks. It was also so mundane and simple. His sole purpose was the endgame. To ravish his mother, to purloin, to impregnate, to discharge his suburban sperm into her weeping body and to fertilise her with a puking baby. David Simmons was a serial rapacious enterer. Probably he had failed to impress more than a score of women in several dating clubs. They had all found him pathetic and wanting, however anxious they were to hook a man. And now his mother was getting well and truly hooked because of her desperation for the man she lost.

"This soup is delicious. Please invite me again." David Simmons said.

The two adults smiled across at each other. Sam dived in to change the wavelength. "Delicious! Mother, I know it's a cliché, but you are the Sabbath Queen. This alone is worth coming home for."

"Darling! You haven't been away yet." She was too happy; too flippant. She had lost herself.

Sam decided to throw a grenade into the works. "David! May I call you David?"

"Of course." The man replied. "I'd be delighted."

God! What a banal idiot. Sam was raging within. He had no choice but to rage without. "David! I believe my mother believes you fancy her, and that you intend to maybe team up with her. How nice. Good luck mate. I don't blame you. Who wouldn't desire her? If she wasn't my mother I would certainly fancy her. But are you sure your union will prove viable?

"But what about me? I mean I do have a say in all this. Where do I fit into this, this sudden need to rush towards an urgent partnership? It's all happening too fast. Surely this sudden urgent desire for my mother's body has also to be discussed, talked about and approved by me? After all, I am a major part in this drama."

Lisa coughed, choked and kicked him under the table. She maintained her suburban Muswell Hill smile, but he could see how furious she was. The soup of truth was out of the cauldron.

And then she burst. "Samuel! How dare you? You are a wicked, nasty youth creature! How could you be so rude? How the hell did I give birth to him? David, forgive him. Don't be angry with him. Take no notice of him. He thrives on this. But he is just another objectionable

264

teenager. Hopefully he will grow out of it one day."

Sam's tears were beginning to roll. "My father loved me. He would never have said that. He never would have broken my heart. Mother! There will be no peace in this house until the urn is emptied."

Lisa hurried round the table and hugged him. "I don't want to hurt you. I don't want to be hurt."

"Mother! We humans are far too cold; it's time we climbed into our refrigerators to keep warm."

David gently tried to soften the situation. "Bravo! I agree. Lisa! He is right. He's perfectly entitled. It affects all of us. We must be open about this important step we are hoping to take. Samuel! I think you are great. And I am not offended. You are original and lucky you can unload your deepest thoughts. That's marvellous. Yes! We have been intending to team up; soon, and we do understand your concerns. I was married to Ruthie for almost twenty years. She was a wonderful woman."

"Where, and how, and why did you dump her then?"

David ignored Sam's retort. "We had, and I still have two kids, a boy and girl, both at university. I'm so glad that I can talk to you like this. Ruthie died. Three years ago. Ovarian cancer. Bad luck! Fate! We have to get on with our lives, no matter what hand we've been dealt."

"I'm very sorry." Sam suddenly didn't hate the man so much. And his anger had been spent.

"So Samuel, what do you intend to do in life?"

"To become a human being; unless it is no longer on the curriculum."

"He's actually applied to do History at Cambridge for his degree," said Lisa.

"Sorry! I've changed my mind. I'm off History. Sorry mother. Will you forgive me?"

She squeezed his hand. "Darling, whatever you feel you must do, remember it's your life." And they all climbed into the refrigerator together and the ice was broken and all smiled with warmth.

"Actually I think I shall read Politics. More soup please, Mother. I'm still starving."

His eyes widened when she ladled more soup and the last two matzo balls.

"But maybe not. Politics is rubbish. If politics changed anything, they would have abolished it long ago."

"What a clever boy you have Mrs Glass." David Simmons winked.

Sam responded. "By the way, I must own up. Someone said it long ago. I do not dislike you anymore, Mr Simmons. And maybe I will come to the understanding that you might deserve my wonderful mother."

"I hope I can rise to the occasion."

"Yes! Conjugalling is a very important facet in any relationship. After all, we are only human, Mr Simmons."

"Please call me David."

"No! Not yet! We may reconsider that after your term of apprenticeship."

Sam turned to Lisa and squeezed her hand. "Mother! You have my blessing, for what it's worth. But please, for all our sakes, it's time we got rid of your husband and my father's ashes from that bloody rotten urn on the mantelpiece."

"Yes. I was only thinking of that a moment ago."

"Thank you both." David said; then he changed the subject, entirely. "By the way Samuel, I hear you are quite an expert on the skateboard."

"Skateboard? Skateboard? Oh yes! My old skateboard."

David continued "I'd love to see your antics at Ally Pally one of these days."

"Sorry David. My skateboard is history. My skateboarding days are over. I left her back in the waiting room in Vitebsk. Or was it Riga? Or was it St Petersburg? Anyway it was somewhere in Russia, when we anarchists assassinated the Jew-hating tyrant, Tsar Alexander the Second!"

David held his hand over his mouth to curtail laughter.

Lisa sighed. "David! Now you can see that my son is quite mad and what we are up against. Now you know what you are taking on."

"I am prepared for the battle. My life of late has been too quiet. It's wonderful to have such an imagination."

Sam stood up. "By the way mother, I've also lost my mobile. It fell from my hands and was smashed to smithereens. Thank you. I must love you both and leave you. Homework! Tons and tons of reading." He kissed her and shook hands with his heavily expectant new father, and went to his room.

He looked into the cracked mirror and talked to himself as his mind whirled. Nothing was easy. His past was still with him and his future was nowhere in sight because he was already within it. "Or maybe, if the fates allow I will take a degree at the Royal Academy of Dramatic Arts and become one of the greatest actors in the world. Oh for the life of desperation, joy and poverty. What could be better?"

They all spoke to him. Actors! Authors! Poets. Drama was about something else, as his master, Anton Chekhov, once whispered. And he knew he was something else. And always somewhere else. His brain had exploded long ago. He knew he had to embrace the person he truly was.

Now he lay in the dark, musing, wandering, recalling events in the past. As the Red Rabbi said, "don't forget to remember the future."

There was a gentle tapping on the door. "Come in Mother."

She came to the bedside and kissed him. "David likes you a lot. God knows how. Thank you for being you. Cos there ain't another like Samuel Glass in this world."

Sam was on the verge, surfing the ocean of tears.

"Thank you for giving me life." He replied. "He seems quite a good man."

"A good man is good enough." She replied.

"Mother! I think you should marry him. Soon! No parties. Just elope. Honeymoon in Bognor Regis or the Seychelles, quietly."

"Yes Sam. I am still comparatively young, so how could I continue for the rest of my life, without someone to talk to; to belong to. To sleep with. The burden would be too much and it wouldn't be fair on you if all my hopes and fears were burdened upon you."

"Mother! You are preaching to the already converted."

"It's been a long journey, and, believe it or not, I am not now tired. David and I are going to the pictures."

She went to the door and blew him a kiss. "Oh by the way, David has invited us for dim sum in Soho, tomorrow lunchtime. Is that alright by you?"

"It's bloody perfect. He's a schmoozer and knows the way to an ageing adolescent's heart."

Sam slid into verse:

And I shall find some girl perhaps,
And a better one than you,
With eyes as wise, but kindlier;
And lips as soft, but true.
And I dare say she will do.

"Katie is a lovely girl. You helped her to slip through your fingers."

"Selah! It wasn't to be."

"Samuel! It's your life."

"Mum! We must do it. Dad's ashes! We must scatter him tomorrow! That urn on the mantelpiece has been stopping me from getting on with my life. Mother I think I know the exact place we can scatter him."

"You're right. You can't be imprisoned by the past when you are looking forward to the future. Goodnight. See you in the morning."

Sam lay musing, stretched out on the carpet. And again he thought could hear the boxcars, far away, fading into the distance. Clanking through intersections into the cadences of his memory; people screaming, shouting to sudden total silence. And now their ashes were shooting up into the clouds above Hoop Lane Crematroium.

He jumped to his feet and played Chopin's sombre Funeral March. Going close to the heart of the music gave him hope.

Chopin was despised and later deified.

Seven wealthy towns contend for Homer dead.
Where the living Homer begged his bread.

Tonight he could sleep, so he pulled off his clothes and

went to bed and soon dived upward, scattering aeons of stars, as he glided into the embracing ocean of endless time. There was a dearth of dream.

The next morning was chilly and bright. It was a London morning. Later they would meet David at the Red Dragon in Gerrard Street, but now they emerged from Westminster Station. The whole journey had been in voluble silence. Sam was miles away, thinking deep and remembering his future. Only now, coming through the exit, did he speak.

"Mother! I haven't told you this before, but certain things haunt me. I'm back home and I'm glad, and I know I have to get on with my life. But I have the terrible sound of boxcars clanging in my head. And the crying of people."

"Oh my God!" She went pale. "I think I hear them too, sometimes. Maybe we need to hear them; to live with them."

"Why?" He sighed and took a deep breath for all the ghosts he had encountered in his odyssey and he smiled at the beautiful woman who had borrowed him from the universe. "Mother? Why are we here?"

"To scatter your father."

"I mean in this life. Why the hell are we here?"

"Why is the most important word in the world."

"Why is 'why' the most important?"

"Exactly!" Now please, leave your mind alone."

They both laughed.

"Here we are. Down these steps we go; on to the Embankment. It was your idea, remember?"

"The River Ganges. We're going on a trip up the river. Great!"

A sudden horrible thought struck. "Where's the urn?

Where's my father urn?"

"In my holdall." She seemed quite serene. He was so afraid she might break down.

"Mother! I've been thinking."

"Terrible disease; thinking! Out with it."

"Is it too late for you to have another child? You're not too old are you? I would love a little brother, or a sister. Or someone in between."

She laughed for a reply and shook her head, meaning what can you do with a son like this?

"I would quite like a little sister. We could call her Suzie or after someone in the Bible, or the Apocrypha. As the Talmud says. "The world exists by the breath of children."

"Sadly it's too late; far too late. Suzie or Agamemnon must sleep on inside. You are more than enough for me." She sauntered over to the ticket box and purchased the tickets. Then they clambered aboard Homer, the creaking, sightseeing puff-puff boat that had seen far better days.

It began to chug its windy way towards Hampton Court. And the sun was streaming gold and soon London was left far behind; and when they reached and passed Richmond, Ravi Shankar started playing his miraculous Sitar over the tannoy; turning the choppy Thames into the eternal Ganges.

"How appropriate." Sam glowed with the thought that life was all one, all beautiful and now.

"Now?" She asked.

"Now!" He replied, taking the lid off the top, and his fingers gently touching, fingering his wonderful father; now no more than grey grain, sprinkling him through all his fingers. The mystery of touch and existence brought a pouring of tears that fell and soaked into the sleeve of his mother's best MaxMara coat. And now they both held the urn high and upturned it. And slowly, slowly, ever so slowly they poured the ashes into the Thames; the hourglass of time.

He cried and she cried. And Sam and his mother Lisa hugged and hugged, and laughed and cried.

As they passed the orchestra of trees, the river started to play the last movement of Mahler's Resurrection Symphony.

Sam remembered Maurice's last words. "Samuel, keep the music going."

He looked around at the green, passing world. Despite everything, life was not such a bad place to find one's self.

And the river flowed on.